C000176965

MR INVISIBLE

DUNCAN BROCKWELL

BLOODHOUND
— BOOKS —

Copyright © 2021 Duncan Brockwell
The right of Duncan Brockwell to be identified as the Author of the Work has
been asserted by him in accordance to the Copyright, Designs and Patents Act
1988.
First published in 2021 by Bloodhound Books
Apart from any use permitted under UK copyright law, this publication may
only be reproduced, stored, or transmitted, in any form, or by any means, with
prior permission in writing of the publisher or, in the case of reprographic
production, in accordance with the terms of licences issued by the Copyright
Licensing Agency.
All characters in this publication are fictitious and any resemblance to real
persons, living or dead, is purely coincidental.
www.bloodhoundbooks.com

Print ISBN 978-1-913942-15-1

ALSO BY DUNCAN BROCKWELL

The Met Murder Investigations

No Way Out #1

Bird of Prey #2

Bad Blood #3

1

The closer he came to the industrial bin the more the stench grew. The fourth of January, and while not typically cold for a Sussex winter, the corpse inside the metal receptacle didn't smell as bad as it would have in August. Detective Inspector David Coates wrinkled his nose beneath the face mask, while covered head to toe in white coveralls. Even his shoes wore white protectors. "Open up," he ordered, the SOCO in front of him lifting the lid. Flies buzzed.

"What do you think, Pat? How long do you think she's been in here for?" He was expecting a lengthy answer from the coroner he worked with on a more regular basis than he wished.

"A couple of days, I'd say," Patricia Rollins said through her mask. "I'm guessing there's no chance of cameras catching this guy?"

Looking around him, Coates noted nothing but fields, and a small recreation park for children. Why was the bin here? The undergrowth almost concealed it. "I don't think so. I didn't see any on the way in. Gary's checking."

With accusatory eyes looking up at Coates, a naked woman – unceremoniously dumped in the container – asked him why, her mouth open in a horrific "O". Coates estimated the woman to be in her mid-to-late twenties. The fact she was exposed would make identification tough, and more so if she didn't have a criminal record. "You think she was raped?"

"I don't doubt it for a second." Rollins pointed at the body. "Bruising and traces of bleeding. The poor woman was bound – those ligature marks on her wrists and ankles are deep. I'll know more after the autopsy."

The first thing he noted when he'd set eyes on her: she had to be around his daughter's age. "What's this town coming to? I used to love Lewes."

"Inspector," came a voice from behind him, "sorry to interrupt."

Turning, he found Detective Sergeant Gary Packard's eyes on him. "Well? Any luck?" He hoped for an affirmative. A shake of his partner's head dashed his hopes. "What I thought." He turned back to the body, his partner joining him. "Looks like we're in for a long one on this."

"Let's start with missing persons," Packard suggested. "Someone must've noticed she's not around. A pretty girl like this... Oh, and we might be lucky with that." He squinted his eyes, studying the ink.

Coates watched as his junior took his mobile out and snapped a photo of the tattoo on the corpse's abdomen. "What is that? A hummingbird?" He attempted to take a closer look. "It's a line of enquiry, I guess. See what you can do with it."

"Will do." His partner pocketed his phone. "I can contact some people if you want? I'm friends with a couple of ink artists locally. And they keep records of their customers. If she's local, she'll be a customer of Wozz's here in Lewes, or Crypt's in Brighton; they're the most popular. If not, I'll research further afield."

"Great! I'll go with missing cases," he said, nodding at the coroner, "and you take that angle." He pointed at the hummingbird. "Pat, how soon can you have the autopsy done?" Trace evidence, if there was any on the body, Patricia would find it. Semen or saliva, blood, whatever, the medical doctor would come through for him. "I've got a feeling she's a good girl." What was it about her? Maybe because she reminded him of his daughter, Hannah.

"By close of play, I hope, but I am backed up I'm sorry to say. If I can't get it done by then, I'm afraid it won't be until Monday." She signalled for one of the SOCOs to join them. Patricia took him by the arm and walked with him away from the crime scene. "If I can complete today, I'll phone the findings through to save you coming in."

"Thanks," he said, the SOCOs busy photographing the area, dusting for prints on the bin and all manner of other evidence-related activities. "You'll give it your all, I'm sure." He took his protective clothing off at the cordon, stooped underneath the tape and handed the clothes to Rollins. Packard followed his lead. "Call me as soon as you have something."

He thanked the coroner one last time, then walked back towards their unmarked white Peugeot, saying "no comment" several times to the press, who were being held behind the cordon by uniformed officers. "Bloody vultures," he grumbled, opening the driver's door and slumping in his seat. "Sell their mothers for a story, most of them."

"Why would anyone want that job?" Packard closed his door and fastened his seat belt.

Coates started the engine. "I've no idea, but most of them would offer out their own mothers. Anything for a story." With the car in gear, he glanced over at his passenger. "Right, let's go find out who our victim is."

2

Friday nights at The Starfish Pub on Bondi Beach were always packed. It may have been the fourth of January, but that didn't stop everyone coming out en masse. Amelia Thomas, having trouble hearing what her friends Georgina and Isla were talking about, gave up. Sat on the last outside table overlooking the sand, she had no clue how they'd managed to snag it. "What are you having?"

A waiter stood by their table holding a handheld till device. Isla ordered a daiquiri, which she contemplated, then decided on a pina colada. Georgina followed her lead, which was unusual; Amelia normally followed Georgina. When the server sauntered off, she sat back and took in the atmosphere, fanning herself. A stunning night, the temperature still in the high teens, the music played from a speaker right next to them. The drinkers out, groups of girls and guys, the majority youngsters in their early-to-mid twenties, Amelia enjoyed the ambience.

With Georgina and Isla busy chatting, Amelia took in the scenery. It annoyed her how Georgina glowed in whatever she wore. Hell, she could give her best friend a sack to wear, and by the end of the night, a couple of thousand people would be wearing one. At Darlinghurst Grammar the girls had mostly followed Georgina, and the boys had wanted to... She tried not to think about it. The number of blokes she'd liked over the years who'd fallen madly and deeply in love with her best friend insulted her. "Thank you," she shouted to the member of staff when he dropped off their cocktails.

Isla, stunning in a low-cut white top and short skirt, interrupted her conversation with Georgina to answer a call. Amelia smiled at Georgina, who went into her bag and pulled out a flyer. "What's this?"

"Which dates can you make?"

"Don't tell anyone, but I'm easy," she quipped, the straw still in her mouth. "I can definitely make the Corona Open in Queensland on 26th March." She read further on. "And the Rip Curl Pro on Bells in April; I can make that, too. Not sure about Margaret River, though; I'll get back to you on that."

"We'll run through them when I've got my diary with me." Georgina, whose skin was annoyingly perfect, not a blemish in sight, was excited. "We're going to have such a blast. I can't wait for Honolua Bay at the end of November. I'm going to wipe Carissa out."

When Georgina laughed, Amelia did too. Her friend didn't possess a bad bone in her body. Georgina could trash talk with the best of them, but she didn't own the killer instinct to win the World Surf League. If Amelia thought for one second Georgina might one day be champion... Well, she wouldn't be socialising with her now. No, Georgina would make money from smaller sponsors and fashion labels, but she would never make the big time.

"The boys are buying drinks." Isla covered the mouthpiece of her mobile. "Are you two all right, or do you fancy another?" She nodded and ordered another round. "Are you going to the Corona Open?" she asked Amelia.

"I reckon! Wouldn't miss the start of the season."

She let Isla take over the conversation, knowing that Kereama, Amelia's boyfriend, was on his way over. Sometimes jealousy of Georgina and Isla took over; they were both talented in their own ways: Georgina being a good surfer and Isla a well-known bodybuilder. Isla had won competitions and, being in a relationship with Oliver King, had solidified her fame – the weightlifters' version of Posh and Becks. Where was her talent? Sure, she could sunbathe, and she wore clothes well, which had secured her a large fan base and three lucrative promotional contracts, but sometimes she wished she could do something better than anyone else. Still, at least she didn't need to work. She made money just by snapping pictures of herself wearing her clobber – especially bikinis – and uploading them to the Chatter app. None of that mattered, not when she had the most gorgeous guy.

A couple of guys approached their table, young, in their late teens or early twenties. The taller fella pulled out a notepad and asked Georgina for her autograph, handing her a pen. Georgina obliged, signing her name, and thanked them for their support. Amelia desired that level of fame; she wanted people to recognise her and ask her to sign whatever they offered her. When her best friend turned back to her, she smiled and slurped the remains of her pina colada through her straw, as the boys arrived carrying their drinks. "Hey!" she said, budging over and letting Kereama sit next to her.

Kereama Tua was a Kiwi, half-Maori, half-white, with long dark hair and a physique other guys would die for. He played guitar in a heavy metal band. Having finished touring only last month, Amelia was looking forward to having him around for a while. And he was the best-looking of all their boyfriends; she thought so anyway. She kissed him in greeting, noting that Georgina looked uncomfortable, left out – Shane wasn't with their guys. Sorry for her surfer friend, Amelia broke away from Kereama and picked up her second pina colada, sticking her new straw in her mouth.

"Where is he?" Kereama asked. "He not out tonight?"

"On his way." Georgina looked around for him.

"There he is." Amelia pointed to the bar.

When Georgina found him, she rose from her chair and thanked her. "No, wait! Your..." Too late, Georgina hightailed it through the throng of drinkers. "Phone." Amelia picked up the mobile and held it for safekeeping.

"Let's see that." Isla's boyfriend, Oliver, reached across and snatched Georgina's mobile out of Amelia's hand. "Cheers!" He grinned, his big slab hand in danger of crushing the flimsy phone. "Bloody hell! She's up to two and a half million followers, mate."

"George gets most of hers through her modelling, not surfing," Amelia reminded him. While Georgina was a famous surfer, the majority of her fans came through her sense of style. "Come on, give it to me. She'll kill me if she knows you've got it."

"Yeah, give it back, Oli." Isla attempted to grab the phone.

Holding it higher than his girlfriend could reach, Oliver winked at Kereama. "Shall we take a look at her messages? I wonder what drongos are following her on here."

Oliver's arms were super toned, his biceps firm and appealing; he was muscular in an attractive way, rather than looking like a balloon about to burst. "Go on, then," she said, giving the go-ahead. She could see Georgina talking to Shane.

"Check out this galah." Oliver chuckled, turning the phone around to show her the account photo of a guy calling himself Elf Man. "Just what I thought, so ugly he can't even upload a picture. Just some stupid snap of a dog."

Amelia shuddered, thinking that Georgina had followers out

there who hid themselves, never posting photos of their faces. "Ew, creepy," Amelia said, feeling sorry for her best friend.

"Do we know anywhere cool for him to visit while he's over here?" Oliver leaned forwards when Kereama beckoned him with his finger.

"Here's as good a place as any, I reckon," Kereama said.

Amelia didn't like where the conversation was going. "No way! Uh-uh! Give it back, Oli." She lunged across the table, trying to snatch the phone. When he rose from his chair and held it too high, she gave up. "You know better than messing with followers."

Oliver perched on the edge of his seat, getting ready to reply. "He could be some sick stalker, you know."

"Behave! He's a pom. He ain't coming over here. He's probably lying in bed cracking a fat one over a picture of George as we speak. Relax! It's a bit of a laugh, that's all."

Amelia sucked on her straw, watching as Oliver typed the text. "Please don't send anything."

"You should come visit us when you're over." Oliver read his handiwork out loud, impressed with himself. "Two hearts, one with an arrow through it." He showed her and pressed "Send". "Too late now, ladies, done."

Isla gave her a look: not happy. Before he could do any more damage, Amelia grabbed the phone from him and hid it in her bag. Oliver grinned, trying to tickle Isla into smiling for him. Kereama put his arm around her.

3

Amelia checked that Georgina was still with Shane when she felt the mobile vibrate in her bag. Her friend was safely wrapped in Shane's arms, talking to another couple Amelia didn't recognise. With trepidation, she took out the phone and saw a message on Chatter from the pom. "Shit!" She opened the app.

"What is it?" Isla leaned over the table towards her.

"Oh brilliant!" Amelia held up the mobile for Oliver. "Nice one, mate. He's just bought flights. This thing's coming here, to this pub." She watched Oliver's face drop.

"Give me that." He grabbed the phone. "I thought he was some pommie drongo. How was I supposed to know this guy would go and buy bloody plane tickets?" He handed her back the phone. "And first class, too."

What was she going to do now? As soon as Georgina took her mobile back, she would guess they'd been playing silly buggers. "I'm going to go tell her," Amelia said, making to leave, when Kereama's strong arm pulled her back. "What? I have to."

"Chill, honey, he's messing with us. He's taken a photo of a boarding pass. He's not coming here to meet George. He's guessed someone's fucking with him, and now he's getting his own back, right, mate?" Kereama asked Oliver.

"I don't know." Oliver shrugged. "Looked genuine to me; it even showed the cost. If it's real, this weirdo's just paid four grand."

Why had she let Oliver send the first message? It wasn't normal for someone to pay for flights on a whim like that; he'd spent a fortune on the trip, although Elf Man might be loaded, she thought. And that made her think: he might be the nicest guy in the world. Then again, he might be a bunny-boiling psychopath. "Come on, Isla, let's go give her the bad news."

To Amelia's surprise, Isla remained sat in her chair. "I'm not telling her," Isla replied, putting her arm around Oliver. "And besides, I agree with Kereama. He's screwing with us. He's not really flying over here, so all this bullshit is exactly that, shit. Tell George there's nothing to obsess about."

"And if he does come here, so what?" Oliver added. "He gives us any shit..." He punched the palm of his other hand. "Between Shane, Kereama and me, we don't have anything to worry about."

"I hope you're right." She sat back down. "I've got a feeling he's going to be trouble." Trying to take her mind off the situation, Amelia picked up her cocktail and took a sip through her straw. She was going to get such a mouthful from Georgina when she asked for her phone back.

"Trust me, he's over there laughing at us." Kereama winked. "So, stop worrying and relax. Guys, are we here to have a good time, or what?" He leaned over and kissed her, licking his lips, feigning he was stealing her drink. "Mmm, pineapple."

Amelia sat there, listening to Isla and the lads talking about a new nightclub opening in town, called Fever. With a great Oxford Street address, the club's online brochure guaranteed a vibrant atmosphere, catering to both older and newer tastes with its myriad of rooms dedicated to varying types of music. Fever also promised the best in live bands which was far more up her alley. Georgina had been sent ten VIP tickets through the post, so they were all going next Friday. "Oh shit! She's coming back." She watched Georgina saunter over, holding Shane's hand.

"Hey, guys!" Georgina said, sitting down.

Shane shook hands with Oliver and Kereama. So far, so good, Amelia thought, hoping Georgina forgot about her phone. When her best friend went into her bag, Amelia brought out her mobile and handed it over. "You left it," she said, smiling, praying Georgina couldn't see the guilt.

Pretending to listen to her friends, she waited for Georgina to view the messages, knowing her friend would go straight for her favourite app.

4

"What the fuck?" Georgina read the messages on her Chatter account, she couldn't understand what happened. "Who's Elf Man? Amelia?" Her friend wouldn't look her in the eye. "Isla? Who's Elf Man?"

The photo of his plane ticket worried her the most. His words and pictures smacked of desperation. Georgina had had her fair share of stalkers, her latest was sectioned at the Seven Hills Clinic. The unstable Sydney local had broken into her home, ransacked her bedroom and filmed himself wearing her underwear. Dread crept in her gut when she went through Elf Man's account. "Here," she said to Shane, who took her phone. "He's anonymous. No photos."

"The hell are you playing at, mate?" Shane hissed at Oliver.

"What? Why do you immediately assume it was me?" Oliver asked.

"After what happened a couple of years ago, you go and do this?" He shook his head in disgust while scrolling through the messages Oliver sent. "Why the hell didn't you two stop him? Isla, I've seen you pull the whip out on him before. Why didn't you take the phone off him? For fuck's sake, this guy's a freak."

The rest of her so-called friends kept their gazes southward. "Thanks a lot, guys," she added. "I thought you had my back."

"Come on, George, Oli was having a laugh." Kereama shrugged. "Anyway, he's not coming over here. He's yanking your chain, trying to put the wind up you. So, stop worrying."

"Just having a laugh?" she repeated. "Would you be laughing if I started messing about with one of your band's fans, huh? If I imitated you and told some random fan you'd meet them, would you find that funny?" No, he bloody wouldn't, she thought, anger bubbling to the surface. Kereama was so serious about his band and fan base, he would spit out his dummy if the tables were turned. He bowed his head. "Yeah, that's what I thought. What the hell happens now? He says he's coming here on Monday night."

"He's not," Oliver reiterated, his tone bored. "George, I'm sorry, all right? I shouldn't have done it. I wasn't thinking. There's no way some weirdo pom's going to fly all the way over here just to see you. I mean don't get me wrong, you're great and all that, but you're not worth a thirty-five-hour journey."

"Gee, thanks, I think." A backhanded compliment was more than she usually received from Oliver, a guy well known for his piss-taking. "You really don't think he's coming?"

"The ticket's real enough," Shane interjected, handing her phone back. "If he does, we'll tackle it."

"You never know, he might be a cool bloke." Amelia lowered her gaze.

"This is getting boring now." Kereama stood, turned to Georgina and said, "He's not coming here, George, believe me. He's fucking with us, probably laughing his head off as we speak. So, let's forget all about it and get drinking. Who's up for another?" He took orders from everyone.

Sitting down next to Shane, she exited out of the app and put her phone in her bag. Trying to put it out of her mind, she listened to Oliver, Isla and Amelia talking and laughing. Giving up, she wanted to see what Elf Man looked like. "Shall I message him?"

"What're you going to ask him? Are you a psycho?" Shane eyed her.

"No!" Georgina replied, oozing sarcasm. "I was going to ask him to post a picture. At least we'll recognise him if he does turn up." She thought the idea was good. "What do you reckon? I could tell him the truth."

She was taken aback when he said, "No way! You're not telling him it was a prank. If he finds out it's all a big joke, God knows what he'll do. Yes, ask him to upload a selfie; it'll be handy to know what he looks like."

5

"All that worrying for nothing," Amelia said, relieved. "He's gorgeous. You might thank Oli for pranking him one day."

Georgina chuckled, the expression on Shane's face a picture. "Aw, don't worry, baby, I'm not replacing you," she teased, ruffling his hair in a playful manner. A weight off – knowing the pom wasn't some freaky stalker guy – she started to relax. "Thanks," she said to Amelia's boyfriend, who placed her drink in front of her. "This is him." She held up her phone for him to see. "Elf Man."

"Yeah, and I'm a champion surfer." Kereama sat next to Amelia. "That ain't Elf Man. I'll put my shortboard on it, mate."

Staring at the picture of the Brit, the thought her Chatter follower might be lying hadn't even occurred to her, that the photo was fake; her new-found relief was suddenly replaced with dread. She heard the girls arguing with him, telling her the picture was genuine, but she didn't believe them.

"You think just because he's good-looking he can't be a psycho?" Kereama said. "Course he can. Not that it matters, because that isn't Elf Man in that photo."

A warm breeze blew Georgina's hair over her face. She leaned across and whispered in Shane's ear, "I think I'm going to go home. I'm not feeling it tonight and I've got an early shoot tomorrow morning." Was she overreacting about this Elf Man thing? Her friends should know how fragile she was after her last stalker managed to enter her home, rummage through her drawers and slip into her underwear. It may have been two years earlier, but they shouldn't be behaving like this.

"Do you want me to come with you?" Shane asked, making to move.

"No, you stay put." She stood and looked down at him. "I'm tired anyway and I'm not great company tonight." She said goodbye to Amelia and Isla, kissing both cheeks, then kissed Kereama on his cheek, leaving Oliver out. When he complained, she turned her back on him jovially, making sure he knew she was angry with him, but not entirely. And as she walked away, Shane chastised Isla's other half, who defended himself with the best of them.

Heading towards the car park, she passed the lifeguard tower and graffiti wall, arriving at her red open-top Jeep in front of Bondi Beach Park. She could hear all the fun in the distance; all the talking, laughter and music blaring out of speakers at Lush, The Bucket List, The Starfish and The Blue Room. If she were honest, she didn't feel like drinking, not because of Elf Man; she hadn't wanted to go out to begin with.

Georgina led a charmed existence. Driving home via Warner's Avenue and Blair Street, she told herself off for being down. She knew millions of girls would kill to lead her life, to look like her, and to be Shane Daley's girlfriend. She appreciated growing up in such a beautiful city with so many magnificent beaches. Sydney was the most amazing place to live.

Cruising along Balfour Road, she thought about how fortunate she was. Her dad had been a professional surfer in his day, which of course had rubbed off on her. Watching him riding those waves romanticised the ocean for her. From the age of five, she'd grown obsessed with the sea, devouring book after book on the subject. On her eighth birthday, her parents bought her a surfboard... And from her first lesson she lived and breathed surfing. She could remember ripping her first wave, that moment of elation.

Catching her first barrel was the biggest rush, even better than sex. Oh, and skydiving topped everything. The first time she'd jumped out of a perfectly good aeroplane, her heart felt like it wanted to leap out of her mouth. The anticipation worse than jumping, once out, falling was exhilarating; she would recommend skydiving to anyone willing to listen. She and Shane loved it so much, they invested in their own diving packs.

Driving along the tree-lined O'Sullivan Road, Georgina put on her favourite heavy metal band, The Deranged. Kereama's group had a bust-up with them, so she had to beg Isla and Amelia to go with her last time. Of course, they'd had heaps of fun.

Fifteen minutes after leaving Bondi Beach, Georgina arrived outside the gates to her house in Point Piper. She was lucky enough to call Wolseley Road her address. Her four-bedroomed home sat next door but one to the Royal Prince Edward Yacht Club, and backed onto Lady Bennett's Beach. A beautiful home, its location was only one draw: its eight-foot perimeter wall also drew her to it. After the breach at their last home, she and Shane wanted greater security.

Pressing a button on her key ring, the gates whirred to life, opening automatically. Georgina drove through and watched them close. Satisfied, she parked outside the house. Then she picked up her shopping bags from the rear seat.

Inside her fabulous house, she closed the door and used voice activation to secure the alarm, always the first thing she did when returning home alone. Once safe, she walked through the hallway and upstairs to the lounge/dining room and kitchen. Four bedrooms were on the second floor, along with two bathrooms and the gymnasium, while the ground floor consisted of another bathroom, a library and her hobby room. In the basement, she and Shane had built a home cinema and games room, complete with full-sized pool table and bar.

In the lounge on the first floor, she ordered the blinds to close, and they obeyed, the whirring her signal it was safe to walk in front of the glass walls. She loved the glasshouse style in the daytime, but when dark outside, she couldn't see through the glass; she could only view her reflection. It creeped her out, so she made sure the blinds were pulled before she entered the room.

Placing her bags on the tabletop, she walked upstairs to her bedroom and unhooked her dressing gown from the back of the door. Shedding her clothes, she wrapped herself up in her soft, comfortable robe and went back downstairs. The lounge messy, she tutted, knowing she and Shane had deliveries from contracts to put away.

She had signed several contracts with clothing designers. All Georgina had to do was wear something sent to her, upload a picture to Chatter and tag the company in. They gave her a promotional code to give her followers, so when her fans bought something, she received royalties. And her top two contracts alone brought her thousands of dollars each month, not to mention her sponsorship deal with Ripped Energy Drink, who she was shooting for in the morning. Ripped were her biggest contract by far.

Diving into her bags, she pulled out a stunning dark blue and white bikini she had earmarked for the next day's shoot. Hanging the top in front of her chest, the mirror told her it was as sexy as she hoped. The air con worked better than it should, so she ordered the thermostat to warm up a little, taking the temperature up to twenty degrees.

After yawning, Georgina decided it was time for bed. Upstairs, after brushing her teeth, she dropped the gown on the floor and climbed under the sheet, getting comfortable with her mobile. It was routine to catch up with her friends' activities on Chatter before sleeping. She smiled, scrolling through her mates' pictures, liking them all, commenting on some. Amelia's page showed a photo from earlier in the evening at Lush: a lovely picture of the three of them. Not being a fan of Twitter, she preferred to "cheep" on Chatter, rather than Tweet on Twitter. She liked the "cheep", and commented, "My bitches".

Georgina didn't know why – she enjoyed catching up with her friends – but she thought about Monday night, possibly meeting Elf Man and she shuddered. Knowing the photo the Brit sent was a fake creeped her out. Did she really have some whacker pom flying all the way over here? She shivered again, knowing she wouldn't be able to sleep until Shane returned home later.

6

It was approaching half five and the police headquarters in Lewes was busy gearing up for yet another Friday night bonanza. DI Coates didn't need to worry about policing boozy nights these days; his worries were far more serious. Instead of controlling pubs, nightclubs and the like, he looked after violent offenders, murderers and rapists. A gruesome job, but someone had to do it.

A number of his colleagues in the office were sat behind desks. Paperwork was an unfortunate necessity of police work. Coates hated the bureaucracy. His monitor displayed a missing persons file; he clicked on his mouse and switched to another folder. "I really thought we'd get lucky on this." Sergeant Packard sat next to him, staring at his screen. "How come no one's worried about her?"

"She might be a prostitute," his sergeant suggested.

"Yeah, I thought that, but even working girls are missed by someone." He clicked another file. "If she was killed a couple of days ago, her family might not have tried contacting her, I guess." He sat back in his chair and rubbed his eyes. Sleep had been elusive the previous night. Focusing on the screen, he asked, "Any luck on the tattoo?"

"I'm running some names now," Packard replied. "My contact at Wozz's remembers doing several hummingbirds. He emailed me the files, which I've sifted through. Two stood out, but photos weren't included."

"We need a break on this one." Coates sighed at the thought of wading through yet more reports. At least he had dinner with his wife, Ellie, to look forward to at The Snowdrop Inn on South Street. The expense was worth every penny.

"I think we might have a match," Packard said, turning his monitor slightly. "Tara Henson, twenty-nine from right here in Lewes. Picked up for solicitation in 2009, charged and sentenced to a hundred and fifty hours of community service, which she carried out. Since then, nothing."

"Well done," Coates said, studying the screen. Holding up a crime scene photo – the likeness spot-on for Tara, although official identification required next of kin, he regarded his partner. "Where does her family live?"

Packard scrolled down. "South Malling, The Meadows. Nice houses in that neck of the woods." There was a brief pause. "Kind of makes you wonder how she got into tricking, huh? If she grew up on that estate, well, opportunity's never far away. Why start selling herself?"

Coates stood and grabbed his suit jacket. "Let's go and find out, shall we?" Discovering the identity of the victim was a huge part of any investigation, whereupon further findings stemmed. They would have an idea of who murdered her, he had faith. "Call through and get a couple of uniforms to meet us there, would you?"

"On it, sir." Packard picked up his desk phone.

While checking he had everything, Coates lifted his own landline phone when it rang. Hoping the coroner, Patricia

Rollins, would be the voice on the other end, he said, "DI Coates," in greeting. Delighted to recognise her voice, he sat back on his seat. After exchanging pleasantries, he got down to business. "So, did you find any trace?"

"Lots. Your suspect, whoever he is, he's sloppy. I mean, we didn't just find semen; we found saliva, a bloody fingerprint, hair, and skin under the victim's fingernails. You name it, we got it!"

Coates had to breathe deep. With that amount of forensic evidence, a name had to surface, surely? "That's great news," he said, something dawning on him. "Although, it would make him either stupid–"

"Or he doesn't care," Rollins finished. "And I know which you'd prefer."

"Dumb every time. And when will we get the analysis back?" It was all very well knowing she'd found forensic evidence, receiving the results could take forever. "Please don't tell me a few days."

"I requested it be expedited. The lab's assured me you'll receive the report by close of play Monday, or Tuesday morning at the latest. I'm afraid we're not working in a perfect system here."

Not believing it would be that quick, Coates thanked her for pulling out all the stops. He could do a lot worse than have her on the case. "You're doing your best."

"How about you? Had any luck identifying the victim?"

"We think so. Gary found her through the tattoo. I drew a blank on the missing persons angle, which surprised me. Anyway, her name's Tara Henson, a local girl, who got mixed up in prostitution by the looks of it, although her parents live in South Malling. We're still trying to figure that one out."

"She could always be a runaway," Rollins said. "Rich girls

turn to tricking as well sometimes, you know, David. Drug abuse, falling in with a bad crowd."

He knew she was right. Interrupting her when Packard tapped his watch, he said his goodbyes, fumbled for his keys in his jacket pocket and walked with his partner through the open-plan office. "Are the uniforms en route?"

"Yes, sir. They'll be there when we arrive."

Coates always met officers in their blues and twos at the next of kin's home. He'd found, through experience, that the bad news came best from an officer in uniform, rather than a detective. So, he let them go in first, until the opportunity arose to commence their interview.

7

"All right, George, here's how the ad's going to go," Lottie, Commercial Director of Ripped Energy Drinks, said. "You're going to paddle out, then come back to shore. You're going to walk up the beach, drop your board and pick up this towel, slow and steady while the camera zooms in on the can in your bag. You're going to dry yourself off, before picking up the can and having a drink. I don't want you looking into the lens until you take a mouthful, all right? Great bikini, by the way; the camera's going to love you."

Not dissimilar to the dozen or so commercials shot for Ripped before, Georgina didn't mind, not when she received handsome payments. The company was only after her followship. Ripped hoped for ten per cent of her followers to buy, and with two and a half million of them, it paid to be nice to her. Georgina handed her phone to Amelia, who looked amazing in a pink bikini. "You know what to do," she said, letting go of her lifeline, her mobile.

Maximising her time and energy, while Ripped filmed her commercial, Amelia would be taking photos of her in her beachwear for a different contract, Foxy Surf Wear, one of

Georgina's favourite brands. She would tag Foxy in on her "cheep". And with the Foxy deal, she gave away a twenty-five per cent discount to her followers, the sales of which she received a percentage of.

This morning's activities – basically twenty minutes' work – would bring her thousands. Every fourth cheep she uploaded, Georgina donated the proceeds to one of her four chosen charities. She'd raised over seven-hundred and fifty-thousand dollars for the animal shelter near her home so far.

Picking up her shortboard, she walked along the sand to the water's edge, waded in and jumped on the board. Paddling out of her depth, she turned around, making sure the cameraman had started rolling. Holding her arm up, thumb extended, she waited for Lottie to give the green light, and made her way back in.

Hopping off her ride, up to her chin in water, she walked the rest of the way back to shore, where she strolled on the sand towards the camera, making a concerted effort not to stare at the lens, every movement she made designed to be alluring and sexy, every flex of her hips pronounced. Her followers expected inviting, so how could she deny them?

Reaching her towel, she bent over to pick it up. Georgina paused while the cameraman zoomed in on the can. Given the go-ahead, she picked it up and dried her wet hair, staring to the right of the lens. The camera lingered on her body, filming her up and down. When ready, the lens back on her face, she lifted the can. Opening it with a fizz, she took a big sip of the disgusting energy drink. On cue, she looked into the camera and smiled, taking another large sup.

"Absolutely stunning, George, as always. This is why we love working with you." Lottie clapped.

After the commercial director and her cameraman left, Georgina sat down on her towel next to Amelia and Isla, who were ready for a day on the beach, which she had promised them. She scrolled through the photos her friend had taken. Camp Cove Beach, Watson's Bay, was beautiful – breathtaking even – and the perfect backdrop to her photo. Georgina found the best picture and prepared a cheep, tagging Foxy Surf Wear and letting her followers obtain their discount. "Done," she said, pressing "Send". "Now we can get on with the rest of our day."

Approaching ten o'clock, the sun beamed down on them. Shane had made her feel better about Elf Man's possible visit earlier, giving her a more positive attitude. Hell, if he did turn up, her friends had her back. Between her boyfriend, Oliver and Kereama, she had nothing to worry about. Shane suggested bundling him into their ute, driving him up woop woop and leaving him out there alone. Although she'd been told not to, she still wanted to come clean with Elf Man, to tell him it was nothing more than a prank. "Where are the boys?"

"Trying to catch some surf," Isla said, the only non-surfer in the group. "Look at it! Flat as. What do they expect to get? I've seen bigger waves at the Icebergs."

The Bondi Icebergs, a swimming pool down the beach, which she and Isla used on a regular basis for fitness routines, didn't have a wave machine. Georgina chuckled at the lack of surf; it was so flat, the boys must've been using the time to chat and banter with one another. "Yeah, looks like a tanning day to me," she conceded. "I could use a down day."

Perfect! Twenty-four degrees at ten o'clock in the morning, meant it would easily make the early-to-mid thirties by two. She and her crew would sunbathe, swim, talk and have a laugh all morning, until one of them mentioned food. Then, they would all walk along Cove Street and Marine Parade until they came to Watson's Bay Boutique Hotel, where they would stop for lunch, and then go back to the beach for more sunbathing and shenanigans.

Georgina took a drink of water, watching the boys in the distance. They sat on their boards, chatting, not expecting any action. Shane, a total barney, was clueless on the board. He only tried to surf to keep her happy. He liked to think he could. In truth, he bailed at every opportunity, a no-no in her eyes.

There were no half-measures in surfing, which was why she'd wiped out so horrendously and publicly at the WSL tournament the previous year. The waves crashed down on her, forcing her to hold her breath until she couldn't anymore. In front of a rolling camera, an organiser-paid lifeguard resuscitated her. The humiliation almost unbearable – save for the support of her family, friends and followers – the only thought that kept her going was knowing she would go all the way this year.

Lying back, feeling the sun's heat, she closed her eyes, listening to the small waves lapping. It was a sound she loved. Georgina couldn't imagine living anywhere else in the world. Sydney was her home; it was where she felt safe. Sure, there were places she could envisage moving to, like Maui, but it didn't have what Sydney had to offer. But she would be going to Maui the next year. She was taking on Jaws, a surf break on Pe'ahi Beach known for its huge waves, where only the truly dedicated surfers went to test their mettle. Jaws was famous for throwing up eighty-foot barrels.

"Is that yours, George?" Amelia asked, shading her eyes with her hand.

The vibration made her rummage through her bag and pull out her phone. It was a message on Chatter. Just when she felt calmer about the Elf Man thing, he went and messaged her again. "Oh God! He's sent a picture of his empty suitcase," she told them. Her friends sat up, while she held her mobile out for them to see.

"I'm so excited about meeting you and your friends, I'm

packing now." Isla's expression fitted the occasion. "See you soon. He is one creepy dude, George. Even if he is good looking. What a desperado."

"I know, right?" Georgina read his message. "And you don't need to pretend. That's not his picture." She shuddered, just thinking about him in his bedroom, packing his suitcase. And then a nasty thought invaded her otherwise-glorious morning: she imagined him lying on his bed... That was enough! "Right, screw this," she said in defiance. "I'm putting an end to this here and now. I'm going to tell him it was all a prank. Yeah, I'm going to fess up and tell him it was a joke. I'll offer to refund his ticket."

The reaction she received from her girls startled her. Amelia snatched Georgina's mobile away from her, while Isla put her arms around her shoulders. "Hey!" Her best friend held the phone above her head. "Come on, Ames. Give it back!"

"Don't be so stupid, George," Isla snapped. "You can't go telling him that. He's already paid for the plane ticket. And most are non-refundable, remember?"

"And hotel, too, probably," Amelia added.

"Right, and hotel too. You don't want to piss off a guy like this, do you? He's flying all the way over here to meet you."

If she didn't know any better, Georgina might say Isla was enjoying this. "Erm, I realise that," she replied, sarcasm oozing over every word. "Why do you think I want to stop it?"

"Stop what?" Shane dropped his board next to her and dripped all over her on purpose. "Come on, tell me!" His smile faded.

"George wants to tell him it was a prank," Isla admitted. "And I'm telling her not to. You don't need to worry about this guy. But if you tell him it was a joke on him, there's no knowing how he'll react."

"Exactly," Shane agreed, bending down and stroking her cheek with his palm. "If he turns up, we'll sort him out. But odds are, he won't. If he does, we'll make him so awkward he won't want to come here again. So, please don't worry, we've got your back."

They were right; there was no telling how Elf Man would react. Even if this guy was persistent, she had Shane, Oliver and Kereama on her side, and a very tough Isla... Oh, and Amelia to a lesser extent.

8

Shane Daley felt the bed move. He heard Georgina's mobile vibrate a couple of minutes earlier. "I thought you'd be asleep by now." He stroked her thigh beneath the sheets, his eyes closed. "What's the time?" When he climbed the stairs to go to bed it'd been half two in the morning. The bed moved again.

"It's him." Georgina sounded nervous.

Bored of all the Elf Man talk, Shane rubbed his face in frustration. With a groan, he opened his eyes to find her staring at her phone. He didn't know why she fussed about it so much. The three of them would easily warn off some pom freak. "I keep telling you not to worry. What's he saying?"

Pulling himself up, Shane sat next to her. She passed him her mobile. Seeing the photo of his first-class seat inside a Qatar Airways flight made it all the more real. A part of him hoped Elf Man was all talk, trying to scare them. "This doesn't change anything, baby," he said, reading the message. "On my way, see you soon. He makes it sound threatening, I'll give him that."

"You all thought he was bluffing, right?" She bit her bottom lip. "He's the real deal, Shane."

"Like I've said before," he started, "this doesn't change

anything. Oli and Kereama will be with us at The Starfish later, so don't worry. The weirdo can't take us all on." Amelia's boyfriend was stacked. Oliver the same, and he could handle himself. If needed, he would call upon his teammates. "You've got to stop worrying about this, George. He's not going to get anywhere near you, all right?"

"You reckon?" She took her phone back and stared at the screen.

"Yeah, I do. Look, worst comes to worst, he's a weirdo. We take him out to the beach and beat the shit out of him. And that won't happen anyway. Most likely, he turns up, I have a word in his ear, and he fucks off. Either way, he's not getting anywhere near you, I promise." He wished she would listen to him. More than that, he hoped she would believe him. "Nothing bad's in your future, honey. You're safe, here with me."

Georgina relaxed.

"Come here, you," he said, wrapping his arms around her like the protective boyfriend. "I'm going to kill Oli," he whispered in her ear. "What was he thinking?"

"He probably didn't expect this guy to buy a plane ticket over here," Georgina insisted. "I don't blame him."

It was just like her not to think badly of Oliver. Instead of telling her so, Shane cuddled her tighter. "This will all be over soon, trust me. Then you can relax."

"Sounds awesome to me." She turned and hugged her face into his neck, her legs entwined with his.

On the one hand she was a strong woman in both mind and body, focused, dedicated. She knew what she wanted and always aimed high. Then, on the converse, he had to look after her. So dainty and delicate, he didn't trust her to defend herself physically. If she went up against a guy, he would destroy her. Isla could handle herself; hell, even he wouldn't go up against Isla. And he wouldn't bet against Amelia either. But not his

Georgina. "Let's try to get some sleep." His body relaxed, melting into the mattress.

From an early age, he'd held a football in his hands. Put there by his footy-mad dad and two footy-crazy older brothers, it came as no surprise to his family and friends that he should take to the sport. And while no one was surprised he lived the game, it shocked everyone when he was scouted at school for the Sydney Swans Under 19s, and none more so than he.

His star shone brightly within the academy. Tipped for stardom by several Swans coaches, his grades at school were his only downfall. The club made a strict policy that team members needed reasonable academic results, in addition to terrific outcomes on the pitch. By the time he'd taken his exams, the head coach had reached an agreement with his headteacher. Shane never found out what the deal stipulated, but by that point he didn't care, he was a fully-fledged member of the Sydney Swans team.

Shane felt like he'd acquired a lifetime of experience by the age of twenty-eight, having started playing for the Swans at eighteen. At twenty-five, he had been selected as captain, and for the past three years his warriors went into battle every week. This year he had no doubt he would take the Swans all the way to the top of the premiership of the AFL, having narrowly missed the number one spot back in 2016 against the Western Bulldogs.

Georgina moved out from his grasp and sat up in bed again. Shane rolled away from her, his eyes closed, drifting off.

Why couldn't she sleep? She kept fidgeting, preventing him from sleeping. With a sigh, he opened his eyes. Her expression told him that she'd done something. "What?" Intrigued by her wide, panic filled eyes, he frowned. "What is it?"

Concerned at her lack of a reply, he sat up and snatched her phone out of her hands. "What?" He read the text just sent to Elf

Man. "You bloody idiot!" His girlfriend had confessed everything, telling Elf Man the original message was a prank, a joke on him. "Why did you do that?" Shane jumped out of bed and paced the room, her phone in his hand still.

"I'm sorry! I had to," she said, in her own defence. "I hate to dupe him like this. I mean, you and Oli were talking about taking him out woop woop and leaving him there. We're better than this, Shane. Don't you get it? Now Elf Man won't come, and he won't be made fun of. It'll be a win-win for everyone this way."

"For fuck's sake, George, we were just fooling around. We wouldn't really do that to him." He was lying; he and Oliver discussed it at length with Kereama at the beach. "Shit, the worst we'd do is tell him to rack off."

Georgina didn't believe him, judging by her narrowed eyes. "You're kidding, right? And how is that any better than me telling him it was all a prank? At least this way he finds out while flying over here, and by the time he lands he'll have calmed down."

She had a point. Shane threw the phone on the bed and rubbed his fingers through his hair, as was his habit when he needed time to think. "Yeah? And it gives him more time to stew on it. Did you think about that before you messaged him? He's no doubt up there contemplating ways he can fuck with us."

"He hasn't replied yet," Georgina said, trying to change the conversation. "That's a good sign, right?"

"You reckon? He's either too pissed to reply, or he's taking his time thinking up the most suitable response." He wouldn't write a knee-jerk reply; he would wait until he had the best possible answer.

"Yeah, well, too late now." Georgina wrapped herself in her dressing gown. "He knows not to bother coming here later, doesn't he?"

"And I told you not to." After she stormed off downstairs, he sat on the bed and thought things through. Now that Elf Man, or whatever his name was, knew what was going on, one of two things would happen: either he would arrive at the airport and avoid The Starfish Pub, or he would still turn up. If he turned up, Shane couldn't say what would go down. Guys like Elf Man were unpredictable. But, he had backup, whereas Elf Man was alone. Shane didn't fancy the pom's chances. "George?" he shouted down the stairs. "I'm sorry! You took me by surprise, is all."

He found her crying on the sofa. Sat next to her, he put his arm around her and pulled her in for a hug. There was nothing worse to him than making her cry. "I apologise, all right? I didn't mean to shout."

"I just want it to be over," she said, hugging him tight. "I didn't ask for this."

"I know you didn't, baby." It was Oliver's bloody fault, Shane thought bitterly. The man couldn't help but cause shit everywhere he went. All Shane wanted was peace and quiet. He wanted to play footy, occasionally watch Georgina surf, come home and chill, in that order. Was it asking too much? He certainly didn't need this aggravation. "Come on, let's go back to bed," he suggested, stroking her cheek and staring into her big weepy dark brown eyes.

Georgina's phone vibrated on the coffee table in front of him.

Shane leaned forwards and picked it up. When he put in her entry number, he could see his girlfriend had received a Chatter message. Wanting to throw the damned mobile against the wall, he opened the app and accessed her messages, feeling Georgina's arm around his waist tighten. He didn't want to read it.

9

Oliver King lined up the black, pocketing it, leaving Kereama with four stripes left. After shaking hands with his opponent, he placed the cue on Shane's outdoor pool table, picked up his stubby and took a sip. Sunday evenings were his favourite; they were so relaxed, chilled. And driving over to Shane and Georgina's place for a barbecue was becoming routine because his host loved to show off his home. "I'm so getting me one of these," he said to Shane, who busied himself with grilling the beef burgers.

Oliver could afford to buy one. His only problem was space, and talking Isla into it. "You've got one indoors," he imagined Isla would say. That and "why do you need one in the garden?" An apt question. He didn't need one outside; he wanted one, and there was a big difference. Why should Shane have all the cool things? While he considered Georgina's boyfriend a mate, Oliver thought him a show-off, always playing the alpha male.

"They're ready." Using tongs to place the burgers on one plate, Shane surveyed his cooking. "George has the veggie options coming."

The backyard was massive, with a large L-shaped swimming

pool, decking with seating for more than twenty people in comfortable sofas and armchairs, a pool table and summer house that had been renovated and turned into a bar. Inside the outhouse, Shane had a marble surface and chrome draught beer taps. A huge poser, Oliver should like him, but he couldn't bring himself to. For Isla's sake, he made the effort.

Wearing a white vest and blue shorts, he walked over to the patio table and sat next to Isla, who looked amazing in a low-cut pink floral summer dress. It was short and showed off her shapely legs. Amelia wore a light skirt and strappy top, which suited her tanned skin, while Georgina carried over a plate of vegetarian burgers wearing a black dinner number. When he found himself thinking how gorgeous Georgina looked, he focused on her flat chest. Shane's girlfriend was very self-conscious about it, and Isla played on it sometimes, being well-endowed in that department.

Soft music entertained them while they ate, Shane's Bluetooth speaker sat in the centre of the table. Oliver put a cheese slice on his burger and squished the patty with the bun lid, salivating at the sight. "This smells amazing, Shane." He noted his host already had a mouthful.

Instead of replying, Shane smiled while chewing.

And it tasted as good as it smelled, the hand-pressed patties moist and juicy. Once the girls had constructed their veggie burgers, everyone sat in silence eating, enjoying the food and atmosphere. A glorious evening, the temperature still in the early twenties, Oliver devoured his meal.

It didn't help that Georgina and Shane threw their success in their faces. It was no secret that she was the most successful of the girls; she had two and a half million followers, and her surfing career. And Shane was hands down the more successful of the guys. Oliver felt a quiet satisfaction that Shane's leadership of the Sydney Swans had yet to prove fruitful. At the start of every season, he prayed Shane's team didn't pull off a win. Petty, but warranted.

Successful enough, having won a number of weightlifting competitions locally, Oliver was a name amongst his peer group, especially after making it to the final of Aussie Ninja Rules, the Australian version of the hit US show, American Ninja, which had contestants competing in an array of physically challenging obstacle courses. He performed well on the televised finale, placing second overall for the season. His followship grew dramatically after that, and a couple of clothing labels came knocking, asking him to model their lines.

In addition, going out with Isla had grown his popularity. Having started with only a few thousand followers prior to competing on the show, he finished up with eighty thousand. But he didn't make the hundred-thousand mark until he began dating Isla. Because she was the Queen of Lifters, she had garnered a huge following of a quarter of a million, but her fans were mainly horny guys, he noted, one night scrolling through them. She was a beautiful person, always smiling and brightening up whichever room she was in, so why wouldn't blokes find her sexy?

A relatively new relationship, he'd only met her nine months earlier, shortly after the show, and funnily enough she'd watched it. They socialised within the same group of friends, which made meeting one another almost inevitable. And when they did, wow!

"These are great, George." Isla spoke with a mouthful. A tiny piece of bun bread fell out and on the floor. "Oops! Sorry!" She giggled.

As much as he loved her, Isla could be such an embarrassment sometimes. Listening to the girls praise Georgina's choice of veggie burgers, Oliver munched on his homemade beef burger. In front of him, his mobile lit up and vibrated. Intrigued, he put his patty down on his plate, and wiped his hands before picking it up and checking who was contacting him. "No fucking way!" He opened his Chatter account. "The pom's messaging *me* now."

"What's he saying?" Amelia asked, placing her food on a napkin.

After opening the message, Oliver scrolled past the photo of Elf Man's plane seat and read aloud. "Quite the practical joker, huh! Feel good knowing you got me? I bet you're having a right laugh at me. Take a bow, Oli, your joke worked... I can't wait to meet you Monday night at The Starfish."

"Hang on, am I missing something here?" Kereama was confused.

"How does he know it's a prank?" Oliver glanced at everyone around the table in turn, starting with Isla, and finishing with Shane and Georgina. "And why does he think I did it?" It wouldn't be hard for someone to figure out he was the piss-taker of the group, he thought, as Shane and Georgina shared a glance. "What?" he asked his host. "Is there something you want to share with the rest of us, mate?"

"What you talking about? This pom's a whackadoo."

Georgina looked guilty, he noticed. "George? Is there anything you'd like to say? Why is this guy so sure I typed the message? And don't even think about lying to me."

Shane stood and glared down at him. "What the fuck did I just say? We don't know why he's saying this stuff. Don't try bullying George, mate."

"It seems a bit suspicious to me," Oliver replied, standing and glaring at Shane across the garden table. "And I saw the look you gave her. What aren't you telling us, George?" He spoke directly to Georgina because he knew it would wind her boyfriend up something awful.

He was forced back when Shane pushed him, hard. If they

were going to come to blows, he would destroy his host, no doubt. The footy captain may be fit, but Oliver was a professional weightlifter and brown belt kickboxer. Oliver took a deep breath, while his mouthy opponent stepped around the table.

"Babe, leave it," he heard Isla say, her voice scared.

"Shane, stop it," Georgina ordered. "Apologise to Oli. He's our guest."

"He's accusing us of something. You can't come to our house and accuse us of shit."

Ignoring his compunction to deck Shane, Oliver puffed his chest out and stepped towards his "mate". "I haven't accused you of anything. Have I, Isla? I just said funny how he's so sure I sent him the message." Oliver was close to Shane's nose. He noted Kereama sat eating his burger, smirking.

"He's guessing. Maybe he's thinking this is all too magical. Who out of all George's friends would be most likely to prank someone?"

Shane had a point. Elf Man could've been speculating, trying to get him to admit his involvement. Still, he saw an exchange between his hosts, a nervous glance from her. They knew more than they were letting on, for sure. "Let me see George's messages," Oliver said to Shane, who'd backed up a pace. "Come on, mate, if you're sure she's innocent, let me see her phone."

"If it'll get you boys back to the table, here." Georgina took her mobile off the table and walked it over to him. "Go through them if you want. I don't have anything to hide."

"Yeah," Shane said, "and you'll apologise after."

Going straight to Georgina's private inbox with Elf Man, Oliver scrolled through the messages, only finding the conversations he'd seen earlier. Shit! he said in his head, hating the fact he was wrong. There were no messages between the two that mentioned him. "Cool! Thanks." He handed the phone back.

"And? Are you going to apologise?"

"I'm sorry!" he mumbled, walking towards his seat. Their food was getting cold. When Shane asked him to repeat his apology louder, he did so, sitting back down. "The fuck are you smiling about?" he hissed at Kereama, who popped the last bite of his burger in his mouth. "You're such a Benny!"

"How pathetic you are. Look at you, getting all stressed over some sad, lonely pom on his way over here. He's just one guy. Why are you all so tense? If he turns up at the pub tomorrow night, we'll beat the shit out of him. He won't come back for seconds, believe me. So, stop worrying and relax, would you?"

"I agree," Amelia said, sat next to Kereama. "Can we please finish our meals? Let's not spoil this gorgeous night, eh!"

Isla's hand squeezed his leg, supporting him. "You're right, *Kerry*," Oliver said, seeing the flash of anger in Kereama's eyes. The Maori hated his nickname, preferring to be called Kay. Kerry was a girl's name. "We'll see him off tomorrow night."

10

"You could've tried harder with Shane," Isla Kelly said, rubbing moisturiser into her cheeks in front of the mirror above her bathroom's sink, "is all I'm saying. I know you don't like him, but you could at least try for me." Her boyfriend and Georgina's boyfriend had almost come to blows a couple of weeks earlier. They'd nearly decked each other when Shane took umbrage at the way Oliver ribbed him about his captaincy record with the Sydney Swans.

"Hey, you didn't see the look they shared, babe." Oliver's voice came from the bedroom. "They know more than they let on."

"She showed you her messages." Isla picked up her toothbrush and squeezed a blob of paste on it. "She hasn't been messaging that weirdo pommie." While brushing her teeth, Oliver grumbled to himself. After spitting out the toothpaste, she walked out of the bathroom in only her long white Ramones T-shirt, to find him lying on the bed in his undies. He had his eyes closed. "Please make more of an effort," she pleaded, getting under the sheet, the air con whirring in the background. "I can't be worrying about this shit every time we meet them.

George and I have been friends for years. I'm not going to sacrifice that for anyone."

"And you don't have to," Oliver replied, his eyes still closed. "You have *your* friends, I can choose *mine*. There's no reason we have to mingle with each other's."

"That's the stupidest thing I've ever heard." She reached across and picked up her tub of CBD jellies. "I don't know why you can't ignore him when he's acting like a moron." The sweets were a godsend, her way of coping with the everyday stresses of life. Delicious. Strawberry flavour. Probably psychological, but when she lay back, her head on her pillow, sucking on the jelly, she swore she felt more relaxed. Except she couldn't be, because it took a good twenty-five minutes for the CBD to take effect. "Want one?" She held out the tub for him. "Suit yourself." She replaced the lid and returned the container to its original position, behind her bedside lamp.

Watching her friends going to work while she headed for her favourite place in the whole world – the gym – seemed unfair, not that she complained. Isla loved the smell, the atmosphere; she enjoyed helping members with their workouts, especially the newbies. Having devoted her entire adult life to building her body, she was now in a position to help others do the same.

Ever since joining Dolly's gym on Macquarie Street when only fifteen, it was a second home. Starting with three sessions a week, Monday, Wednesday and Friday, it was clear to her trainer that she had a spark, a dedication found in few people. Totally dedicated to chiselling the perfect body, Isla became one of the gym's most prolific and talented lifters. She still had the "before" images of her less than impressive fifteen-year-old body, which she often used to show prospective members when showing them around. "Look what you can achieve, if you focus and dedicate yourself," she would say, relishing their awe, as they checked her out now, compared to her younger image in the photo.

At twenty-three, Isla had opened her first Chatter account with only a hundred or so followers, mainly friends and family. Deciding to make it a mixture of her own personal and business blog, where she would cheep about her workouts at Dolly's, it soon became clear to the gym's owner that she was doing something right; their membership almost doubled in three years, and Isla's following went from a couple of hundred to fifty-thousand. Dolly quickly offered her a job as a personal trainer and her book filled inside two weeks.

So, while her friends – not Georgina or Amelia – drove to their offices, or wherever they worked, she was there at Dolly's helping members to improve their bodies, minds and spirits with her own blend of championing, and she did it well. So well, in fact, that only the previous year, the gym owner asked her to set up Gym Dollies, a group of fitness-obsessed models who would help attract visitors to Dolly's in Perth, Adelaide, Melbourne, Brisbane and Darwin through their own Chatter TV show. And Isla accepted the offer with a verve.

She spent a year garnering a following for The Gym Dollies series from a few hundred to over three hundred thousand and growing every day. By the next year, she hoped The Dollies would have a huge fan base. People were crying out for a group of six gorgeous, physically fit and toned health fanatics to show them how to work out.

Her five fellow Dollies were as dedicated to fitness as she was, yet they all followed her lead, no backchat, no disrespecting. In addition to her career as a training instructor, Isla modelled for a couple of gym wear labels, and a manufacturer of equipment. The three contracts were worth over half a million dollars a year. These deals, combined with her healthy salary from Dolly's, and Oliver's income had allowed her and Oliver to buy their four-bedroomed home in Darling Point.

And then there was her CBD jelly contract, which she signed only a couple of months earlier. All she had to do for that was take a photo of herself with a pot of jellies, and inform her following of the health benefits of taking controlled amounts of CBD. Easy peasy. Every month she earned royalties from her sales.

Oliver started heavy breathing, which meant one thing: snoring. Sighing, Isla reached for her ear plugs, when her phone vibrated. Always curious, even at one o'clock in the morning, she checked: Elf Man. "Shit!" she muttered. "Oli!" She shook him until he groaned himself awake.

"What?" he asked, sitting up, yawning.

"He's messaging *me* now," she said, waiting for him to rub his eyes. Once satisfied he was with her, she opened the message on Chatter. "I expect this from the boys, but I expected more from you," she read out, her voice almost quivering. "You disappoint me." There was no liking that comment; it had threatening tones. *Leave us alone*, she typed. *No one wants you here. It was just a joke.*

"You're not sending that, are you?"

"Huh? Why not? It's true." But maybe he was right. Should she reword her response? She didn't want to meet this guy. If she told him the truth, he might back off, she thought, her finger poised over the "Send" button. "Shall I?" she asked Oliver, who was making no attempt to prevent her.

"You decide," he said, no help at all.

And with that, she pressed "Send", immediately regretting it and going to the edit message icon. "Oh shit!" She panicked, remembering that Chatter users could only alter messages started by them. She launched the phone across the room, feeling Oliver's hands massaging her shoulders, followed by his lips on her neck.

"You're so tense," he said, helping her to lie back.

"Of course I am. We're being stalked by some nutty pom." One minute she thought it funny that Elf Man was some saddo, and then she panicked, knowing that he was flying all the way over here from the UK. This wasn't some pathetic loser; he had a tone to him that frightened her.

"It'll be fine, babe." Oliver kissed her neck. "Kerry's right. There are six of us and only one of him. If he tries anything, we'll beat the shit out of him, okay?"

Starting to relax, she let thoughts of Elf Man fade away. And just as she was forgetting their visitor, her phone vibrated over the other side of the room. Trying to forget it, she let Oliver kiss her lips, then pushed him away. "He's replied," she said, getting up and walking over to her mobile. Isla read out the message, "You've just made the biggest mistake."

11

Kereama Tua loved watching his girlfriend; he could watch her for hours. Other guys enjoyed ogling her, too. And why wouldn't they? She was stunning, with long slim legs, a deep tan and a size-six figure other girls would kill for. He adored her smile the most. When he had met her for the first time, at one of his band's gigs, her lips had attracted him first.

Amelia emerged from the sea, walking past a couple of groups of guys, who eyed her with interest; Kereama could tell by the way their heads followed her as she walked on by. She looked amazing in a white bikini, her dark brown skin contrasting with it in the best possible way. "Here," he said, getting up from his towel, picking hers up and wrapping it around her. Some of the guys were still watching. For good measure, Kereama kissed her, opening one eye to scoff silently at their jealous expressions.

After she dried herself, Amelia asked him to rub sun lotion on her back, which he agreed to, gently stroking it in, as she lay on her front. A couple of guys stared at her, walking past them. Kereama made his feelings known with a narrowing of his eyes. They averted their gaze, his muscular frame imposing to the lanky youngsters. They could be two of her huge following.

As Amelia lay on her front, the straps of her top detached, he sat up and watched the comings and goings of Manly Beach. A blistering day, easily in the mid-thirties, a blonde and a brunette, both lovely-looking, walked past him. The blonde's eyes met his and he held her stare until she had strolled past, but not before she gave him the cutest smile. Variety was the spice of a lasting relationship, so long as *she* didn't find out, he thought, watching the brunette's rhythmic hips.

Playing in a band had its pluses, especially on tour. On his last Australia and New Zealand tour, Kereama found a groupie at every gig, and he was often spoilt for choice. These girls threw themselves at him. Who was he to deny them?

He couldn't have Amelia finding out. Having been together for three years, he'd been with her since before the record label signed his band, before his group started making any real money. If he split with Amelia now, he wouldn't trust a new girlfriend. And he was going to be wealthy in a few years. He didn't want that headache in his life; he wanted to focus on his music. Besides, he liked Amelia well enough; he just didn't love her. She let him do his own thing. "You hungry?" he asked her, his stomach growling. "The Pantry's open."

The Pantry, his favourite beachside restaurant, was getting busy with breakfast diners. Great for traditional Aussie fare, the kitchen catered to his tastes, the finest establishment on Manly Beach. Amelia failed to acknowledge him; instead, she lay on her front soaking up the morning rays. "Hello? Ames? Are you hungry, or not?"

"Not yet, babe. Maybe in an hour, or so."

He could wait, he thought, lying back, his shades shielding his eyes from the glare of the sun. Not a cloud in the sky, and it promised to remain clear all day. His band, The Savage Seeds, had struck lucky – a label scout had spotted them at a gig in Queensland little over a year earlier. Since signing, they'd released their first full album, and had completed their first tour, which had earned his group a small fortune, but, of course, had to be split equally five ways. While not millionaires yet, his and Amelia's combined income was enough to allow them to buy a three-bedroomed place on Darling Point. The main drawback: they were only a short walk away from Isla and Oliver.

They were such tools, he thought, smirking at the memory of Oliver and Shane almost coming to blows the previous night. He rooted for them to brawl, and his money was on Isla's boyfriend to win. Shane, a show-off, stood no chance against Oliver in a fight. He thought Isla's boyfriend a puffed up... buffoon. Yeah, buffoon described him well.

He tolerated Shane and Oliver for one reason: Amelia. Although he didn't love her, she was the closest he'd come to loving someone. He'd moved in with her, so that showed some commitment at least. No, too naturally selfish to fully commit to someone, anyone, Kereama knew it was a failing of his, not hers. He couldn't ever imagine being happy with one woman. He was on borrowed time with Amelia. He would continue tasting new flavours while she knew nothing of his indiscretions.

Shade made him open his eyes. Lying on his back, he looked up and stared at a tall, skinny guy staring down at his girlfriend, checking out her arse. Sitting up, Kereama grabbed his phone. "Here, use this to take a picture, mate," he said, holding it up. "It'll last longer." He stood and glared at the blond grommit, who turned away, laughed, and carried on walking towards The Pantry. "Piece of shit! I'll kick your arse," he yelled up the beach.

"Kay, sit down." Amelia continued lying on her front. "You're embarrassing me."

"He was staring at your arse," he defended, glaring at the lanky grommit's back.

"So what? Guys stare at my arse every day. We've been going out long enough. You know that."

Calming his temper, he sat on his towel, resting his elbows on his knees, watching the surf. There were a couple of surfers on the line-up, waiting for the perfect set. She was right: he didn't care that guys checked her out. Why get bent out of shape now, he thought. "Sorry!"

Amelia got up and sat next to him, her sunglasses hiding her eyes. "What's up with you? Are you stressing about tonight?" She elbowed him playfully. "You are! You're aggro about meeting Elf Man."

"What? Pshh! Are you kidding? I haven't given that pom a second's thought." He hoped he didn't sound like he was lying to her. In reality, he thought about Elf Man a lot. What kind of guy went and bought a plane ticket to fly to meet someone they followed on Chatter? A nutter, that was who.

"So, why're you so stressy?" Amelia asked.

Nothing sprang to mind. "Band business, nothing major," he lied.

As she asked him to elaborate, his ringtone interrupted her. Seizing his chance to block her, he took his mobile out of his bag and entered his passcode.

"It's him, isn't it?" Amelia asked.

"Nah, don't panic." When he opened the app, Kereama saw the message was from the pom. "Nah, yeah," he confessed, turning the phone so that she could also see it then turned it back again. "Finally here," he read. "See you guys tonight. Can't wait!"

He was in Sydney. The photo uploaded with the message showed Kingsford Smith Airport terminal's front doors. There was something about this guy; Kereama couldn't put his finger on it. Oliver started all this, he should be the one sorting it, he thought. "Don't worry about all this, okay?" he said, squeezing her shoulder, the fear in her eyes hurting him. "Like I said yesterday, if he turns up, he won't be coming back for seconds."

His mobile ringtone told him he had a message: Oliver, asking if Elf Man had contacted him on Chatter. "Oli," he said to her, tapping his response. It didn't take long to receive a text from Shane as well. Then, he heard Amelia's phone's ringtone. It had to be one of the girls.

Kereama listened to his girlfriend talking to Georgina about how freaked out she was. If Elf Man did show his face, Kereama, Shane and Oliver were going to enjoy kicking the shit out of him. "Come on, let's go get some brekkie," he suggested to Amelia, after she'd terminated her call with Georgina.

12

Georgina was nervous, her stomach so tight she felt nauseous as she drove her Jeep towards Bondi Beach, the potential meeting with Elf Man imminent. Wearing a white top and colourful short skirt, with thongs, her hair blowing in every direction, time felt drawn out. On the dashboard, the clock said it was approaching half seven. Next to her, Shane kept saying it didn't bother him, yet she knew it did. "Switch the station, would you? This is boring." She didn't like the commercial pop tunes.

If she didn't know he hated heavy metal, Georgina would have put on a couple of songs by The Demented, or Disturbed. Instead, she listened to more popular music blasting through her stereo. Amelia and Isla were huge Nicki Minaj fans, but she couldn't bear it. With a following on Chatter of over a hundred million, Georgina would more likely ask Minaj about that than about any of her songs. "And you choose this?" Glancing over at her boyfriend, she shook her head.

With a huff, Shane leaned forwards and pressed the station button again. "Happy?" His question was laced with sarcasm when a guitar heavy song by some band she couldn't identify came through the speakers.

"All right, no need to bite my head off." Concentrating on driving, traffic light along O'Sullivan Road, even for a Monday night, she slowed behind a Nissan. They would arrive at Bondi Beach inside ten minutes. "What's the matter with you tonight anyway?"

He told her not to worry. In silence, she drove them along Blair Street and Warner's Avenue, until she came to Campbell Parade, where she parked on Queen Elizabeth Drive. Killing the engine and stereo, she took the key out of the ignition and put it in her bag. Shane sat motionless in the passenger seat, silent. "It's time." She opened her door. "Let's go meet the others." When Shane didn't move, she stopped and stared at him. "What is it?"

He turned and stared at her. "I want you to be ready, George." He was serious. "Because if this guy does show, we're messing him up, do you understand? We're taking him down to the beach and beating the shit out of him, and I don't want you getting upset... I need you to expect it, that way you won't be begging me not to."

Being half aborigine, her mum's half was a pacifist and deplored violence on all levels, for any reason. That being said, her dad's half was pragmatic and taught her that whackos, like this Elf Man, needed boundaries outlined to them in ways they understood. She didn't know this pom from Adam; she didn't owe him anything. And the fact he'd flown over a thousand miles to be there freaked her out more than she let on, even to Shane. "Do whatever you feel's necessary to get him to rack off; I won't say anything if it gets physical, I promise."

Taking his hand, Georgina walked through the car park, past the graffiti wall and lifeguard tower, her nerves jangling inside her. Still in the early twenties, the heat made her perspire. As she strolled with Shane, watching the passers-by, she glimpsed Amelia and Kereama stood outside Lush, talking to friends. "There they are." Georgina pulled him in the direction of the café.

Amelia, who looked stunning in a white vest top, skirt and had her hair up in a beautiful hive display, saw her and said goodbye to her mates. Georgina didn't recognise them. "Hey! Are Isla and Oli here yet?" Shane and Kereama nodded their acknowledgement of one another, as guys often did.

The Starfish Pub's outdoor tables were at about half capacity, which wasn't surprising given that it was only a Monday night, and only January seventh. Georgina scanned the taken tables for single blokes. Only one she spied, pale of complexion, a balding man who looked to be in his early-to-mid forties. No, he couldn't be Elf Man, she thought, squeezing Shane's hand and gesturing the singleton. When Shane shook his head, she breathed easier.

Amelia and Kereama chose a table closest to the beach, where they could get a good view of the comings and goings of the pub. Georgina sat next to her friend, a nervous expression creeping over her, which she expelled with a smile. The boys asked them what they wanted to drink. Being designated driver, she asked for a Diet Coke, while Amelia asked for a rum and Coke. "I've got butterflies," she said, after the guys went to buy the drinks.

"Same here. I have all day, and this pom's not coming to meet me. I'm so sorry for not snatching your phone off Oli."

"Don't worry about it, Ames." Georgina put a comforting arm around Amelia's waist. "No one knew he'd go and buy flights out here. Hell, even Oli wouldn't have done it had he known. I mean, he's a jerk, but he's not a complete jerk."

"Thanks for not hating me." Amelia rested her head on Georgina's shoulder. "I'll make it up to you, I promise."

Stroking her friend's hair, Georgina replied, "You're here

with me now; that's all the payment I need." She observed the occupants of the other tables, noting that every table had at least two people sat at them. If Elf Man were here, now, he would be at a table by himself. He hadn't mentioned meeting friends. Her heart fluttered at the thought of coming face to face with him. "Here they come."

When the boys returned with their drinks, they got comfortable and attempted to converse with them. It was stilted and obviously so, long silences hanging over the table. Georgina couldn't stop her leg bobbing up and down, even when Amelia put her hand on it. She laughed whenever Shane or Kereama said something vaguely amusing.

"Here they are," Oliver said.

Georgina turned around and smiled, relieved when Isla waved as she walked towards her. "Oh thank God." Greeting her other best friend, Isla stooped down and kissed her on her cheek. "I thought you two bailed on me."

"I've got your back, George. My boyfriend started this whole thing off, so I can at least back you up."

She loved her friends so much, if not their choice in boyfriends. Still, she couldn't have everything. Amelia she'd known since primary school and Isla since college. Despite knowing Amelia a lot longer, Isla had found a special place in Georgina's life. "None of you should blame yourselves," she said to all around her table. "Yeah, Oli did something stupid, but I'm guessing you're never going to touch my phone again, are you?" She laughed at his expression, a hearty laugh for the first time in days. Now that they were all together, Georgina felt safe. With her friends behind her, she could do anything.

Her joviality didn't last long. Before Oliver could ask Isla what she wanted to drink, Georgina's ringtone told her she had a message.

Everyone around the table stopped talking and stared at her.

Taking her phone out of her bag, she glanced at the screen and breathed out heavily at her mum's text. "Thank God," she said. "Just my olds."

After Oliver came back with his and Isla's drinks, the atmosphere palpably changed. Georgina listened to the boys' banter when she noticed it was quarter past eight. With any luck, Elf Man would be a no-show, all mouth and no trousers. It might be wishful thinking, she thought, laughing at Shane's impression of Oliver, because the pom had paid over four thousand pounds for a plane ticket here. Why would he do that? Her fake bravado evaporated when all their phones went off.

"He's here." Shane was the first to open his Chatter account to find the photo of The Starfish Pub's entrance. Some of the customers seen buying their drinks in the photo were sat at the tables in front of them. "I wish this guy would rack off."

Georgina's heart rate increased. Having a gulp of her Diet Coke, she stared at the picture. Elf Man was here, amongst them. With caution, she studied every person around her, in turn. The vast majority of visitors to the pub were in groups, chatting and laughing, enjoying the evening, like they were supposed to be. There were only two single people near them, the guy she spied coming in and an older woman, who was drinking a gin and tonic. "You're around here somewhere," Georgina whispered, watching people in the distance.

There were a number of people walking past the pub along the promenade. Georgina scanned them for a lonely straggler. Shane stood and surveyed the area with her, while the others joined them. And when she lost all hope of finding Elf Man, her phone's ringtone made her jump. "Shit!" she said, her hand shaking.

A private Chatter message from the pom appeared on her

screen. The photo showed them sat talking and laughing together, taken a few minutes earlier, before he sent the picture of the pub's frontage. "The whole gang's here," she read out for them all, before setting the phone in front of them to observe the picture. "Isn't that sweet!"

"This is how you wanna play it, huh?" Shane shouted. "You fucking coward!"

Georgina looked around her at all the curious drinkers watching him and muttering to themselves. She wanted to tell them to mind their business, except she had more important things to worry about. Elf Man was here, hiding. "Let's go, guys," she suggested, her voice small. "I don't like this."

"Don't be stupid, George." Oliver puffed out his chest. "We can handle one guy, can't we, boys? No way some pom's chasing us out of our own pub."

"Oli's right, babe, we'll teach this fucker a lesson he won't forget." Shane stepped out from behind the table and stood in the centre of the walkway, still scanning for their elusive guest. "We'll find you eventually, Elf Man."

Embarrassed for him, the pub's visitors talking about him under hushed words, Georgina joined him in the aisle separating the two rows of tables. The phone in her hand went off again, attracting her friends' attention. And when she opened Chatter, there was a video of Shane shouting, "This is how you want to play it, huh? You fucking coward!" She gasped, seeing that the film was recorded to their right.

"Ah, forget about it." Shane, checking who was to their right, behind the tables of guests, continued, "He's playing with us."

"We're giving him what he wants," Georgina said, holding Shane's hands. "If we go home, we'll deny him all this."

"I'm with George." Amelia held Kereama's hand. "Let's all go back to yours and have some drinks, yeah?"

Another photo came through, taken to their left, of them stood in the centre of the walkway. Georgina checked; there was no one over there. Then, she studied everyone around her, scanning the beer garden for Single Guy.

13

"You sneaky little bastard!" Shane said through gritted teeth. The Single Guy who'd moved tables turned his head and caught sight of him, then quickly turned it back. "George! That guy." He made a move towards the pub. Up ahead, he saw the pub's owner, Nathan, striding in his direction, finger on an earpiece, as if someone was telling him what was going on.

"I thought we agreed to leave him." Georgina walked with speed to keep up with Shane's longer stride. "Elf Man's younger, babe."

Shane reached Single Guy before Nathan arrived, and pushed him so hard, he nearly fell off the bench. "You! You sneaky piece of shit," he hissed at the unsuspecting balding man in his early forties. "Stand up! We're going for a little walk, you and me." Single Guy looked up at him, scared. Shane kicked the wooden table, making it shake, the guy's drink almost toppling over. "Did you hear me? I said, get up."

"Shane! What the hell?" Nathan was a tall thin bloke in his late thirties, with a stupid moustache and normally sunny disposition. "You can't go intimidating my customers like this. Come on, calm down and tell me what this is all about."

Bending over, Shane grabbed Single Guy's shirt collar and pulled him to his feet, the drinkers around him gasping and muttering. "Rack off, Nathan, this isn't your concern, right?" Shane couldn't stand Nathan. He turned his attention to Single Guy. "No, this is between us. You can't go around scaring these ladies."

"Shane, leave him alone," Georgina pleaded. "We don't know it was him."

"Yeah, put him down, Shane. This isn't right," Nathan whispered. "What's he done?"

"Go on back to serving drinks, all right? I'll handle this. Or do you want me to tell the lads to avoid this place in the future? Up to you." The last thing The Starfish's owner wanted was for him to boycott the pub; his team not only spent a lot of money here, they brought in customers, too. The Starfish received a great deal of publicity with the Sydney Swans drinking and eating there.

"You're making a mistake, Shane, but you go ahead." Nathan had his palms displayed in a placating manner. "I'm sorry, I tried," he said to Single Guy.

"I don't know what you're talking about, buddy."

When Shane heard the guy's accent, he gripped the shirt even tighter. Single Guy was a pommie. "Oh, is that right?" He pulled Single Guy out from behind the table and pushed him towards the beach. "You can tell it to my boot in a sec." He had no hesitation in believing this pom was Elf Man. He pushed the scared bloke every time he slowed his pace, hearing Georgina behind him moaning to Amelia and Isla. Oliver and Kereama were by his side, ready. "Let's do this!"

Walking along the sandy beach, Shane forced Elf Man to

stop when he couldn't hear voices coming from Lush, The Starfish or The Bucket List anymore. "Here'll do, mate." He grabbed him and spun him around. "Give me your phone," he said to Single Guy, digging into his shorts and pulling out his mobile. He handed it to Georgina. "Take a look through this. I'd like you all to meet Elf Man."

"Who? Huh? What?" Single Guy stuttered. "Elf Man?"

"Nice try." Shane clenched his fist and landed the first blow to his cheek. It hurt his wrist, but it was worth it, to see the little bastard dazed on the sand. With Elf Man on his back, he went in and kicked him in the ribs, then stamped on his knee, the rage flowing out of him. "Won't be coming back here again, will you, huh?"

"This won't be good for your health," Kereama added, kicking Single Guy in the other side of his ribcage, taking it in turns with Shane.

Oliver kicked him in the balls, as the pom yelped.

"Pick him up," Shane said, breathless. He wanted to laugh in Elf Man's bloody face. "You come near my lady again, I'll kill you, do you understand?" He growled, then lurched forwards and punched the guy in his stomach, knocking the wind out of him. He was about to finish him off with a fist to the face, when he heard, "Stop! This isn't Elf Man. Here, look for yourself."

Grabbing the phone from Georgina, Shane stared at the screen. Elf Man was groaning, held up by Oliver and Kereama, his head down. It had to be him. What were the odds of them finding a single guy at The Starfish, who happened to be a pom? And he'd acted shifty. It had to be him. "Oli, grab his wallet." Going to the guy's Chatter account on the app, the name: Iain French. Not Elf Man. "What's his driver's licence say?"

"Iain French." Oliver shook his head. "He lives in Richmond, UK."

"Shit!" Anger welled up in Shane's gut. He drew his arm back and threw the bloke's phone as far as he could in frustration. Rubbing his hair, he pondered his predicament. He had just beaten up the wrong bloke. He stepped up to the almost-unconscious man. "Hey! I'm so sorry!" The guy's head hung; he was barely conscious. "Right, we need to get him to the hospital. George, call him an ambo, would you?"

"What the fuck, Shane? We've just beaten the shit out of this guy," Kereama complained. "He's going to call the cops on us now, for sure. Plus, there are about two dozen people back at The Starfish who watched us drag him away."

"Don't you think I know that!" he yelled at Kereama, who held the pom upright.

Georgina and the girls went to his victim's aid, gently placing him on the sand.

While they were tending to him, Shane had to think. The only way out of this was to pay the guy off, to give him enough money to not press charges.

He walked towards the ocean, listening to the waves lapping over one another. It was a stunning evening, with not a cloud in the sky. He found the guy's phone and picked it up. The sand cushioned the blow. "What've I done?" Shane asked himself. Then, he turned and headed back.

With the others, Shane crouched and studied the bloke's bloody face. "I'll make this up to you, I promise." He laid the mobile on his chest. "This is all a big misunderstanding. I'll pay you whatever you feel's appropriate." It was falling on deaf ears, the guy almost unconscious. "He's done. Is an ambo on its way?" Shane asked his girlfriend.

"It'll be here in a few minutes." Georgina glanced at the poor man.

"We'd best bolt." Oliver gestured leaving.

"There's no point. We're done. Too many people saw us. No, the only way out of this is to pay him off. We can't leave him here like this." An ambulance wailed in the distance. "And you told them where to find us?"

"On the beach, down from The Bucket List, yeah." Georgina wiped the guy's face with a bandanna she had in her bag. "We're in the shit, Shane."

"No! Really?" It was the most obvious statement ever. Shane's mobile rung in his shorts pocket. Without thinking, he retrieved it and entered his passcode. "It's him!" he said, as Oliver and Kereama crowded around him. Shane read out a message. "Is this the famous Aussie hospitality? Your lot aren't very welcoming. Lol."

A video showed him punching the guy to the sand, then kicking him while down. It was taken from quite a distance, back towards The Starfish. Shane didn't need to watch the video; he needed to find Elf Man. Looking up from his phone, he couldn't see anyone.

Shane took the mobile and ran with it back the way they'd come, positive he would find Elf Man walking away. "I know you're there, prick," he said as he ran at full pace, the sand hampering his speed. And as he approached The Bucket List, he saw a guy strolling away from him, wearing a white shirt and brown khaki shorts.

"Elf Man!" he shouted, still running as fast as he could.

Elf Man turned his head, shocked, then started sprinting.

"Shit!" Shane's lungs burned. He was too far away to tackle him, he conceded, watching the pommie visitor join the crowd of people walking along the promenade. He stooped over to catch his breath, his palms on his knees. "Tosser!" If he'd kept quiet, he might have gained enough ground to stop him. Hindsight was a bitch, he thought.

Once his lungs recovered, Shane headed back in the direction of the others. He could see the ambulance crew had arrived. Trying to forget Elf Man was on the loose, Shane's focus had to be on convincing Iain French not to press charges.

14

"I thought she said Tuesday morning at the latest." Packard glanced at his watch.

Coates turned off the ignition and checked out the row of terraced houses through his window. "You've worked here for long enough, you know what it's like. She says Tuesday morning, but really means Thursday afternoon." It was a good job he had leads to chase down. If not, he would be banging on Patricia Rollins' office door.

After interviewing Tara Henson's parents, who formally identified their daughter, he and Sergeant Packard now knew their victim's history. She had been homeless in London at sixteen, after three long sex-and-drug-fuelled years. She packed a bag and went to stay with her then-boyfriend, Finn. Hooked on cocaine, he introduced her to the wonders of heroin, until three violent years later he grew bored of her and threw her out. Unable to return to her parents, she found a squat with a couple of girls, where she lived for five years, doing whatever it took to buy her precious H.

A common story told to Coates countless times. All it took to corrupt some people was a weak will. Seduced by the sex, and the drugs, it didn't take long for life to spit her out. Alone, selling herself to anyone who had the cash, her father had found her after she flagged him down on a kerbside, mistaking him for a punter.

By this point, she had a pimp, who attacked Mr Henson when he tried to convince his daughter to return home with him. Fortunately, Tara's dad beat her pimp by the kerb, breaking his left femur, right patella, and fracturing his left fibula. He also broke three ribs and fractured the pimp's right arm in three places.

Having taken her away from a life of heroin addicted debauchery, Mr Henson checked her into rehab, where she dried out, and vowed to clean herself up. True to her word, she completed her rehabilitation and returned home to live with her parents.

At twenty-six, she had no qualifications and no work experience, but that didn't stop the pretty girl getting a waitressing job at a restaurant in Lewes town centre, where she worked up until her murder a few days earlier. According to her parents, Tara found a terraced house that Mr Henson put a deposit down on. And for the last three years, she'd lived there happily on her own.

Coates thought it tragic that she should go through such a tough time in her teenage years, overcome those obstacles, only to meet a brutal and violent end after she'd safely navigated her way through. He was certain Mr and Mrs Henson felt the same way too. And interviewing the occupant of the terraced house next door would bring justice closer to the family's reach, Coates hoped. "I'm going to call her after the interview. Now, let's get this done. Stacey Redmond was her best friend for the past three years or so."

"Yeah, I guess if anyone knows anything about her private

life, she will," Packard conceded, opening his door. "Sorry! All this waiting does my nut in."

Heaving himself out of the white carpool Peugeot, Coates regarded his partner over the roof. "And you think I like waiting?"

"You're so calm about everything, I can never tell when you're agitated." He grinned as he closed the passenger door. "I guess that's why they made you inspector, huh?"

"I like to think I'm good at my job." He locked the doors with his key fob then followed Sergeant Packard over the road, through the property's gate and along the driveway. At the door, his partner knocked, while he stood back. A portly woman in her mid-thirties opened it a crack.

"Detectives, please come in." She let them through. "Can I make you a cup of tea or coffee? The kettle's boiled."

In the hallway, she led them to the small – homely – lounge, which was beautifully decorated and adorned with candles. Everywhere he looked in the living room/dining room picture frames held images of wild birds. "Bird lover, I see." He hoped to start building a rapport immediately. "Which is your favourite?"

She thought about it for a second. "Umm, I'd have to say, Mr Robin." She pointed at the picture front and centre, hanging on the chimney breast, above her gorgeous ornate fireplace. "So beautiful, and we get plenty visiting our garden year round."

Their interviewee left them alone, while she went and made their drinks. Stacey brought back three steaming mugs of coffee a couple of minutes later. "Thanks," he said, sitting on the sofa next to Packard, opposite her on an armchair. "Tara's parents tell us you were friends with her, that you would know about her private affairs?"

"Well, only as much as she let on. She could be secretive when she wanted to be. We've lived next door to each other for years now, and she only confided in me about her childhood last year. Imagine living rough for years; it must've left a stain. But yeah, she trusted me. What do you need to know?"

"Was she dating anyone?" Packard asked.

Stacey sucked air in. "She was clean... If that's what you were getting at?"

"No, that isn't what I meant, Miss Redmond, not at all," he reassured her. "We know all about her past, what she did to survive. No, we're interested in her more recent history. We're working a lead that points in the direction of a man she met. Maybe online, or through a friend. Is there anyone like that in her life?"

"Her ex-boyfriend, you mean?" Stacey asked. "I'm afraid I never–"

"Not her ex, no," Coates interrupted. "Her parents gave us him. He checked out and his alibi is airtight. He's out of the country, and has been for over six months. No, we were hoping she might've confided in you about someone new?"

Stacey shook her head. "No, I'm sorry. I can't think of anyone."

Coates, disappointed, hoped she might point him in the right direction. "Has she had any run-ins with anyone? Any confrontations with men? Anything like that?"

"She led quite a simple life," Stacey said. "Some might say boring, but I think Tara had enough excitement in her life growing up. I think she wanted a quiet, dull life." Stacey leaned forwards, staring into thin air. "I tried convincing her to go online dating."

"And did she?" Packard asked, excited.

"Yeah, she joined LoveMe.com. I helped her fill out her application and choose the picture. I wish I hadn't, for all the luck she had on there. Not one date, in over six months. She got talking to a few guys, but they were all losers, desperate and sleazy. I felt guilty helping her."

"Was she on social media much?" Coates asked.

"The usual, Facebook and Chatter."

Before he could ask his next question, his mobile rang in his suit jacket pocket. "Excuse me, I need to take this." He mouthed "coroner" to Packard on his way into the kitchen, away from prying ears. "Hi!" he said in greeting. "I hope you're bringing good news."

"I am, and unexpected."

"Oh? Why's that?" Through the kitchen window, a couple of blackbirds fought over Stacey's feeder in the garden.

"We got lucky on this one. The prints belong to Arthur Peebles." Her voice stopped at the mention of the notorious name. "Dave? Did you hear me? Arthur Peebles. All the trace is his; there's no doubt."

Coates couldn't speak at first. Shock prevented it. "I hear you... But I thought, isn't he in prison?"

"Nope, released eighteen months ago," Rollins said. "I've sent the report over to you by email. You have your suspect."

And he did. "Yeah, great. Thanks, I appreciate you getting this back to me. Have you put this through the scanner a couple of times? You're absolutely certain it's him?" Still in shock, he tried to put it to the back of his mind.

"A hundred per cent," Rollins confirmed.

Coates thanked the coroner and let her go. Staring at his phone, he thought of the ramifications. Shaking away his thoughts, he walked back to the lounge, where Packard was questioning the homeowner. "We thank you for your time, Miss Redmond, but we need to leave."

"But, sir, we're getting somewhere," his partner protested. "Stacey's just told me about a guy Tara talked to on Chatter."

"Brilliant! Stacey, can you send over his account details, please. I've spoken to the coroner. We have a positive ID on our suspect." He saw the sudden rush of excitement in Packard's eyes. "We need to get back to the station."

Finishing his coffee in two gulps, Coates thanked Stacey once more, then led Packard out of the house and across the road towards their car. "Are you going to tell me who it is?" he heard his passenger ask from behind him. After unlocking the car, he got in and waited for Packard to fasten his seat belt. "It's Arthur Peebles." He waited for acknowledgement.

"I'm sorry! Am I supposed to know who that is?"

Coates sighed, letting out a lungful of air. "Oh, of course, you must be too young to remember," he said, trying to hide his annoyance. "You're only twenty-six, I forget that sometimes." He started the engine and pulled out of the space. "Arthur Peebles was given life imprisonment for the rape and murder of Zoe Evans, a minor. He and Michael Ince, his co-defendant, were both fourteen at the time; they were classmates with Zoe. It made all the national press at the time."

"I recall something, Shouldn't he still be in prison? I mean, if he'd been released, wouldn't it have been all over the news?"

"According to Rollins they released him eighteen months ago." Coates pulled up behind an elderly woman driving a Nissan. "Maybe the probation service had to let him go on the quiet, you know? Anyway, Rollins emailed me the file."

"You know, if you had a smartphone, you might be able to read the email right here." Packard sniggered, always one for making fun of his being a luddite. "Or I can pull it up for you now, if you want?"

"Thanks, but I'm not handing you my password." Getting annoyed at the slow speed of the Nissan, Coates honked his horn. "No, I can wait until we get to the station."

15

Oliver loved the hot weather, yet was grateful for the air conditioning at night. He spat toothpaste into the basin and replaced his toothbrush. Wearing a white vest top and khaki shorts, he walked through to his bedroom to find Isla looking out of the window. Their room looked over the road below. "What's so interesting?" He stepped behind her and pinched her bum. She turned and complained jovially. He said, "What's out there?"

"I'm not sure. I thought I saw a guy coming out of our drive, but I think he just walked past. Probably nothing."

Concerned, Oliver pulled the curtains back and gazed out of the window at the street lamp lit road. "Where is he now?"

"Gone. Maybe he didn't come out of our driveway, babe."

A sudden rush of fear enveloped him. "But the Nota's out there," he said, praying it was unharmed. His pride and joy, the Nota Le Mans, was his dream sports car. If something happened to it, he would go mental. He wished they could afford a place with a perimeter wall, like Shane and Georgina had, but they weren't that wealthy. Without hesitation, he rushed out of the bedroom, hearing Isla chasing after him. Downstairs, he found the house's alarm panel and input the code to disarm it.

Outside, the warmth hitting him, he breathed out in relief when he saw his beloved sat on the drive, her red coat gleaming in the street light. "Oh thank God!"

"Why's she out here?" Isla asked. "Why isn't she in the garage?"

"I forgot." He was so relieved "she" had remained undamaged. He had only bought her six months earlier. Being both track and road ready, his Le Mans was the most favourite thing in his life. Everyone's heads turned when he drove past, the way he liked it. "I'll put her away now." He headed back to the house.

"Oli, was this here before?" Isla asked.

He didn't like the way she said it. "What?" As he approached her, Isla was pointing at the driver's side. He crouched down and stared. His eyes widened when he saw it. A white scratch running the length of the car. With his heart thumping, he followed the scratch to the rear, where the continuous line kept going. All the way around it went. Whoever was responsible, had keyed it to within an inch of its life. Oliver wanted to punch something, anything, to dispel the rage he felt inside. "I'm gonna fucking kill him!" Oliver growled, his hands shaking.

"You think it was *him*?" Isla asked.

"Who else would it be?" Oliver hissed. A thought forced him to sprint after Elf Man. He ran into his road, Lindsay Avenue, his thongs not the best for running. If he caught the pom, he would make him pay for scratching his gorgeous Nota.

Oliver ran the length of his road, past McKell Park on the opposite side of the street, turning left into Darling Point Road, where cars lined the street ahead, but there was no sign of Elf Man. The pom could've turned right, yet Oliver had a feeling the

Brit had turned left. He sprinted past cars and lamp posts until he had to stop to catch his breath.

Stood in the centre of the quiet road, his mobile vibrated. Reaching into his pocket, he retrieved it. On Chatter, he had a video message from his tormentor. And the footage displayed before he pressed "play" was the side of his car. "Bastard!" He didn't want to watch. He wanted to wring the pom's bloody neck, with his bare hands. And he could tell Elf Man enjoyed defacing his gorgeous car. "You'll pay for this, you mongrel!"

From behind him came the unmistakable sound of screeching tyres.

Bathed in bright white light, with his phone in hand, Oliver instinctively turned round as two white lights came at him with speed.

Without thought, he dived to his right, almost hitting his head on the side of a stationary Ford. Had his reaction been slower, the speeding car would have sent him hurtling over the bonnet and roof, leaving his broken body lying on the tarmac.

Elf Man had just tried to kill him. He was dangerous, an elusive shadow waiting to exact his revenge. As Oliver picked himself up, the red rear lights of the pom's car disappeared from view.

On his way back, limping, his knee bleeding, Oliver decided not to tell Isla what had happened; it would freak her out too much, and it served no purpose. He would just tell her to be vigilant and keep an eye out for him.

His girlfriend waited for him at the end of their drive. She looked at his injured knee. "What happened to you?"

"Nothing," he lied. "I'm embarrassed. I can't run in these, and fell over. I almost face-planted the tarmac." He showed her his scraped palms. "Lucky I kept my arms out, eh?" She fussed over him, until he told her he was all right. When she ordered him inside so she could tend to his wounds, he said, "I'll be there in a mo; I'm putting her in the garage first. I'll catch you up." As she went inside, he jumped into the driver's seat and started her engine. The garage door opened, and he drove the Nota gently through.

After locking his beloved up for the night, Oliver found Isla waiting for him in their bathroom with the first aid kit. "I'm fine, baby, honest." He rested his foot on the bathtub, allowing her access to his cut. Blood dripped down his leg.

"Why was she left on the driveway?" Dabbing at his knee with alcohol-soaked cotton wool, she waited for an answer. "You can't forget things like this, Oli. You know how many people envy us. They'll do everything they can to ruin it."

With nothing to say in his defence, he nodded his agreement. "I know." He took his phone out of his pocket. "But it was him, look." Oliver inputted his passcode and opened his Chatter video message. She stopped dabbing. "He's out there, so stay alert, all right?" When she tutted, he added, "I mean it, Isla, this guy's dangerous."

"Fine, I promise I'll keep my eyes open." She sighed. "But if you'd put her in the garage like you're supposed to, she wouldn't have been out there for him to scratch, would she?" Isla shook her head. "You're so lazy sometimes."

Not wanting an ear bashing, he tutted. "Oh, here we go," he said, taking his knee back and heading for the bedroom.

Isla followed him. "Hey! Don't walk away from me!"

"Why? I'm not getting a decent convo from you anyway. Might as well go downstairs, the hell away from you and your nagging." He hated it when she got her knickers in a bunch; she could be such a royal pain in the arse.

His walking away didn't improve the situation. Oliver ran down the stairs and into the kitchen. By the time Isla reached him, he had his face in the refrigerator. She yelled at him about being a child. "Well, you chose me, right? You knew what I was like," he countered. But when she shouted at him that Elf Man's arrival was his fault, he slammed the cooler door, a tinny in his hand, and faced her. "Oh, right, now you wanna blame me? I didn't expect the bloke to fly over here, did I? I mean, who does that? Who flies to the other side of the world to meet someone you follow on Chatter?"

"A fucking psycho, that's who!" Isla yelled. "And now he's here, on our bloody driveway, scratching the shit out of your car. And you brought him here." Her hands were shaking with rage. "Right, because you led him to our doorstep, you can get rid of him. I don't care how you do it, Oli, but you do it. If you have to pay him off, or if you have to beat the shit out of him, I don't give a shit, I want him out of our lives, for good. And if you ever pick up someone else's phone again, I swear I'm gonna cut off your hands. Jesus Christ, you make me so fucking angry!"

Oliver stood back, awed at her anger. Her chest rose and fell, the exhaustion of her raging outburst affecting her breathing. "Shh! I know you're scared," he said, stepping towards her, his arms out. "But I'll sort it, I promise. I'll find him, and I'll fuck him up." His voice was calm, given that she'd just yelled the house down.

"Oh, and you're sleeping downstairs tonight," she said, before she flounced off.

"Great!" Anger built up inside. "Fucking pommie bastard!"

———

16

D I David Coates powered up his computer.

DS Packard pulled up his chair and sat next to him.

Although his partner mocked him for his lack of technical expertise, he managed fine. Using his mouse, he opened up his email account and clicked on Patricia Rollins' report, which he had to download.

"You're getting the hang of this."

"You're funny. You won't be laughing when I bust you down to traffic duty." And that wiped the grin off Packard's face, Coates noted, not that he had the authority to enact it. "Come on," he said, agitated, desperate to see the evidence for himself. "Here we go." A file popped up.

"Well, he doesn't look like much. Talk about Mr Average."

Coates ignored his partner's comment. The photo of Arthur Peebles was not very flattering, but arrest photos never were. He had a mop of unruly hair and thin, horrible lips. And even with dark hair, he had a pale complexion that didn't suit him. Coates thought him less than average; ugly. Knowing what he did to that poor fourteen-year-old girl compounded it. "He's more than average in other ways. Let me show you his record."

Using his mouse, he clicked on the Police National Computer, PNC, and typed in Arthur Peebles' name in the search bar. There were eight entries to choose from. After finding the correct one, he pulled up Peebles' file. The picture was the same one used in Rollins' report. "Ugly spod," Coates muttered.

"Why is it redacted?"

He could think of no reason why some parts of Peebles' record should be blacked out, while others were legible. The key details of his arrest, the laws broken, and the facts of the case against him were left intact. "Here we are." He turned his monitor slightly for Packard to read. He remembered the court case well, even sixteen years later. It was all over the news back in the day.

A fourteen-year-old Arthur Peebles was arrested five days after the defiled, naked body of Zoe Evans was found in a shallow grave in woods in Hull, with the help of sniffer dogs. It took two days to secure a confession out of Michael Ince, Peebles' partner in crime, who told police that Peebles had beat her to death with a brick, after they both raped her. Coates heard Packard's disgusted sigh. When questioned, their suspect tried to pin it all on his co-defendant, saying *he* killed Zoe with the brick.

The trial took place six months later and it took two weeks for the jury to produce a guilty verdict, whereupon two days after that the pair were sentenced to life imprisonment, where Peebles spent fourteen years of his twenty-five year stretch, before being released back into the community eighteen months earlier. There was an entirely redacted report from the prison. Peebles and Ince spent their first four years in a young offender's institute, before graduating to HM Full Sutton Prison at the age of eighteen.

"It would help if we could get hold of an unedited copy."

"You're right, it would," he agreed, turning in his chair to scan the open plan office for his line manager, Detective Chief Inspector William Morgan. "Sir," he shouted, waving his boss over, "can we have a word?" Without assistance from the top brass, he and Packard would hit a grand wall of silence. The file was redacted for a reason, possibly by a politician, or some senior officer within the probation service, so he needed to enlist the help of his superiors. He would go to DCI Morgan, who would go on up to Chief Constable Gately, and so on, until the right person spoke to the right contact.

"What's the problem, Dave?" Morgan, a heavyset man in his fifties with a full head of greying hair and a red nose and purple veins in his cheeks, indicative of an unhealthy relationship with whisky, stood by his desk.

"Any idea why this would be redacted?"

"I remember this one. Horrible little bastards, they were. Why the interest?"

"Peebles' DNA is all over the bin body, sir. We've got everything from semen to a bloody fingerprint. All I need to know is what it says on his record. Is there anyone you can reach out to? Don't misunderstand me, I'm not asking for a miracle here."

"No, leave it with me." Morgan pulled his mobile out of his suit jacket. "I'll phone Gately, see what he says. I think he'll help; he won't want Peebles out there causing trouble, any more than I do. But, don't get your hopes up, getting in touch with the right person's going to take time. If I were you, I'd look at different angles to locate Peebles. Try talking to the governor at Full Sutton, see what he has to say."

Coates thanked the chief inspector and went back to his monitor. "Looks like we've got our work cut out," he said to his partner, who took his chair back to his own desk. "I'm going to carry on with this; why don't you go back to Stacey, see if you can locate the guy Tara was online with."

He had a suspect, but locating and apprehending him seemed a long way off. Still, nothing worthwhile was ever easy, he told himself. One question popped into his mind: if Peebles was from Hull, why had a corpse with his fingerprints all over it surfaced here, in the south east? "Let's see what we can see." He clicked on Peebles' record and looked up the parents.

Victor and Ursula, the parents, relocated after their son's incarceration to a village near Hull, called North Ferriby. Coates surmised that they must've found it hard to continue living in the same town, after their son had committed such a heinous crime. The whole country knew how Peebles beat Zoe Evans in the face with a brick over forty times. Forty-six to be exact, before burying her in a shallow grave, and after he and Michael Ince raped her.

An anomaly: on paper, Arthur Peebles had no reason to be a convicted rapist and murderer. He'd had all the opportunities in life. He and his family may have lived in a relatively deprived town, but they didn't want for anything. In fact, the father owned a successful printing company, and the mother a GP practice.

Arthur Peebles had three siblings: two brothers, one older and one younger, and an older sister. Coates ran records on each of Peebles' relatives and not one of them had form, which meant they were all law-abiding citizens. In fact, they weren't just respected citizens, they were all high achievers: his older brother was a GP, like his mum; his younger brother owned a telecoms company which floated on the stock market, while his sister earned her living as a solicitor.

Coates leaned back in his chair, pondering a question: if

Peebles came from good stock, which he clearly did, why had he become a rapist and murderer? Nature vs nurture, he thought. Maybe Michael Ince nurtured him? Coates shook away the thought. By all accounts, Peebles was the ringleader, the alpha, in that partnership.

"Stacey says I can go over there." Packard stood. "Are you all right staying here, or do you want to come with?"

"No, you go ahead. I'm going to do some research on Peebles." His partner left, and he went back to his computer. Abnormal psychology – psychopathy – had always interested him. Why did one become a killer? Was it down to bad wiring in the brain? Or a chemical imbalance? Maybe because Peebles had met Ince, and they'd encouraged one another? Had Peebles been exposed to too many violent movies? Or could he be just plain evil?

Making a note of the Peebles' landline number, Coates picked up his desk phone and dialled it, hoping to set up a meeting with them. The more he could understand about their son, the greater chance he had of apprehending him, hopefully before the psychopath raped and murdered again. "Come on, answer," he said, looking at the clock on the wall: 12:45. Almost lunchtime.

After eight rings, a deep masculine voice answered. Coates introduced himself and why he was calling, only to be cut off. "Hello?" He looked at the receiver. "Hello?" Rude bastard, he thought placing his phone on its dock. The mere mention of their son's name brought out the worst in the family, it seemed. Mr and Mrs Peebles were a no-go.

DCI Morgan's words went round in Coates' mind. Picking up his phone again, he dialled the number for HM Full Sutton Prison, hoping to speak with the governor. Greeted by a female voice, who identified herself as Governor Brian Hicks' secretary,

Coates explained the situation to her, explaining that he needed to speak with Hicks about Arthur Peebles. The secretary told him that the governor couldn't talk. Away on a course until the following afternoon, Wednesday, apparently. Sighing, Coates seized on the opportunity and booked an appointment with the governor.

17

The wind whistled through Georgina's hair as she drove her Jeep along Ocean Drive, heading into Port Macquarie. Georgina and her best surfer buddy, Mingzhu Chan, a tiny Chinese girl she met a few years ago, set off for Lighthouse Beach in the early hours of the morning, attempting to arrive by nine. Looking at the clock, it was five to, and she had been driving for four and a half hours.

Music blared out of the Jeep's speakers. She and Mingzhu were both huge fans of The Deranged. Her passenger hooked her phone up to the stereo. All morning she and her gorgeous Chinese friend had moshed to the greatest hits The Deranged had to offer.

"Are you all right, George?" Mingzhu shouted. "You've been really quiet all the way here. Something up?"

"I don't want to talk about it! I just want to enjoy the ride." Without glancing at her friend, she knew Mingzhu wanted more.

"Come on, out with it. I know when something's bothering you."

Reaching into her bag behind her on the back passenger

seat, Georgina retrieved her phone and handed it to her friend, holding her thumb on the home button so it would clear the passcode. "Open up Chatter. Go into my private messages." Looking out to sea on her right, she waited for Mingzhu to catch up. Ahead she could see Tacking Point Lighthouse, a bright white beacon sat atop a cliff. The closer it came, the closer she was to surfing. "I'm being... We're being stalked."

"Who is he?" her friend asked, reading her messages. "It says he lives in the UK."

"He's a pommie," she clarified. "Oli was mucking about on my phone Friday night, and this is the result. This Elf Man guy, he sent me a message on one of my cheeps, and Oli replied as me, telling him he should come visit... He has. He bought a plane ticket there and then."

"What an arsehole! I can't believe Oli did this." The wind rushed through Mingzhu's long black hair. "I don't get it, what's the problem? You meet him, say hello and move on."

"The boys wouldn't have done it; they'd have taken the mickey. So, I told him I didn't send the messages, that a friend was fooling around."

"Oh shit, George." Mingzhu's expression grave, she continued. "Let me guess: he didn't take it too well. So, what, he's stalking you now?"

Georgina nodded. "Uh-huh! You got it. We went to meet him on Monday night at The Starfish, as agreed, but he didn't turn up. So, I thought he was all talk, right? Wrong! He filmed us from a distance, which spooked the crap out of Shane and he goes and beats the shit out of some pommie guy sat by himself thinking he's Elf Man."

"Holy crap! So, what's he doing about it? He can't be seen beating people up, not if he wants to keep his job as captain of the Swans."

Getting excited at the lighthouse approaching, Georgina

shook her head. "He paid the guy off, gave him a few thousand dollars as an apology. He's not pressing charges. Last night, this Elf Man scratched the shit out of Oli's new car."

"Not the Nota?"

"Uh-huh! The very same. He's heaps pissed."

"Yeah, I can imagine."

Keeping her eyes ahead, slowing down on Matthew Flinders Drive, Georgina turned right into Tacking Point Surf Life Saving Club's car park. With the music off, and hardly any cars parked nearby, she chose a space closest to the pathway leading to the beach. She pulled up the handbrake and glanced at Mingzhu. "I've come here to forget all about this guy, honey. Can we just go surfing? Please?"

"Your wish is my command, my queen."

Georgina loved Mingzhu so much. Of all her close friends, she was the most loyal and trustworthy. She might have known Amelia the longest, but she often got the impression Amelia hated her success. Whenever she mentioned surfing, her supposed best friend would change the subject to something centred on her. Over the years, Georgina learned to ignore it. With Mingzhu, it was different, she guessed because they had similar interests. Her slender surf mate was as genuine and fun-loving as they came. "Thanks, babe, I appreciate it."

Outside, she and Mingzhu picked up their shortboards and bags. Georgina put the roof back up, leaving her phone and wallet inside and locked the car. "Right, let's find a blinding set," she said, her bag on one shoulder, the board under the other. Wearing short denim shorts, and a white vest top over a dark blue and white bikini, she walked with Mingzhu along the pathway in her thongs.

At just gone nine in the morning the north beach had the best waves. Georgina put her bag and board down and slid her shorts off, then took off her vest top. On the line-up, a couple of guys caught their first barrels, one of them bailing as the crest of the wave rolled into a barrel. What a barney, she thought.

It was going to be another scorcher, in the mid-to-late thirties, with promise of a huge storm that night. Georgina didn't regret leaving her wetsuit behind. Determined to get a superb tan while carving up some waves, she bent down and picked up her Firewire board. "Are you ready?"

She watched Mingzhu slip off her shorts, revealing a stunning floral bikini. The five foot three inch Chinese girl had the tautest abs. Shane often joked that she was so tiny that a strong gust of wind would have her away, yet he couldn't argue her fearlessness and dedication to the surf. Mingzhu almost defied the laws of physics on her Stevenson board. "I can't wait to get out there," she said, the rush of adrenaline spiked as she ran along the sandy beach into the sea.

Holding Mingzhu's hand while running, Georgina laughed as her feet hit the water. The perfect temperature. When she was knee deep, she threw the board in front of her and jumped on her front. Paddling with her arms, she traversed some high waves getting to the line-up, where the same two guys were waiting for the ideal wave. In the distance, to her right, she could see the bright white beacon on top of the cliff.

The fellas said hi, and she and Mingzhu chatted with them while they waited. The alpha of the two seemed competent enough. Georgina didn't think the same about his mate. "You know, he might be better off down shore. The waves aren't so intimidating."

The barney objected, telling her his foot slipped on his last wave, that it could happen to anyone. She nodded at Mingzhu and started paddling, a swell pushing her board along, until she jumped up and both feet landed on it simultaneously.

When the wave was at its highest, she cascaded down its surface and carved right, taking her into the newly formed barrel, her long hair hitting the water as she zoomed along the inside of it. When she came out of the tube, Georgina went against the wave and flipped her board on purpose, not wanting to be dragged back to shore. Treading water, her board attached to her, she found Mingzhu and paddled back to the line-up.

While sat on her board, her lower legs dangling in the water, she laughed with her friend. Alpha and Barney had moved further over, towards the gentler waves. Georgina searched the shoreline for her bag, when she saw a bloke bending over their belongings. "That guy's right by our bags." Waving her arms, crossing them over one another, she yelled, *"Hey! Those are our bags."*

The guy rifling through her stuff wore long khaki shorts and a blue T-shirt. He stood, looked at her and waved, like he was a friend of hers. "It's Elf Man."

Without hesitation, Georgina went with the next wave, jumping on her board, heading for the shore, all the while watching him, as he turned and strolled towards the car park.

Georgina hopped on her stomach and paddled to shore, Mingzhu by her side. "My keys are in my bag," she told her mate. At knee depth, she jumped off her board and ran in the water to the beach, where she raced to her belongings.

"Has he stolen anything?"

Scrambling to find her keys, she turned her bag inside out, praying they were hiding from her. "Shit!" she cried, conceding defeat. "He's taken my keys." She got up, picking up her bag and board. "My Jeep," she said, running towards the pathway leading to the club's car park.

Georgina yelled out, angry and frustrated at the empty parking space. She wanted to cry. "What the hell am I going to do?" she asked Mingzhu, tears rolling. "He's got my baby."

"He's got our phones, too. We need to call the police, George. Come on, we'll phone them from the club."

With her bag on her shoulder and board under her arm, Georgina walked with her friend to the front door of the lifesaving club. She knocked frantically on the glass door. It was only 09:45. "It probably won't open until later," she said, knocking again.

"Someone's in there," Mingzhu said, peering through a window.

A guy in his early thirties, fit with dark hair and a healthy tan, unlocked the door and opened it. "What's all the noise about?"

Georgina explained the situation and asked to use the phone. She spent a good hour trying to connect, and another waiting for the police to arrive. At almost midday, she told all to the female officer stood in front of her at the club's bar. The staff member who'd let her in asked them to sit down at a table to allow members to order their drinks and food.

While she and Mingzhu were explaining the situation, a male police officer walked up to their booth table. "A red Jeep, you said?"

"Uh-huh!" He rattled off her registration number. "Um, yes, that's it."

"It's right out there," he said, pointing to the front door.

Mingzhu grabbed Georgina's arm and pulled her to her feet.

Outside, in the car park sat her beloved Jeep.

"You can go in now, Inspector Coates," Nancy, Governor Brian Hicks' secretary, said. "Apologies for the delay." She stood and walked to the governor's office door.

Coates checked the time on the clock above Nancy's desk: 12:35. Hicks had kept him waiting for thirty-five minutes, and he arrived fifteen minutes early. There was no need for such tardiness, he thought with resentment. He stood and met Nancy's stare. "Thank you," he said, sarcasm hanging on every syllable.

The door opened and a rather tall man in a brown suit strode up to him and held his hand out, his shake firm and strong. "Detective Inspector David Coates," he said by way of introduction, after Hicks introduced himself with a genuine smile.

"I can't apologise to you enough for the hold-up, inspector." Hicks let go of Coates' hand and walked him through to the spacious office. "We had a power cut literally a minute before I was due to meet you. As you can imagine, it's a serious threat to this institution... I had to be on hand to supervise; I hope you understand."

Hicks had stormed past him at midday. The excuse sounded plausible. "Of course, governor. These things happen."

Hicks stood behind his mahogany desk and gestured a chair in front of him. Without hesitation, Coates took him up on his offer. The tall prison manager sat on his leather upholstered seat and leaned on his desk with his elbows. If Coates didn't know any better, he would say Hicks was trying to intimidate him. He almost laughed.

"Nancy tells me you're here wanting information on an ex-convict of ours?" The fingertips of both hands met. "I'll help in any way I can, inspector."

"Thank you, governor." He relaxed into his leather seat. "I was hoping you might fill me in on Arthur Peebles' time here?"

Hicks' eyes, upon hearing the name, grew narrower. "Why? What's he been doing?"

Professional courtesy made Coates pull his mobile out of his pocket and open his photos. Once he found a photo of Tara's body, he handed the phone to Hicks, who looked down at it, his eyebrows raised. "We have Peebles bang to rights for this," Coates started. "There's no margin for error here, either. The coroner has every type of evidence going that he's the responsible party. We know he's guilty, the only problem is–"

"He's no longer Arthur Peebles, am I right?"

Coates nodded, then waited for the governor to explain.

"I knew it wouldn't be long," Hicks confessed. "A guy like that wouldn't change. He sure didn't try changing in here, the little *bastard*. At his probation hearing, I tried. I told them he hasn't changed, that if anything he's ten times worse than when he arrived here. But would they listen? No, they sided with Peebles' solicitor, and released him early. Hell, Ince didn't do half of the things he was charged with, and he's still here."

"Why do you say that? How bad is he?"

Getting up from his chair, Hicks walked over to a filing

cabinet behind his desk and flicked through folders, until he found one in particular. It was marked Peebles. Back at his table, the governor sat and regarded the report, pulling out two photographs. "Now, I'm not showing you these, do you understand? If you so much as mention their existence, I walk away, never to be seen again, understood? This is highly classified... I'm trusting you with this."

"You *can* trust me, governor." Coates waited for the first picture. "Look, all I want to do is catch this guy before he kills his next poor victim, all right?" He reached out and took the first photo.

Bloody and brutal, the photograph showed a muscular naked white man spreadeagled on the shower room floor. The man's face bore the brunt of the wounding, stabbed several times by the look of it. At the time of the picture being taken, the victim's blood was draining away. There were a couple of stab wounds on the convict's belly and neck. "Peebles did this?" Confused, Coates said, "Forgive me for asking, but why release him? He should've received another life sentence, right?"

"Evidence, or lack thereof, should I say. We had our own internal investigators on this, and they couldn't find anything on Peebles, even though I knew it was him."

"So, how did you know?"

"Gripper hated Peebles; he loathed rapists and nonces. Not that I witnessed it, but apparently this beast made Peebles' life hell here, and who stood to gain the most from Gripper being shanked in the showers? He did. And his life became far more bearable after Gripper's departure, until that is, this prisoner came here six years ago."

Hicks handed him the second photo. Coates had to hold the picture away from his eyes. Again, brutal, it showed a black guy sat on a chair, his head back and a long deep gash in his throat. Fully clothed, the once-larger-than-life prisoner's life force had soaked through his prison issue overalls. The felon's eyes were wide open in terrified disbelief. "Where was this taken?" Coates asked the governor.

"The projection room. Again, the investigators couldn't find any evidence against Peebles, but he stood to gain the most. Hector took an immediate disliking – or rather hatred – to him. Every chance he got, he beat on the child rapist and murderer. Until that fateful afternoon, when Hector's corpse turned up."

"And life improved for Peebles here after that?"

"Oh no end. The rest of the inmates were too afraid to even speak to him, much less anything else. They didn't want to be found with fifty-five stab wounds to their faces. No, they let him be. In fact, they let them both be. Two rapists, just allowed to walk around like they owned the place... Made me sick, turned my stomach, watching that, all because we couldn't prove his involvement. And without proof, we couldn't use the murders against him at his probation hearing either. That's how he was released, that and having an exceptional solicitor."

One thing bugged Coates. "These are both big boys, right?"

"Oh yeah, I wouldn't mess with them."

"Then how did Peebles manage to get to them? He's no match for these guys. Only what, five-nine? Maybe ten or eleven stone? How does an average Joe like that take out two strapping lads like these, hmm? It doesn't make sense. And this Gripper, the one in the shower, did Peebles creep up on him, or what?"

Hicks shrugged. "It sounds far-fetched, inspector, but I know Peebles killed them both." He reached across the desk and took the photos back. He shook his head, his eyes sad. "And now he's gone and murdered that pretty girl."

Coates popped his phone back in his suit jacket pocket. "I'm afraid so," he said in condolence to Hicks. "What matters now is catching this bastard. Where is he?"

"How the hell would I know? I'm a prison governor,

inspector; I don't follow ex-convicts after they're released. You'll have to take that up with someone at either the Ministry of Justice, or probation service. Once he's out of here, he's not my problem."

Coates nodded his understanding. "I don't suppose you have contacts at the Ministry of Justice, do you? I could really use some help on this. I need to find out why Peebles' record has been redacted."

"I'm afraid not. He was sentenced as a minor, right?"

"Right, so?"

"The probation service will have given him a new life somewhere. A new name, in a place they can keep an eye on him. You're from Sussex way, yes?"

"Lewes, yeah," he said, slowly understanding. "And you think he was relocated to the south east for his protection?" It made sense, he supposed.

"They did the same for Venables and Thompson."

Coates was beginning to think he would never find Peebles.

19

K ereama Tua leaned across and kissed Amelia goodbye on the cheek. "I'll be back by five," he said. "See you later. Have fun shopping." He opened her car door and picked up his rucksack from under the dash. "And try not to worry about this bloody pom, all right. I'm telling you he's all piss and wind."

After waving her off, he stood outside the entrance to the Central Metro Station, put his bag by his feet and took out his pack of cigarettes. Lighting one, he leaned back against a wall and inhaled, relishing the smoke hitting his throat. Amelia hated him smoking. A stupid and costly habit, he earned enough and told himself he could quit anytime he liked.

Packed on the pavement outside the underground with commuters trying to travel to work on a Friday morning, one woman caught his attention. She wore a suit and a killer smile, with long blonde hair tied back in a ponytail. He blew a plume of smoke above people's heads.

Wearing a pair of blue jeans, a Led Zeppelin T-shirt and a light leather jacket, he stamped out his cigarette and picked up his bag. Kereama would normally drive to the recording studio in Cronulla, however his car was having its yearly inspection. The Metro would be packed, until he reached the outskirts of the city. By the time he got to Sutherland, he might actually grab a seat.

Squeezing through the pack of travellers, he found himself walking with the crowd towards the escalator down to the platforms. He'd organised his ticket online, so he didn't need to pay at the booth. With his eye on the blonde in front, he stood two steps above her, taking in her strong, yet sweet perfume. She smelled divine.

Having stepped off the escalator, about to approach her, the tall woman turned left and disappeared, catching a train going in the opposite direction. "Bugger!" he mumbled, then shrugged and carried on.

It didn't take him long to find another beauty. On his platform, he stood among the crowd, locked in like cattle, when a black woman in her early twenties caught his eye in front and to the left. She beamed healthy white teeth at him from between commuters, but had to turn her head to find him. He smiled back.

Onboard the train, he had to stand, holding a vertical handrail, his bag by his feet. A woman stood next to him wrinkled her nose in disgust. "I smoke, lady, bite me!" he said with a sneer. He was a fucking rock star; he didn't take shit from an arsehole like that. When she huffed and turned away, he chuckled to himself, the black girl in front of the doors laughing with him. He mouthed, "Snooty bitch". And she laughed again. While stood there, he imagined ripping her clothes off. He wondered what she hid beneath the office attire.

Disappointed, he watched as the black woman turned when they started to slow down pulling into Carlton Station. Movement, as people squeezed past him. He saw her disappear.

Gutted, he breathed in, letting more commuters pass him, when he felt a stabbing pain in his side.

He groaned and placed his right hand over his ribs.

When he stared at the palm of his hand, warm sticky blood made him gulp. His hand red, blood dripping from it, he went cold.

People were still piling out of the carriage.

He stared at his blood-covered hand.

A scream came from behind him.

Sweat trickled down his temples; he felt queasy and needed to exit the train before the doors closed.

When he went to walk forwards, the commuters in front took steps to the side, forming a pathway.

Holding his side, his palm covering the wound, he staggered one weary step after another until he was on the platform. He heard the bleep of the doors closing.

With blood dripping on the concrete, Kereama scanned the area for a first aid station, all the while commuters looked on in horror. "We need to get you to the hospital, mate," he heard some guy say, as he felt hands helping him towards a seat. "Someone call an ambo, please?"

Before he knew what was going on, he lay on his back, a crowd of people gathered around him, concerned faces peering down at him. Then, the mob seemed to disappear, and he saw a male and female paramedic above him in their dark blue uniforms.

20

Fridays in Westfield Shopping Centre, Market Street, were busy. Being early January wasn't putting off the shoppers, it seemed to Amelia, who hated crowded stores. "Let's try Zara," she said to Bronwyn Mason, needing a top for the opening night of Fever. "My feet hurt."

Bronwyn, Amelia and Georgina had met on the first day of primary school and had remained close friends up until the age of fifteen, when Georgina became obsessed with surfing. Pretty, with a size six figure, Bronwyn was far more suited to shopping than anything else. Amelia always chose her to shop with.

The only thing Amelia wanted to do was sunbathe; she lived for it. If she had her way, she would spend every day lying on the golden sands of Bondi Beach, listening to the waves gently lapping over one another, taking in the scent of salty air and suntan lotion. Even holding a lovely top up in front of her, she daydreamed about being in a bikini, slowly turning a darker shade of brown. "I might've found a winner." Her watch told her it was almost midday. If she bought the garment, she might go home, grab her things and be down the beach by half one.

"You're going to the opening of Fever tonight, right?" Bronwyn asked.

Amelia took the top and continued scanning the rack in front of her. "Yeah, George got us tickets. Why? Are you?" Judging by the sad expression on Bronwyn's face, no. "Shall I ask if she has any spare? I think she had ten posted to her."

"Ah, would you? I haven't really spoken to her in months. I don't want her to think I'm using her."

With another gorgeous top in front of her, Amelia smiled. "George isn't like that," she said, deciding against it and putting it back. "She'll give you tickets if you ask. But I'll ask her for you this time, okay? I wish you two would make up. I don't even know why you're not talking."

Bronwyn sighed. "If I'm honest, neither do I."

It was a lie, though. They both understood why: jealousy. The more famous Georgina became, the more distant Bronwyn grew. By the time Georgina turned pro-surfer, Bronwyn was on the periphery, an occasional friend. And just after Georgina wiped out so spectacularly at the WSL Championships, Bronwyn reappeared, there to give Georgina her condolences, which Georgina took very well, Amelia thought. Anyway, none of that mattered now. In need of a top for the opening of Fever, the hippest club in town, she made a decision.

"Right, this one it is." She had plenty of outfits in her wardrobe from her modelling contracts, but wanted to buy something special for herself. Knowing she made more money than Kereama, even with his recording contract and tours, made her happy. "Come on. Let's go pay. Then we can go to the beach, or The Icebergs."

"I reckon I'll be staying in town, babe. And anyway, I still need to find something to wear for tonight."

At the till, she paid for her new top and handed over her credit card when her ringtone told her she had a call. Reaching into her bag, she pulled it out and answered, only to be told she was speaking to a police officer.

"I'm afraid he's been injured. He's in surgery, but it would be advisable to come along if you can?"

She gasped, her shaking hand covering her mouth, tears welling up, and stared at a concerned Bronwyn, then at the cashier. The policeman told her that Kereama was stable prior to commencing surgery at Sydney Hospital, over on Macquarie Street, a short walk from the mall. If she ran, she would be there inside five minutes. Amelia hung up after informing the officer that she would be there.

She apologised to the cashier for bailing on her and took her card. "I've got to go, Bron," Amelia said, putting her purse back in her bag. "Kay's been injured. He's in surgery." And without warning, she searched for the correct exit and started running.

Behind her, Bronwyn chased after her. "Wait for me, Ames."

Amelia ran along Market Street until she had to cross the road and cut through the north end of Hyde Park, following a path that led to Macquarie Street. From Macquarie Street it was a short run up to the hospital, where Kereama would have been taken straight to accident and emergency, before being wheeled to surgery. "We made it."

Panting, she walked through the automatic glass doors.

After a long to and fro between her and the receptionist, Amelia finally received directions. With Bronwyn in tow, she found the waiting area and asked the nearest staff member wearing a white coat how he was doing. The kind doctor, nurse, whatever, said he would find out. Alone, with only Bronwyn for company, Amelia sat. She needed Georgina by her side.

Bronwyn asked her if she wanted anything to drink. When she said yes, her shopping friend left, leaving her enough time to phone Georgina and Isla, who both dropped everything to join her. With a half-smile, Amelia accepted the plastic cup of coffee and sat back, imagining the worst.

It took Georgina twenty minutes to arrive. Standing up, Amelia hugged her longest, dearest friend, ignoring an uncomfortable Bronwyn behind her. Georgina asked what happened. Even Amelia didn't know. With a shake of her head, she answered Georgina's question. "All I know is he's been hurt. I left him at the Metro."

Isla came rushing in all concerned. Amelia hugged her and cried. Having her two best friends present meant the world to her and helped when two doctor types appeared with two police officers in tow. "Oh God, no, please don't tell me he's dead."

"Relax, Miss Thomas," the taller of the white coats said. "He's fine. He was brought in with a nasty stab wound we had to deal with, and he lost a lot of blood, but he's going to make a full recovery. We've sewn him up, so he's going to be sore for a while."

Amelia gasped through the tears. "He was stabbed? But he's going to make it?" Her girls, her sisters, hugged her. "I don't understand. Where? Why?" When the doctors shook their heads, she asked, "Can I go in?" She needed to see his beautiful face.

The doctor told her that he might be out for an hour or so, to wait until a member of his staff gave the all-clear. "In the meantime, however, the police would like to talk to you," the shorter doctor said.

"Me? Why? I don't know anything."

"Routine procedure with stabbings," the female officer in her light blue shirt and grey shorts replied. "But please, Miss Thomas, it's nothing to worry about, I promise."

And so, Amelia stood in the centre of the waiting room answering a barrage of questions from Sydney's finest, until she'd had enough. After the police left, she asked Isla and Georgina, "Where's Bron?"

"Rude!" Isla said.

The tall doctor appeared and told her she could visit Kereama, although only for a short time; he was groggy and needed quiet to recover. Excited, Amelia took her friends' hands and walked through the corridor until she stood outside Kereama's door. Taking a deep breath, she opened it to find him lying on his back in bed, his eyes closed, his cut dressed beneath a hospital gown.

Hooked up to a drip – which was normal apparently – he smiled.

"You scared the shit out of me." Amelia's face crumpled as she rushed to his side, his eyes widening when she touched his bandaged wound. "Oh, I'm so sorry! Are you all right, baby? I didn't mean to."

"What the hell happened?" Georgina asked.

"What do you think? Elf Man." Kereama grimaced. "I was on the packed Metro. We stopped at Carlton Station when I felt a stabbing pain in my side. I hobbled out onto the platform and I must've passed out, because the next thing I remember is seeing the paramedics around me."

Amelia put her hand in her bag when her mobile dinged. Taking it out, she went straight for her Chatter app: another private message from Elf Man, with a photograph. Listening to Kereama talking to her girls, she read the text. "This the kind of man you want?"

The picture made her want to throw her phone at the wall. Anger rose, itching to escape and hurt him. It showed Kereama eyeing up a very attractive black girl in a suit, whose eyes were devouring him whole. She stood out because she was taller than most of the commuters around her. "You piece of shit! You absolute, you total bastard!" She shook the phone.

"What? What've I done?"

She threw the mobile at his chest, catching him off guard. When he flinched and said, "ow", she glared at him. "Go on! Look at it! There I was worrying about you, crying over you, thinking you were dead, and you were eyeing up some skank on the train? I've fucking had it with you. Always making an idiot out of me. Well, no more, *Kerry*!"

Kereama tutted. "Wait! I can explain."

Had Georgina and Isla not been there to pull her back, she might have flown at him. He actually thought she didn't know that he had all these groupies on tour, any girl who'd have him, more like. And as she stood staring at his ridiculous, speechless face, she realised that if she didn't shed him now, she probably never would, and he would forever be making a fool of her. "Well, explain then, you useless mongrel."

"Nothing happened with her."

It didn't matter. It was the way they were looking at one another, the way the black woman devoured him with her eyes. If he'd met her on tour, or at a bar in town, they would end up back at hers, ripping each other's clothes off, laughing at silly old Amelia, back home waiting up for him. The final straw. For too long she'd put up with it. And to think he wanted to do away with protection. Before she exploded, she turned and left the room with her two best friends by her side.

"Ames, come back!" he shouted. "Please!"

21

"Are you sure you want to go to this tonight?" Georgina asked. "We don't have to. We can stay here if you want. Let's dial in a pizza, the boys can grab some coldies."

"I appreciate what you're doing, George, but I'm not letting him ruin my night out. Fuck him! I don't care."

Fiddling with her hair in front of the mirror in her hallway, adding some finishing touches, with her girlfriends stood behind her, looking stunning in their chosen outfits, Georgina thought all three of them looked amazing. Amelia wore a cute top and short skirt, while Isla sported an unbuttoned shirt over a vest, with denim shorts. With Amelia's mind made up, Georgina thought her friend was making a mistake going out. "You're sure?"

"Yes, I'm sure. Can we go now? Please?"

She took one last peek in the mirror. "Let's go!"

The boys were waiting outside in the cab. Even with Elf Man on the loose, he didn't scare her; she was with her best friends and boyfriend at a nightclub cram packed with people. Georgina gathered her girls and locked up the house.

The lads looked and smelled amazing, particularly Shane,

she thought, who wore black trousers and a white shirt with four buttons undone. His body visible through the flimsy material, she smiled.

Not missed by anyone other than Amelia, Georgina thought Kereama was a sleaze. She'd tried broaching the subject of his infidelity with her friend on a couple of occasions, but fell short for fear Amelia would accuse her of jealousy.

The drive to Fever, on Oxford Street, only took seven minutes. At half past eleven on a Friday night, traffic around the city was busy. Oliver and Shane exited first, turned, and waited for them. In front of a huge throng of revellers queuing, Georgina, the last to leave the cab, took Shane's hand to a chorus of approval from the crowd. She loved the fame, loved everyone knowing who she was. If that made her a vain person, or a narcissist, to hell with it, she thought, she also raised loads of money for four charities. When she waved, the crowd cheered.

A suited man approached her. "Georgina? Will you and your guests please step this way. We have your VIP area waiting for you."

Georgina took Shane's arm and followed her friends inside. Feeling a little guilty at queue hopping, she focused on walking in her new heels. Tripping in front of all these people would be as embarrassing as being resuscitated live on TV, she thought, concentrating. Once in the foyer, she relaxed a little, knowing if she tripped, most partygoers queuing would miss it.

The bass of the music reverberated through the floor: disco, her favourite for dancing to. While she loved heavy metal to her core, Georgina had a soft spot for disco after her dad made her listen to it when growing up.

Fever, situated on Oxford Street, just up from Hotel Centennial and across the road from Centennial Park, benefitted from a genius location, because it was the only nightclub in the area, and it would attract customers from all around. Fever boasted lots of rooms, where music styles would vary in each room. With two floors, it promised to be a lively and vibrant venue.

The club manager walked them through to the main room, along the huge dance floor and up a flight of stairs to an impeccably decorated VIP area, sectioned off with a cordon consisting of two stainless steel posts and thick red rope.

"This zone is for you and your friends. Champagne and canapés are over there. If I can help in any other way, don't hesitate in calling me over."

Georgina giggled when the boys and her girlfriends descended on the drinks table, like locusts finding food after a long day's flying. "Save some for me." She joined them and accepted a glass of champagne from Shane.

Taking Amelia by the arm, Georgina walked her over to the railings and observed the revellers in front of the bar below. The dance floor was empty, but given an hour or so, would be jumping when the DJ turned up the volume and started playing the great disco tunes. Georgina, up for a dance, wanted to forget about Elf Man for the night. "I'm so sorry about what's happened."

"Why? You're not to blame for him being a mongrel." Amelia leaned her cheek on Georgina's shoulder. "I feel so stupid. I mean, I knew he had girls on tour, of course, but he's never looked at anyone else before, at least not in front of me, or, well... I would physically grab his testicles and rip them off."

The intensity with which her friend described castrating Kereama, told Georgina she meant it. "Here's hoping I never piss you off, eh!" Amelia downed her glass of champagne in one huge gulp. "Careful, babe, this stuff'll knock you on the floor if you drink it like that." And have her crying on her shoulder, no doubt, she thought, shaking her head when Isla gave Amelia a second flute which she drank in one gulp as well. "Going to be like that, is it? Great!"

Georgina had Amelia on one side and Isla on the other, all watching the activity below them. A group of lads huddled on the dance floor looked up at them. Georgina groaned when Amelia tugged on her arm. "Might be best if you stay up here, Ames." Amelia wanted to go down and chat the guys up. "You'll only regret it tomorrow. You still love Kay; I know you do."

Georgina's mobile bleeped in her bag, the glow of her screen catching her attention. She had a message from Elf Man on Chatter. "Shit! It's him!"

"Shit! He's here." Shane stood behind her, his hand on her waist.

The photo in the message was of the foyer, a non-too-subtle hint that he had entered the building. Georgina couldn't believe the guy's nerve. She thought she would have a safe outing tonight. "For fuck's sake," she puffed. "When's this guy going to leave us alone?" She wanted to shout at Oliver. The frustrating thing: if she'd taken her phone with her at The Starfish, none of this would be happening. Kereama wouldn't be staying overnight in hospital after being stabbed; Oliver's car wouldn't have been keyed; her car wouldn't have been stolen, and then returned; and Shane wouldn't have had to pay thousands of dollars to the guy he beat up. When was this nightmare going to be over? "We've got to get the hell out of here."

"No way! We just got here," Amelia said, having downed her third glass. "Let's go and say hi to those boys!" Her eyes were glazed.

"Elf Man's here, Ames. The dude who stabbed Kay's here. We need to leave." Shane grabbed her phone. "Hey! What're you doing, babe?" She peered over his shoulder as he typed a reply to the pom. She read out aloud for the group. "What's your problem, mate? We've already apologised. What do you want from us?"

Shane sent the message and handed her the phone.

"What do you expect to get from that?" she asked.

"I don't know, to open a dialogue maybe?"

The mobile vibrated in her hand and the screen lit up. "Here's his reply." She held it up. Amelia was too busy waving at the boys below. "To be your friend. But you blew it. You had to go thinking you're so much better than me." And before she finished reading it, Oliver had it in his hand.

"I'm fucking sick of this." He quickly typed a reply, reading it aloud as he did so. "And why should we be friends with you? Why do you deserve to be our friend? We're all high achievers, what've you done? Give us one good reason why."

"No! Oli, please don't send that; you're only going to make it worse." But he turned his back on the group before she got to her phone. And her spirit sank when she heard him say, "Oops!" Staring at Shane for support, she grabbed her phone back and glared at Oliver. "You just can't help yourself, can you? You idiot! You've gone and made it ten times worse! I'm sorry, Isla, but enough's enough."

"No, you're right, George." Isla slapped her boyfriend. "You never behave. This isn't a joke, you moron. This guy stabbed Kereama earlier today, remember? We're not dealing with some socially awkward pommie here. You make me so mad I wanna thump you sometimes."

Georgina jumped when it vibrated again. "Oh God! He's replied." With Chatter open, she checked her messages. With one eye closed, she pulled up the picture: of them stood by the railing, taken from below them on the dance floor. She gasped, then glanced down, hoping he would be down there looking up at them.

"What've I done? Ha! You'll find out soon enough," Shane

read. "And high achievers? Don't make me laugh. Shane's the captain of a third-rate football club. The Swans are useless since he took over. Congratulations, Shane, you've taken them from top flight to bottom of the premiership. And Oli, second place on some reality show, really awe inspiring, I guess, for losers. Kerry's the guitarist for a totally shit 'heavy metal band' and looks like an aftershave commercial model, yeah, rocking. Amelia lives on the beach and gets paid to wear clothes – what a role model! Your mum must be so proud. Then we come to Isla, with all those muscles. Wasted your life on vanity, well done. And finally we come to the lovely Georgina: wiped out mid-competition. Resuscitated on live TV. Model and Chatter royalty. Why the fuck are you with this mob of losers? You should ditch them and come with me. I'll love you and treat you like the queen you are."

The venom in those words made her shudder. "Please can we leave now? Let's go home and call the police, report him," she pleaded. There was so much hatred in Shane's eyes. "What're you thinking, Shane?"

"George, you take the girls home," he said, taking her phone from her. "We're going to have it out with Mr Elf Man here, tonight."

Georgina begged him not to, but after he'd baited Elf Man, she decided against arguing. Instead, she kissed him goodbye, forced Amelia to join her and Isla and walked down the stairs to the dance floor, where she kept vigil, scanning the busy room for the pommie. No loners, only youngsters out enjoying themselves.

Outside the foyer doors, queues of revellers waiting to go inside, she hailed a passing cab and helped Amelia into the back. With Isla taking charge in front, Georgina stared at the entrance for Elf Man. No one appeared as the taxi drove away.

22

The view from the railing of the VIP room was panoramic of the club. Partygoers were filling up the dance floor, while more introverted guests sat around tables and chairs at the side. Elf Man, if he obsessed over Georgina as much as Shane suspected, would try to follow the girls. He ordered Oliver to search for the Brit downstairs. "Shit! He didn't go for it," he said into his phone to Oliver. "He's still here, mate. Give it a reccy, would you?"

With Oliver hunting for the pom, Shane leaned on the railing and watched the crowd below, his leg jigging up and down to the music. He wouldn't admit it to Georgina, but he enjoyed disco; he loved dancing to it, especially with fit girls grinding on him. Yeah, he loved that. The new football season was almost upon him, which meant parties. They were legendary, the Swans parties. The women, my God, the women, he thought, watching a couple of hotties dancing. They smiled up at him.

"Bugger!" Oliver sidled over to them. Shane could foresee what was in store for him. Oliver would walk the ladies up the stairs, palm one of them on him, whereupon he would start chatting to her and end up kissing her. From his vantage point, he spotted at least three covert photographers, all out to get their lenses on something juicy to sell to the tabloids.

Four of his fellow teammates emerged from the bar carrying drinks. He caught their attention, and summoned them up to join him in the VIP area. Behind them a group of hot women traipsed, a mixture of blondes, brunettes, white, black and Asian. He waved them all up and shook their hands in turn. "Ladies, help yourselves to the champers."

Oliver joined, holding hands with the two girls from downstairs. "No sign of the Elf," he said, walking the girls over to a table and settling down.

Shane, in deep discussion with his rover and ruck rover about the upcoming season, forgot about Elf Man. Being captain of the Sydney Swans he tried to treat everyone equally and made it a matter of pride to get along with each member of the team on a personal level. Out tonight, he had his rover, left forward pocket, a ruck rover and centre half-forward. The conversation was lively, taking his mind from Elf Man.

And he lost himself even more when one of the entourage joined them, her hands all over him. Valerie, a brunette, six feet tall, with a killer hour-glass figure, demonstrated intentions he didn't need to read into. As the conversation went on, he talked less to his teammates, and enjoyed more of her touch, until she moved in.

Valerie was a superb kisser. After five minutes, Shane opened his eyes and checked on Oliver. He grinned when he saw a blonde head going up and down behind the table, Oliver's eyes closed, his expression one of bliss. Valerie's fingers on his chin, he turned his head back to her.

"Shall we find somewhere a little more comfortable?" she asked, her hand on his chest, sneaking underneath his open shirt. "So strong."

"I'm game." He kissed her again.

The vibration in his trousers caught him off guard. Taking his phone out of his pocket, he answered it to the sound of Georgina's voice. "Hey, babe," he said, putting his finger up to shush Valerie. "Are you all right?" He breathed a little easier when she confirmed they were home safe. "No, we lost him. Tell Isla we'll be back when we've dealt with him. Don't wait up, okay? And don't worry; we've got this." He winked at Valerie, who played with his belt.

On his way to find somewhere more comfortable, he glanced at Oliver's table. The blonde woman's back hid Oliver, but by the way she was grinding on him, fully clothed, Oliver wouldn't stop her, even if he wanted to. "Good boy!" he whispered, spotting a lonely table. Good enough for Oliver, good enough for him, he thought, excited to sit and acquaint himself with Valerie.

Getting comfortable, Valerie on his lap, Shane let her unzip his trousers, as he kissed her deeply. Then, he heard raised voices in front of him. When he leaned to the side, three guys with cameras pointed them at him. His heart lurched, his mind immediately playing scenarios where Georgina found pictures of him with Valerie in the national newspapers. Luckily, his teammates were trying to bar them from entering the VIP lounge, but two of the three paparazzi weren't having any of it; they attempted to push past, to take more photos of him with Valerie. Shane cursed, then threw Valerie from his lap and got up. "No fucking way!" He moved with purpose towards them.

When he approached the first photographer, he grabbed his camera and looked through the pictures, deleting all featuring him, while his teammates held him by the scruff of his neck. "Now, fuck off, you vulture." He handed the camera back. "Go find a real job, one that matters to people."

"Oh, like yours? Playing a game for money? And badly," the photographer countered.

Moving on to the second paparazzo, he resisted and Toby, his ruckman had to punch him in his gut. Shane prised the camera from him and flicked through the photos of him, deleting them as he went. "You lot really do need to get a life!" He gave the camera back, looking over the vulture's shoulder for the third guy. "Where'd he go?" he asked his teammates. "He was right there. There were three of them."

Toby shook his head. "Nah, mate, only two."

His other workmates agreed with Toby; there were only two photographers. "No, three, the third guy at the back, behind the other two, where is he?"

Oliver shrugged, too busy with his blonde to notice at the time.

"And you're no fucking help!"

In the centre of the dance floor, a man trying to make his way to the front doors, squeezing through the throng of revellers, carried a camera, Shane noticed. The pom turned around and grinned up at him, then fled. "Elf Man! Get him!" Shane yelled at Oliver and the Swans. "I need those fucking pictures!"

Feeling sick, he raced down the stairs to the dance floor. Once there, he tried to remain polite, asking people to mind themselves. He couldn't move for dancers. Annoyed, he started pushing people, shouting at them. Oliver by his side, Shane sprinted for the foyer, where the beefy doormen greeted them. "A guy with a camera just came out of here," he barked. "Where'd he go?"

"Keep your knickers on. He went that way."

Following directions, Shane ran to the left, along Oxford Street towards Queen Street. There was no doubt he would kill Elf Man, wring his bloody neck, or better yet, beat him to death with his bare hands.

Shane and Oliver carried on past the turning for Queen

Street, until they came to Wallis Street, opposite Centennial Park, where Shane stopped to catch his breath. Looking around, he couldn't find Elf Man, only randoms walking to and from their chosen destinations. "Shit!" His phone went off in his pocket.

"Let's see the damage."

Shane hesitated. "He'll fuck everything up."

Oliver waited with expectation.

"If George finds out, I'm a dead man." Swallowing his fear, Shane opened Chatter. "You don't deserve her," he read out loud. "He's going to use them." The three photos were bad. In one he was barely visible; it mostly showed Valerie's back. The other two were horrendous, his face clear, with her on his lap. "I'm so fucking dead."

"Ask him what he wants," Oliver suggested.

"Why bother?" Hope vanished. "He wants George."

"Doesn't mean you have to hand her to him."

Taking Oliver's advice, Shane typed out the message and sent it. With late night drinkers walking past them, he waited for a response from Elf Man. Nothing.

"You have to fight for her, mate," Oliver said.

Putting his mobile away, Shane started back towards the club. "Let's go home, while I still can."

23

D I David Coates knocked on the door of the five-bedroomed country house and stood back, listening for signs of life inside. The house sat in an acre of land, surrounded by trees and bushes of varying types. He took in the home's surroundings. At the rear of the garden to his right he spotted an ornate pond, which if he investigated, he assumed would hold fish of all descriptions. "All right for some."

A woman's face appeared through a small gap. "Yes?"

"Mrs Peebles?" Upon hearing her confirmation, Coates reached inside his suit jacket and retrieved his identification wallet. "Detective Inspector David Coates, ma'am," he said, to her irritated expression. "Before you close the door, please hear me out."

"I told you, I don't want to talk about him," she snapped. "Go away. We don't want to know him, or what he does." She slammed the door.

Coates sighed. "Even if he's killed again, and you can help me find him?"

Nothing. She might have closed the door on him, but he knew she was listening. "Please, Mrs Peebles, he'll kill again."

"I can't help you, I'm sorry."

A step closer to the door, he leaned forwards. "Can I ask why not?"

"Because I, we, my husband and I, the last time we spoke to him must have been a year and a half ago."

"Please, can I come in and talk to you about him?" The first couple of droplets of rain landed on his coat. Dark grey clouds promised to soak him any minute. "Please, Mrs Peebles."

The door opened. Ursula Peebles sighed. Then she stood to the left and invited him in. "You're in luck. Victor just put the kettle on."

Coates took her up on her offer and asked for a cup of coffee. The first thing he observed about Peebles' mother: her age; she had to be in her mid-to-late seventies, and slow moving. He followed her through to the huge kitchen, where she offered him a chair behind a long table big enough to seat twelve. "Milk, one sugar, please." He examined the surroundings.

North Ferriby was situated off the A63, a few miles away from Hull, the Peebles' hometown. Coates had set off from Lewes four hours earlier; he was grateful for the pick-me-up. "Thanks." He sipped his beverage.

Unexpectedly, Ursula Peebles started their conversation. "I apologise for shutting the door on you. You must understand that Victor and I have grown a tough skin over the years. After his arrest, people would yell at us from outside. Everyone seemed to blame us. Strange how our lives are split in two: before it happened, and after."

Trying to imagine her pain, Coates put on his most sympathetic face. "I'm sorry for your loss." The Peebles had disowned their son, which must hurt, he thought.

"So am I. He was such a lovely child. He loved his family, his brothers and sister; he would do anything for them." Her face changed to sombre. "Until he fell under Ince's spell. I swear he caused all this. None of this would've happened, if Michael–"

"Who's he murdered?" came a male voice from behind him.

Turning in his chair, Coates eyed Victor Peebles for the first time: a short, squat man, balding, with an air of intelligence about him, stood in the hallway. Peebles' narrow, suspicious eyes were on him, waiting. "Her name's Tara Henson; she lived down south in a small town called Lewes." Coates took out his phone in case his interviewees wanted to view their son's handiwork.

Mr Peebles walked inside the room and went to the sink. "Well, we haven't seen Arthur in over eighteen months. So, how can we help you find him when we don't know where he is? He's dead to us now. If I'd had my way, I wouldn't have paid for the solicitors, but she made me."

Coates couldn't understand their mentality. He liked to think that no matter what Hannah did, he would support her. There were limits to unconditional love, he guessed. "You could tell me about him, what he was like growing up, that kind of thing. Any input will help."

"And you don't have any doubts he's responsible?"

"None. All we need to do is apprehend him. Forensics picked up so much trace evidence, semen, saliva, hairs, skin and a bloody fingerprint." He heard Mrs Peebles' gasp at his mention of semen. "I'm afraid he... Before he murdered her."

"You can say it, detective. Our son raped that poor woman."

"He's a monster," Mrs Peebles whispered.

He couldn't argue with her. Monster described Arthur Peebles well. By all accounts they'd given Arthur the same opportunities as his brothers and sister, who had all made something of themselves. No, they weren't responsible for Arthur's sickness, not that that stopped people from thinking so. "Don't blame yourself, Mrs Peebles. Look at how the rest of your children turned out. And you didn't treat him differently, did you?"

"Of course not. She knows this, detective."

He needed more from them. "He's been out of prison eighteen months now, Mr Peebles. I don't suppose he's tried contacting you in that time, has he? Please, if you know anything, even his assumed name, it'll help, sir."

"Is that why you came here?" Mr Peebles asked. "Even after I made it clear we don't speak to Arthur anymore."

"We saw him at the parole hearing, where I told him we never want to see him again. We paid his legal expenses against Victor's better judgement." Mrs Peebles' voice broke, strained.

Mr Peebles unfolded his arms and stepped towards the table. "You're upsetting my wife, detective. You need to leave now."

Coates held his hands up, palms displayed. "I didn't mean to." He delved into his pocket when his mobile saved the day. "I'm sorry! I need to take this." Mrs Peebles wiped her eyes with a handkerchief. Asking the caller to wait, Coates stood, then followed Mr Peebles to the front door. "Again, my apologies." Taking out his cards, he handed one to his interviewee.

He cursed under his breath at the closed door. Turning, he put the mobile to his ear. "Sorry about that, sir." He walked along the driveway. "I was interviewing the Peebles. What's new?"

"I set you up a meeting with someone in the Ministry of Justice. He's an aide to Richard Luckland, the Justice Secretary. He agreed to meet you after I explained the situation. From what I gleaned from our brief conversation, Luckland wants Peebles brought in quietly. I get the impression his arrest will be a source of embarrassment for both the MoJ and the probation service."

"Now that I can do. You can let the aide know we're on the same team."

"No need. You can assure him when you meet on Friday."

Disappointed, Coates said, "Friday's four days away, sir," he moaned. "Peebles could kill again at any time."

"The best I can do, inspector. How's Sergeant Packard getting on with the tattoo angle?"

"We're in talks with the victim's neighbour." Coates sighed. "But, like you say, we've other leads we can follow up until Friday. Thank you for reaching out, sir."

After hanging up, Coates opened his car door and slumped heavily in his seat. Why didn't they understand the gravity of the situation? Politicians were such dicks, he thought, closing his door, and switching on the engine. Releasing the handbrake, he set off on his long journey back to Lewes.

24

Georgina was nervous. "Is this necessary?" Pulling into the car park of the Dover Heights Gun Club, she waited for a reply. Everyone in her family, including her dad, hated guns. After her stalker managed to penetrate their previous home's security, she allowed Shane to buy a pistol and keep it in the house. "I hate those things." She spotted a space and parked her Jeep.

Shane reached behind him and picked up the two cases, one bigger than the other. "Football season starts soon, babe. That means I'm not going to be around as much, so I need the peace of mind you're safe. This is the only way. It's easy, George. Honestly, you make sure the magazine's loaded, you take the safety off and pull the trigger."

She exited her Jeep, still not convinced. Shane knew how to shoot. A member of the club and regular user of the firing range, he was licensed, adding to the other two million permitted gun owners in the country. The previous day he'd brought home the second, smaller gun. When he handed her the Beretta 21 Bobcat, the weight of the tiny pocket pistol surprised her. "Let's go!" She met him at the front of the Jeep.

"You might enjoy it." He took her hand and walked towards the gun club entrance.

Since he and Oliver had returned in the early hours of Saturday morning, Georgina thought Shane was acting strangely: quieter than usual, jittery. Whenever she asked him what was wrong, he shrugged it off, gave her a kiss and told her not to worry. Georgina knew better. Something happened on Friday night at Fever, she could tell.

Inside, Shane went to reception while she waited, listening to the gunshots in the distance. When he came back, he carried two sets of noise dampers, which looked like headphones. "For me? Oh, you shouldn't have," she quipped. "And in my colour, too."

"Nice." He led her through to the firing range stalls.

Through a pair of thick wooden doors, Georgina found a new world, a world run by weapons fanatics. Following Shane past stalls filled with both men and women firing their pistols at targets, Georgina entered an empty stall. "Is this it?" She scanned the area.

"This is it," he shouted back. He put the cases down and opened them, taking her Bobcat out first, followed by his Beretta M9.

She noticed the size difference between his huge M9 and her handbag filler. He handed her the Bobcat and showed her how to eject the fully loaded magazine. Then, upon his instruction, she pushed the magazine in, and held it down by her side. "What now?" Shane pressed a green button on the wall of the stall, and a whirring noise made her turn and face the target. It moved towards her. "Really? You want me to shoot that?" His confirmation made her raise the firearm and hold it with both hands.

He nudged her feet further apart with his own. "Remember,

squeeze the trigger, don't pull it. It will recoil some, even that tiny thing." He stood behind her.

Georgina closed her right eye, focusing on the target ahead. When she squeezed, the gun bucked a little. The paper shaped like a person moved when she fired, so she assumed she hit it. "And again?" She hoped he would say yes. With a nod from him, she took the stance once more.

Several rounds later, the pistol's dark grey grip hot, she stepped back as Shane pressed the button to bring the target up to them.

"Not bad for your first time, George." He sounded surprised. "Every round hit." He stood forward, his M9 down by his side, waiting for her to finish whirring the new target away. "How far do you want it?"

Georgina kept her finger on the green button. "You've had heaps of practise. This evens it out a bit." Letting go only after the target had finished whirring, she grinned. "There. Try that." Shane had experience. Taking another step back, the headphones over her ears, she watched as he squeezed off ten rounds. "Are you done?"

"Yeah, I think so. This magazine only holds ten rounds."

Just as she suspected, his clustering of shots were better than hers, every bullet hitting the centre of the target's chest or forehead. How he could be that good, she had no clue. Shane didn't sleep with his gun, at least she didn't think he did. Georgina thought she would have known by now if he did. "Hook up another." She waited for him to pin a target up and send it away from her. "That'll do."

Closing her right eye, she squeezed off six rounds in fairly quick succession, loving the recoil; she could see now why people enjoyed guns. "All winners. Maybe not as tightly grouped as yours, but they're all on target."

"You're a natural," he encouraged. "But this isn't a

competition. I just need to know you have the tools, if this pom freak comes for you and I'm not there. Will you feel safer knowing a gun's in your bag whenever you go out? Remember, you can shoot someone in self-defence only, and you'll need to prove you were fearful of your life in court."

"Great! Comforting! I feel so much safer." It didn't matter; she would never shoot Elf Man. She lost her thoughts when her mobile bleeped twice. "Probably one of the girls," she told him, retrieving it.

"Please no." She opened Chatter. "Elf Man!"

Georgina gasped at the sight of her parents stood smiling at the camera on Elf Man's message. "No!" Without thinking, she ran from the gun club to her Jeep in the car park.

25

Kereama was grateful Amelia let him stay at the house. His girlfriend overreacted at the hospital, as she always did, about everything. "Drama queen" suited her. Insanely hot, every guy wanted a piece of her, but he sometimes wondered if she was worth the aggro? He'd never touched the girl on the Metro. He smiled at her, sure, but he didn't think it a big deal. Amelia did.

Saturday lunchtime he'd left the hospital after much begging. Amelia had relented and came to pick him up. When she arrived, she allowed him to stay in the house. He would be sleeping in one of the spare bedrooms. Unable to argue, he agreed. Back home, she helped him inside and vanished, leaving him to fend for himself for the weekend.

Tuesday morning, Kereama lay on the couch when the doorbell rang. "Ames! They're here!" He winced as he pulled himself to his feet from the sofa. Every time he moved, the stitches stung. "Don't worry, I'll get the door."

At the front door were two police officers, the same two officers who had spoken to him at the hospital. "Please, come in." He let them in, showing the way into the living room.

Amelia came walking down the stairs. Kereama noted her nonchalant expression. "Have you identified him yet?"

The male police officer, Senior Sergeant Scott Kennedy, spoke first. He produced a photograph taken at Carlton Station. A busy photo with hundreds of travellers in it, circled in black pen he saw a face, or rather half a face. The person highlighted wore a baseball cap. "Is this it? Is this the sum total of days of effort? It could be anyone."

"We don't think he's just anyone, do we, Janae?" The sergeant was sat on the sofa, wearing a light blue short-sleeved police shirt and shorts, carrying a sidearm holstered on his hip. He looked like he enjoyed visiting the gym and had blond hair. "After interviewing Miss Thomas, we believe you know him. Random stabbings are rare, Mr Tua. Extremely. As in they don't happen at all."

"If you tell us what you can, we'll try to locate the suspect for you." Incremental Sergeant Janae Willis, a fit and healthy ginger woman in her early thirties with her hair tied in a ponytail, went on. "But we need your help. If not, more than likely he'll slip through our net, I'm afraid."

"I've told you everything," Kereama complained. "I was standing inside the train when I felt a stabbing pain in my side. I couldn't see shit because heaps of people were getting off. All I've got; I'm sorry!"

As suspected, they couldn't help him locate Elf Man, and Kereama didn't want to involve the police in this matter. He sat there, answering questions as well as he could without giving anything away. For a good fifteen minutes, he and Amelia nodded or shook their heads at the appropriate times. When they concluded their interview, the female officer stood first, followed closely by the senior sergeant. Kereama matched their move.

"As you're no doubt aware, the New South Wales Police

Force takes knife crime very seriously, Mr Tua. And in doing so, we'll keep looking into this for you until we apprehend the suspect. Please, if you think of anything else that might be useful in identifying him, give me a call. My line's open day or night."

After showing Sydney's finest to the door, and promising to contact them if he thought of something helpful, he closed it, hoping they didn't suspect anything. Elf Man knew too much about them; he could get them in a whole heap of trouble. "Thank God they're gone." Kereama leaned against the wooden door. "I think that went well."

"They suspect." Amelia looked airy and cool in her open shirt, bikini top and skirt over her bikini bottoms. "They're not stupid. Why else did he make that point about random stabbings?"

"I don't care. They can't prove anything, and until they can, we're safe. All we need is Shane and Oli to come through for us and we're set." He didn't hold out much hope. "Nothing to it."

Amelia sighed. "Come on, I'll give you a hand."

Accepting her offer, he let his girlfriend-for-now take some of his weight, easing the pressure on the stitches, and hobbled back to the living room. "I am sorry." His voice was low, quiet. "But I only smiled at her, Ames, honest. Nothing happened."

Amelia helped him to the sofa. "Look, I overreacted, I'll admit. But I'm not ready to forgive you yet. I saw the look in that girl's eyes; she was eating you all up, which means you must've at least encouraged it. And what about your tour girls, huh? And don't lie to me, Kay, you fuck one at every gig."

"Ames, who told you that?"

"Save it! If you're going to sit there and lie to my face, I'll go back upstairs. Otherwise, we can talk, like grown-ups. We can get past this." She perched on the coffee table in front of him and reached out for his hand. "If we do, it has to be me, and only me, baby. I can't be hearing whispers that you're fuckin' your fans."

No use. Futile even, to argue his innocence. Amelia had him. When he was about to speak, Amelia's mobile rang.

"We'll be right there, George."

"What's going on?" Kereama attempted to pull himself up.

"We're driving over to George's parents' house," Amelia announced, helping him to his feet. "Elf Man's over there, apparently. George wants us as backup."

26

The sun beamed down on Georgina as she turned right onto Bando Road. On any normal day, she enjoyed the drive over to North Cronulla Beach; not this time, though. The thirty-minute journey along the M1, A1 and The Grand Parade in her Jeep while worrying that Elf Man had done something to her parents made her nauseous. "I swear if he's touched them." She let the end trail off. If Elf Man had hurt her mum, Georgina would tear him apart with her bare hands.

"And I'll be by your side," Shane said, holding on for dear life.

Georgina let out a huge lungful of air upon seeing her dad tinkering with his car. He had the bonnet up and his head inside the engine. A massive smile formed, as she pulled up outside her parents' driveway. Welling up, she scrunched her eyes and wiped her nose, breathing deeply. "Oh thank God!" She opened her door.

"I thought we weren't seeing you two until Sunday?" her dad said.

Letting out a laugh, she opened her eyes to find her old man walking towards them, cleaning his oily hands with a cloth. He wore a really old pair of dungarees over jeans and a black Rip Curl T-shirt. "Hi, Dad!" she said, getting out of her Jeep and hugging him, a little tighter than normal. "We were nearby and thought we'd drop in."

She stood back and let Shane shake her dad's hand. They had a good relationship, her dad being footy mad, and a lifelong Swans fan didn't hurt. "Where's Mum?"

"In the garden pruning, I think." He invited them inside.

Having walked through the house, Georgina found her mum outside with her pruning shears. "Hi!" she said, hugging her even tighter than her dad. When asked why she stopped by, she lied and said they were in the area. And to her delight, her parents invited her and Shane to stop for lunch.

Happy that they were safe and well, Georgina went into the house with her mum and found her dad and Shane sat at the kitchen table tucking into Tim Tams and drinking turmeric and lemon myrtle tea, her mum's own version of the recipe. "There had better be one left, Shane. I want a biccy, too," she said, going into the cupboard, only to find the Tim Tams gone. "You're so selfish, honestly."

Breaking a Tim Tam, he offered her half.

"Leave him alone, George!" her mum scolded. "If you want, Anzac biccies are in a tin at the back of the cupboard. I only baked them yesterday."

"A bit early for these, isn't it?" she asked. "Not that I'm complaining." She reached in and pulled out the mentioned tin, lifted the lid and inhaled that coconutty, golden syrupy and oaty goodness. "Mmm, I love your Anzacs."

"So does your dad." Her mum was fumbling at the counter. "I've been baking a batch a week to keep him happy."

Being an aborigine, her mum had some terrific recipes, which Georgina grew up on. Shane loved eating at her parents' house. Outside, came a long beep.

Kereama and Amelia are here, she thought, rushing out front to find them parked behind her Jeep. "They're fine," she told them, a big smile splattered across her face. "Come inside, Mum's making us lunch." She didn't need permission to invite them. Amelia might as well have been their second daughter. "And she's baked her Anzac biccies."

Once everyone had said hello, Georgina sat her friends at the table. She made them all drinks. And after they'd helped themselves to food, she plated herself some seared kangaroo fillet and salad. "So, anything exciting happened recently?" she asked, trying to elicit the correct response.

When her parents shook their heads, she asked, "So, you haven't had visitors?"

Shane and Amelia glanced at her.

"Ooh, we had a friend of yours come say hi." Her mum seemed pleased with herself for remembering. "Such a lovely young man, so polite. He said you gave him this address, so I assume you must've known him for some time. He wanted your current address, but I said no. He understood, didn't he?"

Her dad nodded.

"Oh? Did he leave a name?" Acting normal was the best course of action, Georgina decided, not wanting to alarm them.

"And what did he look like?" Shane asked. "Do I need to worry?"

Kereama winced when he laughed at Shane's joke.

"Danny, I think he said," her mum said. "Yeah, but I can't remember his surname."

"The only Danny I recall from a while back is Elfman." She hoped the name would register. Her mum's face lit up, and she confirmed it. "What does he look like now?"

The question puzzled her mum. "How would you describe him, darling? I don't know, an unruly mop of dark hair I wanted to brush for him. I could tell he was a pom, his skin pasty white like they all are. And he had these thin lips. He was nicer to talk to than look at, poor fella."

"He seemed all right," her dad added.

Georgina, happy that her parents were safe, finished her food and then helped her mum clear the table, while everyone else sat chatting around the table. This could have been any normal day, Georgina thought, if only. Washing some plates in the sink, she smiled at her mum, who started drying up, as her mobile bleeped. "Shane, can you answer that?"

"We've got to go, babe," he said. "Thanks for the delicious lunch."

Georgina asked her parents for permission to leave. Her mum said "fine", that she would finish up. "You're the best." She gave her a kiss on her cheek. From Shane's abruptness, she took that the message involved Elf Man. After drying her hands, she walked with Shane, Kereama and Amelia to their cars out front. "What is it?" Shane had her phone in his hand.

The photo showed Shane and Georgina's swimming pool. Elf Man had taken the picture from their back garden, trespassing. The only way in for him without a key to the front door was over an eight-foot wall. It creeped her out to think Elf Man had scaled their razor wire-topped wall. "Right, we're phoning the police."

Shane snatched her phone. "No, we're not. Don't be so stupid. He has things on us, George, and we'll probably end up in the shit ourselves. I can't afford to get arrested, can you? Hmm? Do you think the World Surf League will want you to participate if you were involved in beating up some pommie guy? He has photos of that, remember."

"So, what do you want to do, Shane, huh? Shall we just sit around and wait for him to make a move? I thought you and Oli were fixing this on Friday? All I've had since you got back from the club is you skulking around the house, jumping every time your phone rings. Is there something you want to tell me?"

"Guys, we need to go." Amelia walked towards her car. "We'll meet you back at yours."

Getting in her seat, Georgina took a couple of deep breaths and started the engine, her red Jeep waking immediately. She drove in silence. Instead of being nauseous, anger enveloped her. She had not confronted Shane about his behaviour over the weekend. "So? What happened on Friday, huh? And don't tell me nothing."

She reached Brighton Le Sands Beach, travelling on The Grand Parade. "Nothing. We found him, chased him and lost him again. Am I not allowed to be annoyed?" He crossed his arms and huffed.

"Really?" He didn't answer her. Silence sat between them for the rest of the journey. Upon reaching their house, pulling up behind Amelia, she and Shane exited the Jeep and walked up to the front gate. Shane held his Beretta down by his side. "Put that away, or our neighbours will see."

"No way! Better to have one and not need it," he said, opening the gate and stepping inside. "Stay behind me."

Georgina did as instructed, hearing Amelia and Kereama behind her. Four against one, she liked the odds. They reached the house, went inside, and searched each room. Nothing. Her underwear drawer remained untouched.

They all agreed Elf Man had not breached the house. Outside, they checked the garden. Nothing. No signs of his presence, other than the photo. "I still think now's the time to involve the police."

"Are you mad?" Shane holstered his pistol in the back of his jeans. "We're handling it ourselves."

"Handling what? Are you kidding me?" The threat of her parents was too much for her frail nerves. "He's in control here, not us. He knows everything about us. And what do we know about him, huh? Nothing. You aren't dealing with this, Shane; he is!"

Palms out, she said, "Sorry! I shouldn't have snapped. It's not your fault." *Again, Oliver's to blame*, she thought.

He hugged her. Amelia and Kereama made their excuses and left them in the garden. A hug turned to a kiss. And when she calmed down, Shane suggested they have a quiet afternoon lounging by the pool, which sounded like Heaven to her. Some light music on, a couple of glasses of wine, sun loungers, the occasional dip; her idea of bliss. "You're on, mister," she said, standing up before heading to their bedroom to change into a bikini.

27

"Come on." Amelia got up from the sofa. "I'll help you up to bed."

"You mean I can sleep in our room again?"

After having a long talk with him, she made her mind up. "Don't get me wrong, Kay, I'm still pissed at you. But, I believe you when you say it won't happen again. I just don't want to be a laughing stock, that's all." When he nodded, she could tell he was serious. People made mistakes, although by all accounts Kereama had made many mistakes with many of his groupies. "So, yes, you can sleep in our bed. But no funny stuff, Kay. I'm not ready for that yet."

"Hey! You have my word."

As much as she hated him for what he'd done, Amelia still loved him. And if she threw their relationship away, she would be left with nothing. Georgina had Shane, who adored her and wouldn't dream of cheating on her, while she had Kereama, who couldn't keep his in his pants. So, not only did Georgina have the looks and talent, she also had the doting, gorgeous boyfriend. Life sucked! "Come on, bedtime."

She helped him upstairs to their bedroom, where he sat and

started taking off his clothes. She'd redressed his wound earlier. He would be having the stitches out the following afternoon, and she agreed to drive him there and back. And as she began her bedtime rituals, she thought about how unfair life could be. Even Isla had a better life than she did. Sure, Oliver was an idiot, a joker, and she didn't understand what her bodybuilder friend liked about him, but he didn't cheat on her.

In the bathroom, she wiped her make-up off, moisturised and brushed her teeth. When Kereama came in, he relieved himself. "Why do you always have to do that when I'm in here?" she snapped.

"What? I'm only having a piss."

Turning back to the sink, she continued brushing her teeth, listening to him mumble. Amelia spat out the toothpaste and placed the brush in its mug.

She kicked herself for not braving up to him sooner, for not acting on the rumours the previous year. At first she didn't believe that her gorgeous guy would betray her. Why would he want anyone else? The envy of half a million followers, women everywhere wanted to be her, to look like her, to live her beach babe lifestyle. And then there were the guys. After every cheep she put out on Chatter, a flood of compliments from blokes all over the world gave her the confidence she craved. Most were in English, yet some comments were in Spanish, German, French; she had some in Arabic and Chinese, too.

So, why then, did Kereama feel he needed to cheat on her? They had an active, bold, and interesting sex life; he didn't go without. Amelia was adventurous in that respect, having initiated it on the Metro one time, and in a nightclub's men's toilet cubicle.

In their bedroom, she changed into her bedwear, a long T-shirt that went down to her knees, and fussed about with her hair in front of her mirror. Kereama lay on the bed, staring at the ceiling. She wondered what he was thinking: probably about some tall, leggy black girl on a train, Amelia thought, fixing her hair. She chided herself.

"Oh shit! We forgot to lock up."

Getting up, she said she would go. He would take ages hobbling down the stairs; it made more sense her locking up.

Darling Point was one of the safest neighbourhoods in Sydney, she'd been told by the estate agent, which, after Georgina's ordeal, was why they'd chosen a three-bedroomed house there. And she fell in love with her new home on sight, badgering Kereama into liking it as well. After a painful two weeks of nagging him, she managed to force him to relent. The next day they put an offer in. Residents locked their doors only at night, before they went to bed, and sometimes forgot. Yeah, she adored her house and the neighbourhood. Having Isla around the corner, and Georgina in the next suburb over made it home, the icing on top of a delicious cake. Life didn't get better than this, she often said to herself, although not so much after hearing of Kereama's extra-curricular activities.

Downstairs, knowing she had secured the back door, she headed to the inner door to the porch, which remained unlocked because they locked the outer door at night. A door inside the porch led to the double garage. It was unlocked. Stepping inside the garage, she checked the metal door was secure. How long had it been unlocked for?

Amelia walked back upstairs and found Kereama under the covers snoring. She would have a few words with him about not locking the garage in the morning. Instead of waking him, she pulled the covers back and slid in beside him.

After putting her earplugs in, Amelia lay on her side and closed her eyes, too pumped to drift off. Her brain fired in a thousand directions. Had she brought this on herself? Had she made him cheat on her? Without him acknowledging his behaviour, how would she ever know? And she couldn't blame the other women for finding him attractive.

Attempting to remain optimistic, Amelia told herself she still had her modelling contracts, and she didn't need to work a day job, ever. She got paid to post cheeps on Chatter. How many people could boast that? So, if everything went south with him, she would be fine. And her next bloke might be a vast improvement on Kereama.

He fidgeted a lot. The mattress moved. "Stop fidgeting, Kerry," she scolded, not bothering to turn over. "Go to sleep, for Christ's sake."

He grunted next to her.

Ignoring his noises, Amelia tried to fall asleep, closing her eyes and letting her body relax. Kereama still fidgeted.

"Ames," she thought she heard, "run."

Turning on her back, she opened her eyes to find a shadow hovering above him.

It took a couple of seconds for her brain to register what was happening.

"Run, baby."

The shadow fought with her boyfriend.

It had something in its hand, a weapon, long and sharp.

The weapon, thin and pointy had a handle.

Amelia saw him grappling with the intruder, one hand around his neck, the other clutching one of Shadow's wrists.

Shadow was choking Kereama.

An ice pick – Shadow held an ice pick.

She gasped when Kereama yelled out.

The ice pick opened his cheek up in a torrent of crimson.

And Shadow's arm went up and down, each time striking at her lover's face.

She screamed at all the blood.

Curled up in a ball, unable to move, time seemed to slow.

Kereama's struggle with Shadow stopped abruptly and his arms fell by his side, his body limp.

When Shadow yanked the ice pick from Kereama's eye, she knew her boyfriend was dead.

Amelia screamed.

Upon seeing Shadow – Elf Man – every paralysed part of her body moved.

She whipped back the covers and flew from the bed towards the door, closely followed by her assailant.

There were footsteps right behind her.

Her feet barely touched the carpeted stairs.

As fast as she was, Elf Man kept up with her.

When she saw the inner porch door, she remembered locking it.

A sharp stabbing pain hit her in the centre of her back.

Amelia almost face-planted, something wedged in her back.

Reaching behind her, she felt a handle: a knife.

Upon realising this, her breathing laboured, she tasted the coppery warm blood filling up her mouth.

Screaming – or rather gargling blood – a foot pinned her to the floor. Then an immense pain wracked her body as her attacker pulled out the blade. "No! Please, I don't want to die."

Elf Man rolled her over.

Knowing she was dying, blood pooling beneath her, she stared up at Elf Man, who mounted her and sat on her stomach, a satisfied smile slapped over his ugly face. She now knew what he looked like: awful wiry dark hair, pale complexion and horrible thin lips, just like Georgina's mum had said. "Please, don't do this."

"Not so cocky now, are you, Ames?" Elf Man pointed the blade at her from above. "You talentless bitch! *You* think you're too good to be *my* friend? You know, you might be beautiful on the outside, but you're so ugly on the inside."

Pure hatred in his stare, his eyes black holes, she gasped when he put the knife to her neck.

Amelia breathed in, as though the act itself would protect her.

And then the cold metal blade sliced into her skin when Elf Man yanked to his right, tearing a gash in her throat.

With every breath came panic; she couldn't breathe. If the blood loss didn't kill her, the asphyxiation would. Her eyes grew heavier with every passing second.

28

Georgina finished her reps with the dumb-bells and replaced them in their rack, next to the larger bells Shane used. Unlike Isla, she didn't want to gain muscle; she liked her body toned and slim. Her workout intensive, sweat clung to her vest and joggers.

After showering and changing into a bikini, she walked downstairs, leaving Shane getting ready for his day. In the kitchen, she forced herself to eat a bowl of porridge and drink a glass of orange juice. "Do you want some OJ?" she bellowed up the stairs, glancing at the front door. No reply came from upstairs. The door ajar, she thought maybe he came downstairs without her hearing.

"Babe?" she said, poking her head outside.

Nothing. Not on the driveway, or on the lawn, a pang of fear hit her. Back inside, after closing the door, she returned to the stairs. He appeared. "Have you been out this morning?"

"What're you talking about? You saw me in bed just now."

"So, you mean to tell me the front door was open all night?" His expression changed to disbelief. "I came down just now and it was ajar. So, unless you were out there this morning, it was left open all night."

Shane walked past her and inspected the door. "It's shut, look," he said, turning to her. "I didn't forget to close it last night. At least I don't think I did."

"Which means you did forget. Bloody hell, you know he's still out there. I know you were wasted last night, and maybe I should've locked up, but we can't afford to get complacent." Her stalker had gone quiet. Since Tuesday's scare with her parents, she had not made contact with him, or Amelia, come to think of it.

"I'm sorry! I don't know what happened," Shane said. "It won't happen again, I promise." He came in and hugged her, as if trying to get her to forgive him.

She never could stay mad at him for long. "Please don't forget in future," she pleaded to his nod. "He's gone quiet on us, but he's still out there, I know he is." And with that, she forgave him, letting him wolf his breakfast down before he had to leave for work. He had to get to Sydney Cricket Ground for the first official day of training.

Sat outside on the decking scrolling through her messages on Chatter, the sun already bright and strong, she thought about Amelia, and how she hadn't seen her for a few days, since Tuesday afternoon. Hearing the pool calling her, the water enticing, she typed a text message to her best friend. "*Hey! You still around? Miss you.*" Amelia texted her, or Isla, most days, at least every other day. "Your turn," she mumbled.

Stood on the edge of the pool, she bent over slightly and dived in. The water magnificent, even at nine o'clock in the morning, she swam. Swimming was her favourite form of exercise, bar surfing of course. It hands down beat going to the gym, or running; she only took part in them because she liked the variety.

Treading water, her elbows resting on the edging tiles, Georgina heard her text ringtone. Hoisting herself out of the pool, she walked over to the table, picked up her towel in one hand and her phone in the other. After opening her text reply from Amelia and placing her mobile on the table, she started drying herself while reading it. "Hey! I'm fine. Been busy with modelling contracts," she read out loud. "We've gone away for a few days, you know why."

Why the hell would she take off now? What a time to up and leave her! "You bitch!" An inner rage boiled inside. *"Where are you?"* she typed.

The reply came back promptly. *"Up north."* Not terribly informative, the north a vast area. Why wouldn't her best friend tell her? Wanting to speak to her, Georgina picked up her phone and dialled Amelia's number. Straight through to voicemail. "Yeah, it's me," she said, her tone confrontational. "Where the hell are you? I can't believe you've just taken off like this and didn't at least tell me first. You're supposed to be my best friend. Thanks a lot!"

Anger made her jab at her mobile to hang up. For once, she welled up, the thought that Amelia could desert her like this almost too much to bear. Wiping her face, she picked up her phone and sent a text to Isla informing her of Amelia's disappearance. *"Just like her; she's so selfish"*, came the response.

Sitting back down, Georgina opened Chatter and looked up Amelia. Scrolling through her account, the last cheep her friend posted was on Tuesday afternoon, a picture of her wearing a bikini in her back garden. She thought Amelia must have taken the photo after the drama at her parents' house. And she looked amazing, radiant, tanned, sexy. "Three days," she said, scrolling through Amelia's thousand plus pictures.

The longest her tanned friend had gone without uploading a cheep, looking now, was two days. And sometimes her friend would send two or three cheeps in a twenty-four-hour period, especially at the weekends. Too early to freak out, she may be having troubles with Kereama, she thought, exiting the app.

The time on her phone: approaching ten o'clock. With hours to kill before she was due to meet Mingzhu at Bondi Beach, she got up and wandered over to one of the sun loungers by the poolside, spreading her large towel out.

Attaching headphones to her mobile, Georgina opened Spotify and shuffled her mixed playlist, which consisted mostly of heavy bands, like Pantera, Avenged Sevenfold, System of a Down, Disturbed, and of course The Deranged. And a couple of tracks she liked by Kereama's band, The Savage Seeds.

With the sun turning her an even darker brown, she couldn't help thinking about her supposed best friend. How could she desert her now? Amelia should be begging for her forgiveness, not running off at the first sign of trouble. Even the heavy guitar riffs of The Deranged couldn't drown out Georgina's disappointment. "You can just rack off!" she said to Amelia, opening her eyes.

She sat up suddenly, a foreign shape at the top of her wall made her take note.

Perching her shades on the tip of her nose, she squinted.

The object moved, then disappeared behind the wall.

Terrified, she grabbed her phone and flew from the sun lounger into her house, sliding the glass door across and locking it. Elf Man was outside. How long had he been there? Had he spied on her swimming? She shuddered at the thought.

Safe now that he couldn't reach her inside, she glanced through the glass, curious to see if he remained, or if he ran off. Even more, she wanted to see his face.

A mop of dark hair appeared by her tree, the only one in her garden. Through the razor wire, she made out a head. Even with perfect vision his features were blurred, although she could see he had a pale, almost ghostly, complexion. "We're gonna get you, you mongrel," she whispered, wanting to take a photo.

He watched her through the glass.

Georgina felt his stare boring into her.

She shouldn't be standing there in only a bikini, she thought, stepping sideways and hiding behind a curtain.

Elf Man was out there. Turning, she looked for her bag. "Shit!" Having her pocket pistol nearby made her feel safe. Slowly, she made her way into the kitchen, reaching inside her bag and retrieving her gun, which had a full magazine inserted and the safety on.

A text message awaited her attention, she noted. "*Sorry about last night, by the way. Think I might've left the front door open. Soz.*"

She almost dropped the phone.

"*Had a fantastic night, though. You were such a gracious host. Lol.*" The messages kept flowing in, too fast for her to cope with. How did he have her mobile number? He'd been messaging her via the Chatter app up until now. How did he know the door was open overnight?

Unless... Unless... She didn't want to say it out loud.

Unless he was inside this house!

"*You were so accommodating. And you're so sweet when you're asleep.*"

Panic took over. Georgina picked up her bag, put the handle over her shoulder and ran for the front door. Her hands shaking, she rummaged around for her keys, found them and fumbled for the right one. Finding the correct key, she unlocked the door and ran out to her Jeep, the keys in one hand and her pistol in the other. The gun she kept raised and pointed at the front door.

With the gates opening automatically, Georgina reversed her Jeep out of her driveway, turning until she was at the right angle to drive straight. She pressed her thong on the accelerator. The text messages were still pinging through. Each time she heard the tone, she jumped, dreading what they would say.

She couldn't hear anything, just her heartbeat. Georgina glanced at her mobile on the passenger seat. With one hand on the steering wheel, she reached across and put it in her lap.

"Damn you, Shane! Pick up, please." She pulled up behind a Ford of some description. A drop of sweat landed on the screen of her phone. She wiped her forehead with her wrist.

She needed to speak to Shane.

29

"You're all gonna have to do much better than that if you want to win the league this year!" Shane shouted, his breathing laboured from so much running. The first day back after Christmas and the New Year and he had to confess to being out of shape. The blazing sun didn't help either, although he was glad his side were skins and not shirts. "Let's run the play again, and this time get it right, for Christ's sake. I'm sick of us losing every season, aren't you?"

Playing ruck rover – as to be ruckman he needed height – he handed the ball to his ruckman and turned to face his second-in-command's ruck rover on the shirts' side. Shane, the ruckman and rover were all followers, which meant they followed the ball around the pitch more than the other positions. They had to be in tip-top physical condition. As he got into position, he held the ball and caught their attention. "Are we going bring the cup home this season?"

A semi-enthusiastic chorus of yeses came from his team.

"My grandma can shout louder than that. Are we bringing it home this year?"

A more confident and convincing "yeah" reverberated around the cricket ground.

"I can't hear you! Again, are we bringing the cup home?"

"Hell yeah!" They all yelled.

And as he watched his ruckman, a guy named Larry, who measured six feet eight inches tall, hand the ball to the umpire, Shane readied himself for the fourth repeat of this play. The team seemed incapable of getting it right. Determined to master it before the end of the session, one complaint he caught commentators making was that his crew didn't work well together. Most of them blamed him for it, and he aimed to remedy that criticism. The fact the Swans had not won a competition, or made the semi, or quarter finals since he'd taken over, only added weight to their comments.

Glad to be back, footy took his mind off Elf Man having an incriminating photo of him with Valerie. He spent the previous weekend and the rest of the week waiting for Georgina to confront him. Shane wished he knew what Elf Man was anticipating; why he dangled the video in front of him?

On Sunday night, Shane had tried telling Georgina what happened on Friday night, about how he met Valerie. When he sat Georgina down, and she smiled at him, he couldn't go through with it; he couldn't face the thought of her hating him. Sometimes, he kicked himself for his stupidity.

Today was the first day he didn't feel jumpy. He lived for football, for the plays and tumbles. Hell, even if she found out and they broke up, he would still have footy, still have wild after-game parties to attend.

"Hey, Shane, is that George over there?" the umpire asked.

Squinting into the sun, Shane found Georgina waving him over, wearing only a bikini and thong shoes. Upon closer inspection, she was crying. He excused himself from the play, running over to her. Up close, she looked awful, tears streaming.

"What the hell happened? I left you at the house less than two hours ago." He pulled her in for a hug, which she looked like she needed.

"He was in the house."

Pulling her away from him, he stared into her wet eyes. "You what? Bullshit. He wasn't in our house."

Georgina handed him her phone. He saw that she had a dozen or more text messages from Elf Man. "How did he get your number?" Shane asked, expecting her to show him Chatter texts. The first text made him so angry, he wanted to punch a wall.

"*Sorry about last night, by the way. Think I might've left the front door open.*" Elf Man had to be winding them up, had to be. He couldn't have been in their house. Then Shane read the second: "*Had a fantastic night, though. You are such a gracious host. Lol.*" And the third: "*And you're so sweet when you're asleep.*"

The thought of the pom being in their house, watching Georgina sleep, made Shane want to throw up. "He's fucking with us, George. This fucker's lying."

"He was spying on me from behind our tree just now." Tears streamed down her cheeks. "And he has my mobile number. How did he know the door was left open?"

Shane couldn't answer. The thought of Elf Man being in their house truly frightened him. Elf Man couldn't know about the door being left ajar... Unless... He didn't want to say it, even in his head... Inside their house. While he snored off the copious amounts of stubbies drunk, Elf Man was wandering around his house.

"Sorry to interrupt, Shane, but are we running through this play, or not?" The umpire backed away, his palms on display. "No, you're right, we'll muddle through without you."

Shane waited until he turned and walked back to the oval-shaped pitch, where his team were watching them. He turned to

Georgina. "You said he was in the garden just now?" When she confirmed, he took her hand and pulled her in the direction of the main doors back to reception. "Is your Jeep outside?"

He tried comforting her on the way back home. Furious didn't do his mood justice. This psychopath had crossed a line. "I'm going to get this mongrel," he said in a low, quiet and determined voice.

"How?" Georgina asked, sat in the passenger seat for once. "He knows everything about us. And we don't even know what he looks like." She dabbed at her eyes with a tissue. The tears had stopped.

The journey home via Moore Park Road and Ocean Street took ten minutes. Pulling up outside their front gate, Shane pressed the "open" button and waited while they obeyed, before driving inside and closing it. He walked up to the door and stood back as Georgina used her key. "Let's see if he's still here." Shane ran upstairs and retrieved his Beretta from his bedside cabinet. "Elf Man? More like dead man!"

With his pistol in hand, he descended the stairs and joined Georgina at the sliding glass door leading out to the back garden. She stared at the tree.

"Is he still here?" He unlocked and opened it. "Elf Man!" Shane bellowed, stepping outside. No answer.

Shane ran at the wall, grabbing the top bricks and hoisting himself up. He had to dodge the razor wire. While there, his arms keeping him up, he noticed a chunk of wire missing behind the tree. "Son of a bitch! That's how he's getting in." He could kick himself for not noticing on Tuesday. Razor wire wouldn't work with this guy.

Georgina screamed. Shane jumped down from the wall and ran over to her. Taking her phone from her shaking hands, he stared in disbelief at the dark video inside their house. Elf Man had brazenly tried their front door. He felt sick at the thought that if he hadn't fallen asleep without double-checking, they wouldn't be watching this sickening footage now.

The single torch illuminated each room. The footage showed him inside their cinema room and games room. Elf Man used the pool cue to pot the black. The video shone in the living room and kitchen.

Stay downstairs, Shane thought, please. His prayer went unanswered when the video went upstairs, slowly, deliberately, Elf Man excited, giggling.

"He's a snorer," Elf Man said in delight.

Shane gulped when he saw himself under the covers asleep. His hand shook. Elf Man slid a blade out and rested it on his sleeping neck. Checking his throat, Shane heard a whispered voice say, "Wake up. Please."

Then the knife disappeared, and the camera moved, backed up and crept around the bed to Georgina's side. He wanted to throw the phone; instead, he held his girlfriend's hand, as the video zoomed in on her sleeping face. "There you are," the voice a mere whisper. "You're so beautiful."

And a hand pulled the covers back, revealing Georgina lying on her side, naked, her arms folded over her breasts. "I can't believe what I'm seeing. You're so fucking gorgeous."

Georgina hugged Shane tight, not wanting to watch any more. A stronger man may have switched off, but he didn't. Shane held her, while Elf Man continued his visual assault on her.

Elf Man's voice grew more excited when she turned and lay on her back, her naked body on display.

Speechless with rage, Shane's hands shook.

The camera started shaking and Elf Man groaned.

Georgina ran away, crying. Instead of going after her, Shane watched as Elf Man's groans intensified, until a final moan told him his intruder had finished. "Oops!" Elf Man whispered in a laboured voice. "Left a bit of a mess."

If Shane could have reached inside the screen and strangled Elf Man, he would have. "I'm going to fucking kill you with my bare hands," he growled, watching as the video showed Elf Man leaving via the front door. Shane launched Georgina's phone across the garden, regretting it immediately. "Fuck!"

After retrieving the mobile from behind a bush, he went inside and upstairs to find her lying on the bed, crying.

He could only imagine how she felt. Stroking her back, he tried to think of something to say. "I'm so sorry! If I'd checked the door, this wouldn't have happened."

Georgina's sobbing subsided. "Call the police, Shane." Her face buried in the pillow, more sobs escaped her. "He was in our house; he had a knife against your throat."

Shane nodded gravely. "All right, I'm calling them now."

Picking up her phone, he dialled 131 444.

Georgina got up and looked at him. "Why aren't you dialling 000?"

"Why? You only dial that when you're in immediate danger."

"What do you mean? He was in this room, Shane."

"Yeah, but he's not in the house now, is he?"

He finished his conversation with Georgina when a female voice greeted him.

30

The camera loved Isla Kelly, or it could be the other way around. Either way, she knew she was the perfect choice to lead The Gym Dollies in their march for Chatter TV's health and fitness superiority. Her five Dollies were professional, and had become firm friends of hers. Having six Dollies, her included, made it easier for pairing up during the workouts. "And next week we'll be giving you our top ten core burn tips, so make sure you tune in."

Staring at the camera, her arms around two of her ladies, Isla stared at the lens. "Until next time, from Queenscliff Beach, New South Wales, take care, and we'll see you all at Dolly's."

Giving her widest, most gorgeous smile, she waited for the cameraman to signal the terminated transmission. "Great job, Dollies." She hugged each of them in turn. Fridays were her favourite, no doubt. She got to work out on Queenscliff Beach, near Manly, in front of both the camera and adoring fans in the morning, followed by a televised session for her own Chatter show in the afternoon. Isla had her own followers to satisfy after all.

As she finished hugging the last Dolly, she turned to find

three girls in their mid-teens stood waiting with pens and pads in their hands. When they asked for her autograph, she feigned shock. A bit of humility never hurt anyone, she always said. Each girl wore a bikini, and looked like they kept themselves in shape. "Great to see you're so keen on health and fitness," she said, handing the last pen back. "Keep up the good work, ladies." She waved them off, knowing she and the Dollies had given them a damned good workout.

Isla lived in bikinis during the summer. What better way was there to show off her gains? Her biceps rock-hard, her abs and thigh muscles the same, while her shoulders and back were solid, and so they should be, for she spent the majority of her life at the gym, either lifting, or coaching others to lift. "Who's for brunch?" she asked her fellow Dollies after their fans had dispersed.

The beach was stunning, the sand golden in the relentless sun, and in the distance Isla could see yachts and powerboats going about their business. One of her Dollies walked to the car park and retrieved her cool bag, while Isla and the rest of the girls found the perfect spot and put down towels. Dawn, a blonde with her hair in a ponytail, returned with the cool bag. "I could really go for a couple of egg sangers."

Reaching into her bag for her mobile, Isla saw she had several messages. With the rest of the Dollies opening up the picnic bag, she checked the messages. The clock on her phone said: 11:03. She took the package from Dawn.

"Your egg sangers, honey."

Isla placed the sandwich between her legs on the towel. Scrolling through her messages while munching on her sanger and listening to her girls laugh and joke, she opened her Chatter app, only to find a photo message from Elf Man. She stopped chewing and read it. "Son of a..." Putting the sandwich down, she stood, scanning the beach. The picture was of her and her Dollies sat on their towels, taken a minute ago. "He's here!"

"Who's here?" Willow asked, a stunning black Dolly with long braided hair, and abs to make even Olympic medallists jealous. She, like Isla, wore a white bikini.

"Ah, no one," she answered, not spying him. A number of visitors walked the length of the beach, but none of them stuck out. She looked for single men, reasoning that a psycho like Elf Man would ride alone, rather than as part of a couple or group. "Don't worry."

"Who's taking photos of us, Isla?" Dawn asked from behind her.

"No one," Isla replied. "You don't want to know, trust me."

No escaping her friends' interest, they all whined and begged her to tell them who was filming them. After a chorus of pleases, she relented. "All right, I'll tell you, if you promise to stop whining." She received a good solid laugh. And she turned around and regarded her five gorgeous weightlifting friends. "My mates, George and Ames, we're all being stalked by some pommie bastard."

Isla heard their gasps, followed by murmuring. "Oli, the stupid jerk, he teased one of George's followers on her Chatter account, and pretended to be her. He invited this guy to meet us for a joke, and this pommie went and bought a bloody plane ticket. Anyway, he found out it was a prank, and now he's out there stalking us."

"Bloody hell, honey," Willow said. "You should've told us."

"I know. But I didn't want to scare you all." She knew that at least three of her Dollies had been victims of stalkers. "He stabbed Kereama on Friday morning. And scratched the shit out of Oli's car." Isla found her place on the towel and sat down, feeling Elf Man's eyes on her.

"You know what?" Willow stood and helped Isla back on her

feet. "Let's go find this mongrel and send him packing. We'll make him regret coming over here."

When the rest of the girls stood, Isla felt energised, invincible. "Come on, Dollies, let's fuck this guy up." She wouldn't want to be on the receiving end of this, she thought, wondering how ferocious six muscular bikini-clad women looked striding up the beach. Already getting worried glances from beach visitors, she told herself she wanted people to move out of her way when she approached.

As she and her Dollies reached the top of the sand, they had to cross a piece of green land before they arrived at North Steine. The length of North Steine Road was lined with parking spaces, even running through the adjoining Manly Beach. "He's around here somewhere, chicks. Fan out, we'll find him quicker. Keep an eye out for a sad, pasty, lonely and pathetic-looking mongrel, and call out if you find him. And when we do, we're going to kick his balls so hard they'll be internal."

And she meant every word. Waiting for Shane, Oliver and Kereama to sort it out was futile. No, when she wanted something done, she relied on herself. And when she got hold of Elf Man, well, he would regret messing with her. "I know you're around here somewhere, you arsehole."

With the rest of the Dollies in pairs off looking for him, Isla walked along the tarmac, scanning the cars, keeping an eye out for him. If he had seen her strutting up the beach towards him, Elf Man would want to get away. Walking next to the powerful Willow, Isla thought her friend should be an athlete competing in the Olympics.

"Found him!" Dawn shouted in the distance. "He's jumping in a car. What do you want us to do?"

Excited, Isla sprinted towards her friend. "Grab him, pin him down if you have to. Whatever you do, don't let him leave."

Unfortunately, Dawn and her partner, Ruth, were too slow.

Elf Man's door closed, he started the engine and shot out from his space, missing Ruth by centimetres.

Isla and Willow ran into the middle of the North Steine, watching as Elf Man's small car came hurtling at them. "Out the way!" Isla yelled at her friend, jumping one way as her friend jumped the other. Elf Man's car shot off past them. Lying on the ground, bruised and grazed, Isla slammed her fist into the tarmac in anger. "We almost had him, for fuck's sake."

Willow hobbled on one leg, stooped down and helped her up. "He would have run us both down, baby." She pulled Isla to her feet. "It's not worth it. You need to phone the police about this guy; he's a crazy white boy."

"I will when I get home." With her knee bleeding, using each other as support, Isla and Willow walked back to their spot on the beach and finished their brunch. She fought her girls off, telling them that she and Oliver would call them later.

31

"You all right, mate?" Oliver's gym buddy, Jake asked. "You look pale."

On any normal day, Oliver would tell his best friend and workout partner almost anything. Not today. He'd just finished a call with Isla: she and her Dollies narrowly missed cornering Elf Man. Sat on the bench, he imagined the mess they would have made of him, had they caught him. Elf Man would have lost his balls for sure. "I'm fine." Taking his vest off and lying back, Oliver assumed position, about to attempt his heaviest lift. "Add another five either side, would you?"

After Jake had placed the additional weights, Oliver prepped himself mentally, telling himself he could do it.

"You do this," Jake said, "and it's a new PB."

Oliver smiled at the thought. Lifting 210 kilos would be his personal best. Other members had lifted more, but they were monsters. "Are you recording this?"

Having mainly worked on his legs and core – saving his upper body for the one rep, a deadlift of 210 kilos – he was ready.

"Can I have your attention?" Jake called, standing next to

him, his biceps bulging when he folded his arms. "Oli's going for his own record. Drum rolls please."

"Buckley's chance, mate!" someone shouted.

"It's only ten kilos more than last time," another member said. "Come on, Oli, you can do this. Make us proud."

The initial raise and lowering of the bar easy enough with aid from his spotters, he held it up with all his strength. With all the energy and anger he could muster, he lifted the barbell, his mind focused on a faceless Elf Man, as his whole body tensed. He thought about what he would do to him when they came face-to-face: tear him apart limb from limb, with his bare hands.

One final push, one last roar, and his arms were fully extended, shaking.

With help from his spotters and Jake, the bar was returned to its rack. Oliver could feel his muscles burning, especially in his chest and biceps. He found it funny how Georgina modelled for Ripped Energy Drink, when she was just skin and bone; she had no muscle definition. He should be filmed for their adverts, not her, he thought, standing to the adulation of his fellow members. Oliver raised his arms, accepting the praise, the clapping and cheering. "Thank you." He wanted the adoration to continue.

"Right, I'll put you down for 220 next week," Jake joked, attempting to massage Oliver's shoulders. "Well done! I thought you were going to crash on me. You wobbled a bit at the start."

Oliver laughed, picked up his vest and put it on. All the members went back to their workouts, either on the machines or using free weights. There weren't many as big as him there, although they were mostly younger. Lucky bastards, he thought, standing up. "I'm off home," he told Jake. "Something happened with Isla. I'll see you here tomorrow." He shook hands and strolled to the changing rooms.

After showering, Oliver walked naked to his locker, pulled

out his clothing and bag, and said hi to a couple of other members, before pulling his pants on. His mobile told him he had a text message. Knowing Elf Man only communicated via Chatter, Oliver checked.

His eyes widened when he saw a video of himself sat behind a table, his head back, arms stretched out. Blonde hair bobbed up and down above his crotch, while loud music played. "Fucking bastard!" he growled, his hand shaking with both fear and anger.

Another text came through: "*Someone's been a naughty boy. You don't deserve Isla, just like Shane doesn't deserve George*". He wanted to throw the phone at the wall. Holding back, Oliver managed to type: "*What the fuck do you want?*"

He dressed himself while waiting for a reply. When he walked out of the gym, and through the car park, the mobile went off in his hand. "A million dollars," he read out loud. "You got to be kidding me!" While walking to his car, he pondered: why would Elf Man ask for that amount? Everyone knew it wasn't that much these days.

Sat in his Ford Mustang, having left his Nota in the garage, he typed: "*A mill? I don't have that kind of money*". Before he turned on the ignition, a text came through.

"*Bullshit! Between you, Shane, Kereama and the girls you have a million dollars. You want me gone, it'll cost you this much!*"

"*You promise you'll fuck off if we hand you the cash?*" he typed, then sent.

"*You have my word. You don't really think I want to be where I'm not wanted, do you? This is fair. I'll contact you nearer the time, and we'll do the drop-off on Monday*".

"I can't believe I'm agreeing to this," Oliver said as he typed. He would need to speak with Shane, Kereama and the girls, but he didn't think they would put up a fight. They all wanted this guy gone.

Half an hour later, he arrived outside Shane's gates, and parked inside the complex after the doors opened, then closed after him. He'd told Shane to meet him, that he needed to talk to him privately. His "friend" appeared, walked up to the passenger side, and got in. "Is George in the house?"

"Yeah, upstairs sorting herself out. We had to file an incident report with the police."

"What kind of incident?" he asked, not wanting to know. Oliver listened as Shane explained how Elf Man had managed to get inside the house, and how he'd satisfied himself in their bedroom, while watching Georgina sleep. "Jesus Christ!" Oliver could only guess how she must have felt. "I'm so sorry! We should've called the police ages ago."

Conversation dried up. Shane stared out of the windscreen. Oliver picked his mobile up and showed him the video that Elf Man sent through. "He's got us by the short and curlies," he said, taking it back and handing his "friend" the text messages. "Read from the top, down. Believe me, I've thought of everything, but this is the only way I can think of to get rid of him."

Shane scrolled through the chain of messages. Up and down, up and down he went, reading them, and re-reading them. After a good five minutes, he handed the phone back and sighed. "And you believe him? You think if we hand him heaps of money, he'll rack off?"

Oliver shrugged. "I can't be certain, no, but this is the only way. If we don't try this now, I'm afraid of what he might do. He's already stabbed Kereama. This pom's a fucking psycho. Maybe, we pay him, and we never see him again." Oliver leaned over, closer to Shane's ear. "And besides, if we want to keep the girls, we can't have him sending the pictures and videos he has on his phone. I don't think we have a choice."

"And you think Kerry will go for it?" Shane asked. "Because without splitting the money six ways, I can't afford half a mill, mate. I can personally go a hundred and fifty thousand, tops, maybe. George will match what I put in. What about you?"

Oliver had thought of little else on the drive over. "I don't know, if Isla chips in, three-fifty, maybe. I'll need to check with her, but she earns more than I do." He noted Shane's smug expression. "So, are you in? Because there's no way I can do this alone."

With reluctance, Shane agreed, stipulating only if Kereama contributed as well. The deal had to be a three-couple split, or nothing, to which Oliver shook on. "I'll sort it out with Kerry." Shane opened his door. "I'll be in touch over the weekend, once this bastard's texted me the place and time."

32

David Coates grew more impatient by the minute. Already sat a table reserved for two in a lovely family-run Italian restaurant on Vauxhall Bridge Road called Il Posto, his dining partner was ten minutes late. Coates hated London with a passion, and visited as rarely as his job required. "Come on! Where the hell are you?" he muttered to no one. "What a waste of time."

Since meeting with Arthur Peebles' parents, the trajectory of the investigation had flatlined. Sergeant Packard, no nearer finding a suspect searching Tara Henson's online activity than he had been a couple of days earlier, kept trying. He and his partner thought Peebles might have contacted her through the dating site using his new name. Their victim had been on three dates with guys, however their alibis all checked out.

Usually identifying a suspect would take them days or sometimes weeks, and then they might not be a hundred per cent certain. The investigation frustrated him because they'd identified Peebles almost immediately. No, politicians and their agendas caused the delay in this case.

The door opened and an elderly couple entered. They were

greeted by a friendly and professional waiter, who showed them to their table. Coates sighed; he wanted the name so he could pass it on to Packard, who would search it on the PNC and start investigating. As soon as they acquired a home and work address, he would set uniforms on them. He would travel to one location while Packard travelled to the other.

When the bell rang, and the door opened, a tall man in a suit stepped inside, waiting to be greeted.

"Finally." Coates raised his hand. The friendly waiter spoke to the politician's aide, turned and walked his guest to the table. Only quarter of an hour late, Coates thought, as he shook hands with the justice secretary's confidante.

Up close and personal he looked younger than from a distance. Coates put him in his early-to-mid thirties, maybe. Well-groomed with combed hair and an expensive light grey suit, the aide, Bennett, obviously bought his from a boutique shop rather than a high-street store. "Please have a seat," he said, sitting down himself.

The waiter asked them what they would like to drink. Coates ordered water for the table to no objections from his guest, and waited for Bennett to start proceedings. He listened as the aide talked about the political mess his boss might be involved in if his theory proved correct. If the news outlets sniffed a high-profile recently-released prisoner going on and murdering again, they would have a field day at the justice secretary's expense, and the home secretary's and prime minister's as well. They were part of a scandal waiting to erupt.

"Look, I understand your position." Coates leaned forwards, elbows out. "You don't want this to explode in your boss's face, and I don't want that either. If you want me to bring him in quietly, fine. I'll be as quiet as I can, I promise. Please, I just need a name."

"And you're sure? You're certain that it's Peebles?"

"A hundred per cent. We have so much forensic evidence, the defence won't try to refute it. As far as the CPS is concerned, they've already said they'll process the case. All we need is Peebles in custody. We've got semen, blood, and saliva samples. We've got trace coming out of our ears. Hell, we've even got a bloody fingerprint, and you know how hard they are for the defence to argue."

As he suspected, Bennett asked to see this overwhelming case. Coates had come armed with the investigation dossier. He stooped down and picked up his briefcase. Impatiently, he handed the file over, drumming his fingers on the cloth.

"Please stop that."

Coates stopped and leaned back in his chair, folding his arms. Why didn't the aide just give him the damned name? Why mess about reviewing the bloody file? "Overwhelming, irrefutable evidence," he said. "If you give me his new name now, he'll be in custody by lunchtime, and processed by dinner."

"Whoa there! Slow down, would you?" Bennett said, handing him back the dossier. "I think you've been misled, detective. I don't have access to that information, I'm afraid. This is a preliminary meeting I was asked to attend by Mr Luckland. He asked me to ascertain if Peebles really is the suspect, or not."

With anger rising to the surface, Coates took a deep breath. "What? I've been waiting since Tuesday for this sit-down. And you don't have a name to give me? Are you fucking kidding me?" He went to stand.

"Sit down, detective!" the aide hissed. "You don't want me calling your chief, do you? Let's keep it civil. I understand you're disappointed, but this is bigger than you or I. Mr Luckland will take up the mantle, if I tell him there's sufficient evidence. The truth is, Peebles' new identity is only known by a few top-level staff within the probation service; that's who he's going to have to deal with to get you your name."

Coates couldn't help but show his frustration. Every hour they didn't have Peebles in custody, he could be making more victims. "You're going to make me wait for how long? He's out there, Bennett. Did you know he murdered two men inside? He slit one's throat from here to here. The other one he knifed multiple times in the showers. Do you really want this psychopath free to roam the streets? Because I don't."

"Oh, and you have evidence of this, do you?" Bennett retorted. "You expect me to believe they would release him if he had murdered two inmates? Don't make me laugh."

Coates had nothing to swing back. "I'm only going by what the governor told me."

"Look, you've shown me enough to tell Mr Luckland we need to find Peebles. This afternoon, I'll make sure he starts phoning the right people in the probation service. I'm sorry!"

"And how long do you think I'll have to wait for a result?"

"A few days, maybe?" Bennett stood.

Instead of showing his frustration, Coates extended his hand. "Thank you for your time," he said through a smile and clenched teeth. He wanted to pull the aide in and headbutt him.

"You're disappointed, detective," Bennett said. "I would be too. But we're merely pawns in a bigger game. The sooner you get used to that idea, the better. I'll be in touch as soon as I can. You have my word."

His last hope of finding Peebles walked out of the restaurant without ordering anything. The waiter arrived at Coates' table carrying a card reader. "I'm sorry! He had to leave." Out of politeness, he paid a nominal fee for wasting the waiter's time.

33

"Oli's outside," Shane said, bending down and kissing Georgina. "I'll lock the front door if you make sure you lock this one when you go inside. And I'll call you when the drop's been made, when this is all over."

Georgina smiled up at him. "Be careful," she said.

And with that, he left her in the back garden, sat at the table with her book. The past couple of days were far more relaxed. Knowing that Elf Man was more interested in money than her made her feel more relieved than she could ever put into words. When Shane had explained the situation to her, the relief was obvious; she agreed to pay her hundred and fifty thousand straight away. "Are you sure about this? You think he's only after the money?" had been her two questions.

It seemed that Elf Man was holding up to his end of the bargain. She had not heard from him since racing over to her parents' house, and neither had Isla, since the incident at North Steine. Perhaps he would disappear after receiving the money.

Georgina would glance up at the tree, half-expecting Elf Man's face to appear. The thought of him at her bedside, satisfying himself, scared her. The thought of him watching her sleep made her shake before going to sleep.

Trying to focus on her book, the evening sun cooled her brown skin. Wearing shorts and a vest top, she put her feet on an opposing chair and tilted her head back. The last of the rays, she thought, closing her eyes. Georgina had not received any texts or calls from Amelia, either. Her best friend had not cheeped.

Shane kept telling her she was being paranoid, that Kereama and Amelia were probably taking time for themselves. They'd upped and left for woop woop before. Only the previous year, they'd packed their ute overnight and disappeared. Of course, her best friend contacted her almost every day. And she'd cheeped pictures and texted regularly.

Sitting up, staring at her phone through dark brown lenses, Georgina picked it up and opened a text to Amelia. She needed to test whoever replied. *"Are you going to be home soon? Your mum's birthday's next week."*

The lack of cheeping and messaging forced her suspicions, that and the wording of the texts themselves. For time memorial, her best friend abbreviated everything. Amelia always wrote in text format. Scrolling through Amelia's most recent messages, she'd replied using complete words and sentences.

Settling back in her chair, Georgina waited for her phone to bleep. With her glass of orange juice in hand, she took a sip when it bleeped. Interested in what reply might come, she picked her mobile up and read aloud to herself. "Bit busy now. I hope to be, but Mum knows I might not be back in time. Speak soon. Xx."

If Georgina went to Shane and explained the situation, he wouldn't be receptive. He would tell her to stop being silly, that Kereama and Amelia were away on holiday. He chastised her for being paranoid too.

Deciding to investigate, she got up and went inside, remembering to lock up after her. Fetching her keys from her bag, she walked out to her Jeep and got in.

With the roof down, she drove over to Amelia's house on Darling Point. It only took her five minutes to drive there via New South Head Road. At first glance, all appeared sound. Georgina got out of her Jeep and marched up to the front door. After knocking twice, she tried to walk round the side of the house.

Fortunately, she had met most of Amelia and Kereama's neighbours, so when she scaled their fence, she didn't expect too many raised eyebrows, if any. In the garden she checked every room on the ground floor by cupping her hands around her eyes to peek through the windows. All was as should be, no sign of a struggle, nothing broken or out of the ordinary. Frustrated, she wanted to take a reccy inside. She betted she would find evidence of foul play. Georgina worried for her friends more than before.

She couldn't think of any reason for Amelia's strange behaviour. If her best friend took off for a few days with her boyfriend, why would she ignore her? And her complete change in style of writing her texts.

Why hadn't Amelia given her a key to her house in case of emergencies? She had given Amelia a spare key to *her* house. With nothing more she could do, Georgina decided she would speak to the police officers when she saw them next. She scaled the fence with ease.

Still believing something had happened to her friends, she jumped in her Jeep and drove home in silence, trying not to think the worst. It creeped her out, imagining all manner of scenarios, most of which involved that psychopath, Elf Man. One suspicion popped in her mind: Amelia replied she and Kereama would contribute too readily, without objecting once, which was totally out of character for her best friend; she always protested when asked to put her hand in her purse.

Back at her house, the gate closed behind her. She let herself in and locked the front door. Safe in the knowledge all doors were secured, she turned on the TV and sat back in her reclining armchair. Nothing decent on, she noted, flicking through the channels.

Georgina couldn't concentrate. She lay back, thinking about Shane and Oliver out there, handing a million of their hard-earned dollars to Elf Man. The situation made her angry, and calmed her: angry because they shouldn't have to do the drop at all, and calm because once the drop was made, she and her friends could go back to normal, the boys bickering like they used to.

34

Shane wasn't impressed with the police's response to Elf Man's home invasion. Upon arrival at their house, Senior Sergeant Scott Kennedy sounded negative, saying they would look into their case, but not to expect too much. According to Incremental Sergeant Janae Willis, they could do little about stalkers. When he and Georgina showed them the video of Elf Man in their home, they said they had enough to start with. Having little confidence after the meeting, Shane didn't bother informing them of their money drop-off. No, the best course of action: drop the cash off themselves.

Sat on the rear seat of Oliver's black Ford Mustang GT, his suitcase filled with twenty-dollar notes, he reached behind him to make sure it still existed. He, Oliver and the girls had agreed to chip in Kereama and Amelia's contribution, meaning that between the four of them, they had to check out half a million per couple, which had almost cleared Oliver and Isla out.

"What do we do if he takes the money and comes back?" Oliver asked, focusing on the cars in front. "Who do we go to then?"

A good question. "What are you saying? Do you want to cancel tonight?" Oliver didn't turn his head; he kept watching the road. "I can call the cops back, let them know what we're doing."

"Nah, I'm just thinking out loud. Ignore me. I'm jittery about the drop-off. That's a lot of money in that briefcase."

Shane and Georgina earned more than Oliver and Isla, and their friends felt the squeeze when the time came to withdraw the cash from the bank. "This whole situation fucking sucks. At least you'll be getting your share of Kerry and Amelia's third back, that'll be a hundred and sixty-six thousand."

"Yeah, like I said, ignore me." Oliver slowed down at a signpost for Barton Park. "Here we are."

Shane reached behind his seat and put the briefcase on his lap, securing the money. He and Oliver devised a plan. Elf Man chose Barton Park because of its isolation in the evenings. They were to leave the case under a certain bench at nine o'clock. Then, when he thought Shane and Oliver were safely out of reach, the pom would retrieve said briefcase. "We'd better hope there are trees and bushes nearby," Shane said to Oliver, who found a parking space off Eve Street. They planned on hiding until Elf Man fetched the cash, then pouncing on him and beating him to within an inch of his life.

Once parked up, Shane and Oliver walked through the huge park, passing only a few visitors, until they found the bench stipulated. Shane knew they had the correct bench because it overlooked a large decorative pond at the north end of the park. Under other circumstances he might be inclined to sit and admire the view, he thought, sitting down and placing the briefcase on the floor between his legs.

"Nearly time." Oliver glanced at his watch. "I'm not sure about this. That's a fucking lot of money, Shane."

"We can still back out," Shane said, wanting to cancel the

drop-off because the nearest trees and bushes were a hike away. They wouldn't be able to sneak up on Elf Man from that distance, not with the amount of open space between them. "Just say the word."

A lengthy silence fell over them.

"I need an answer, Oli," he said, sliding the briefcase beneath the bench, "or we leave it here and hope for the best."

His "friend" remained silent, making his mind up.

"Yay, or a nay, mate?"

"No, let's go for it."

"Hope for the best," Shane said, apprehensive at leaving the briefcase full of money. He turned and followed Oliver towards the bushes. They were more of a hike than he realised; he understood why Elf Man chose the bench. Even the fastest runner wouldn't be able to catch him from that distance.

After finding a good bush to hide in, Shane knelt and observed from behind leafy branches protecting him from view. Oliver followed suit. With the pond, and by extension the bench, being so isolated, Elf Man would find it as difficult to hide as they did. "Where are you, you mongrel?" he whispered.

"You don't think he can see us here, do you?" Oliver asked.

"If he can, he'll know we're too far away to catch him."

Wanting nothing more than to be face to face with the pommie, Shane fantasised about little else. How he would destroy Elf Man. If he got the chance to punch him, he would, aware he wouldn't be able to stop, and he didn't think anyone in his group would want him to. "Why's he keeping us waiting?"

He checked his phone: 21:20. No way Elf Man would be this late to pick up his million dollars. Shane felt something: dread. "Something's wrong."

"He should be here by now. What are we going to do?"

With one last glance at the bench, Shane stood. "First things first." He stepped out from behind the bush. "We go and get our money." And as he walked in the direction of the cash, he could see no one coming. His mobile bleeped. A text message from Elf Man: A picture of Georgina taken in his back garden through the living room window. "That piece of shit!" Shane spat, showing Oliver. "He never intended accepting our money; it's a fucking ruse!"

Shane sprinted to the bench, picked up the case and legged it back to Oliver's car, trying to keep up with him. Surprised at how much the briefcase weighed, he arrived at the car and sat in the passenger seat, breathless, as Oliver pulled out of the parking space.

A normal twenty-minute drive took a mere twelve in Oliver's beast. The Mustang parked up outside his gates and Shane shot out, opening them with his key ring. They couldn't open fast enough for him. Running at full pace, he reached the front door, only to find it locked. Images of Elf Man hurting Georgina leapt to the forefront of his mind. "George!" he yelled, Oliver right behind him.

If he had his gun, Shane would have had it out as he went from room to room looking for his girlfriend. Not finished searching the ground floor, he heard Georgina's voice, and his heart jumped for joy at hearing such a wonderful sound. She appeared on the stairs, confused.

"What's all the shouting about? Is it over?"

He didn't need an invite, Shane ran up and grabbed her, pulling her in for the longest hug. "I thought I'd lost you," he said, looking at her beautiful face, her cheeks warm to his palms.

"Are you all right?" she asked. "What happened?"

"Elf Man didn't show. We brought the money back with us."

Happy that Georgina was safe, he invited Oliver upstairs to the living room.

While making them all tea, Shane noticed Oliver's pale complexion. "You all right?"

"What if he wanted us to come here first?" he said out loud, picking up his car keys. "What if Isla's his target?"

35

Not caring that he lost Shane and Georgina along the way, Oliver drove his imported muscle car at almost twice the speed limit through his suburb of Darling Point, screeching to a stop in front of his driveway. Hearing a car in the distance, he got out of his Mustang and ran up his drive. "Isla!"

His heart lurched at seeing the door open a crack. When he left to pick up Shane, he was positive he'd closed it. Opening it wider, he peered in and shouted, "Isla!"

No answer. He stepped inside as his friends appeared outside. "He's been here," he said, the words soaked in fear. "I closed the door when I left."

"You don't know he's been here; you might've left it open." Shane put a hand on his shoulder in support. "Let's find her, before you go blaming yourself."

Blaming himself? How could he not? He was responsible for everything. Hell, Elf Man scratched his car because he thought taking the piss out of one of Georgina's followers would be funny. Kereama had been stabbed because of his "joke". No, he couldn't blame anyone else. He walked through his house, scanning each room for signs of life.

And every room he visited on the ground floor looked untouched. With no sign of a struggle, he felt hopeful. Oliver would have fallen to pieces had he seen broken furniture, or pictures, crockery, and whatever else might break during a disturbance. "Isla!" he yelled.

He climbed the stairs, scared he might find blood spattered on the walls, or pooling into the carpet. "Baby, speak to me!" he said, his voice quiet, Shane and Georgina behind him.

On the landing, all appeared normal, no blood, no broken possessions. One foot in front of the other, he was either going to find Isla alive and well, or the bedroom covered in her blood. "Where are you, baby?" he whispered, pushing his bedroom door open. "Please be alive," he said, "please be alive."

Nothing. Their bedroom immaculate, he closed his eyes and let out a deep relieved breath. "Thank God!" he told Georgina. "I thought I was going to find her in a bloody mess on the floor." Backtracking, he entered the spare room and let out another sigh of relief.

When he stopped outside the bathroom, he heard a sound he adored: Isla's version of singing. She was alive! Oliver saw the smirk on Georgina's face. A terrible singer, that didn't prevent his girlfriend from joining in with her Spotify playlist. With a grin, he opened the door to find her in the tub, surrounded by candles and bubbles.

Isla jumped and screamed when she stopped singing to find Oliver, Shane and Georgina smirking at her. Taking the earphones out, she sat up. "What? What's happened?" She sank lower, making sure they couldn't see her breasts. "Will you all stop grinning at me and tell me what's going on, please?"

Without an invite, Oliver rushed over to the tub, bent down and hugged her. "Thank God!" he said into her ear. "I thought he came here and hurt you."

"Why? I thought you were out paying him off?"

"He didn't show," Shane explained from behind Oliver. "So, if either of you have any ideas on how we proceed from here, now's the time to tell me."

Staring into Isla's stunning eyes, he replied, "We'll think on it."

Georgina whispered to Shane that they should leave.

Grateful for her intervention, he turned to his friends. "Thanks for coming." He followed them downstairs and thanked them again for driving over there. He remembered to lock the door. And as he walked back upstairs, he tried to remember closing it before he left.

In the bathroom, he sat next to the tub while she finished bathing. "Did you go out front earlier?" he asked, in more of a muse than a question.

"Uh-uh." She lathered her leg in bath soak.

Isla drove him wild. When she asked why, he said, "Oh, no reason. Just that the door was left ajar. I could've sworn I closed it."

Ignoring his musings, she beckoned him with a crook of her finger. "Are you going to take me to the bedroom, or are we going to sit around talking all night?" she asked, her voice soft and enticing. "Well? Come here then!"

Oliver didn't need to be asked twice; he stood at her command. When she held her hands up, he pulled her to her feet, bubbles sliding down her wet toned body. Isla put her arm around his neck, as he stooped down and picked her up. He carried her to the bedroom, and deposited her gently on top of the sheets. He didn't care that she was dripping everywhere.

"I want you so bad," she said, writhing on the bed.

36

Isla rolled Oliver over. For such a fit and healthy guy, he snored a lot. Satisfied with his heavy breathing instead, she lay on her back staring at nothing in particular, the ceiling, whatever. She regretted not catching Elf Man. If they had managed to corner him, he wouldn't be out there stalking them; he would be in hospital, or worse. She dreamed of hurting him.

Of her fantasies, the most rewarding would be for her and her Dollies to surround him and keep kicking him until he stopped moving, stopped groaning in pain. That, or her and her friends pounding on him, although the enjoyment wouldn't last as long with Oliver, Shane and Kereama joining in. Knowing Georgina, she would try to stop them, being the Buddhist of the group. Isla loved her to bits, but Georgina could be a liability sometimes.

Being a sufferer of insomnia for the past ten years, she sat up and opened the drawer of her bedside table. She took out a tub of CBD jellies, unpeeled the lid and stuck a couple in her mouth, tasting the strawberry flavouring as she chewed on them. Swallowing the juice, it wouldn't take long for the CBD to work its magic, for her muscles to relax and help her fall asleep. Worked a charm every time.

Lying on her back, she closed her eyes and attempted not to think of anything, to empty her mind, like her self-help books had taught her. Sod's law, whenever she tried, thoughts invaded her. Sometimes they were good, positive thoughts, other times negative. The reason she worked out so hard every day was to quieten her negativity.

A lifelong quest for Isla, having the perfect body meant everything to her. She started with two or three workouts a week like any regular member would, until she noticed the gains, and increased it to five or six sessions weekly. Eating a healthy balanced diet was also imperative. A year after joining the gym, she had abs, the holy grail.

Drifting off, her eyelids heavy, Isla's body almost melted into the mattress, her head following suit. The best feeling in the world. It wouldn't be long until she fell into the sweet land of slumber, her favourite place to be, where anything could happen. The laws of physics didn't apply in her dreams.

A loud bang forced her to sit up.

It had come from downstairs.

After listening for a while she figured she must've dreamed it.

Her heart rate slowing, she lay back down.

Another loud bang, only closer.

"Oli, wake up." She shook him. "Wake up, baby. I think someone's in the house."

After shaking him awake, she watched as Oliver threw back the sheets and walked over to his wardrobe. He fetched a wooden baseball bat and swung it a couple of times. "Are you going to put some clothes on?"

Isla pointed at his pants on the floor and he obeyed, sliding them up his legs. "Be careful." She wished she had dreamed the noises. "Switch on the light."

Flicking the switch, Oliver cursed when nothing happened.

Begging him to be careful, he opened the bedroom door and stepped out onto the landing, closing the door behind him. While listening for noises, she took out a pair of knickers and a black T-shirt from her chest of drawers and put them on.

Stood by the door, she pressed her ear to the wood.

Oliver screamed.

Several loud, hard crashes and thuds made her spy through a crack between the door and frame. "Oli!" she whispered after making up her mind to investigate.

Out on the dark landing, she stood at the top stair and saw her boyfriend lying unconscious at the bottom, his legs at awkward angles. "Oli!" She ran down the stairs so fast her feet barely hit carpet. Kneeling by his side, attempting to wake him up, she felt cold metal under her chin.

She looked up to find an unfamiliar face peering down at her. Georgina's mum was right in her description of Elf Man: thin lips, unruly hair, and pale complexion.

"Hello, Isla," Elf Man said. "We meet at last. I've waited for so long, I can't tell you."

Fight or flight. Those were her two choices.

Before she had the chance to choose, Elf Man pulled her hair back, exposing her throat.

Isla couldn't speak for fear of him slicing her.

"Are you going to be a good girl?"

Daring to open her mouth, she said she would.

"Good girl. I want you to tie your hands together. Here, use these plastic ties. Can you do that? Or do I stick your boyfriend with this now?" He raised the knife.

"No! I'll do it. Please, don't hurt us. I'll do whatever you want, I promise."

She picked up the cable ties and tied one around her left wrist, then threaded the second beneath the first and around her right wrist.

"You're a strong girl, aren't you, Isla?" Elf Man asked. "Drag Oli into the lounge, please." He walked ahead of her, his knife itching to play, she noted.

Even with her wrists bound, she could slide Oliver along the hallway carpet and into the living room, where two chairs were placed facing one another. Continuing to drag her boyfriend, she stopped next to one of them.

"Now put him in it, or I'll slit his throat right here."

"I'll need your help; he's too heavy," she argued, hoping to get Elf Man close to her so that she could tackle him. "He's a deadweight."

Elf Man declined. He told her she either lifted him into the chair herself, or he would stick the knife in Oliver's ear. Somehow, she managed it. Getting Oliver into it took a few minutes, with the pom's verbal encouragement.

Gesturing the opposing seat, Elf Man told her to sit.

With little choice but to obey, Isla sat while he tied her ankles to the wooden legs with cable ties. Every time she moved, the plastic restraints dug into her flesh. "Please, you don't have to do this," she begged, tears streaming down her cheeks.

He stuck the knife between her hands and cut the plastic cuffs, freeing them. Then, he took two more ties and wrapped them around her wrists and the wooden arms of the chair. Helpless, now Elf Man could do whatever he liked to both of them. "I'm begging you, please. Oli didn't mean anything by it, really. Please, you have to believe me."

Oliver groaned. The slow movement of his head scared her.

Elf Man stepped up to her disoriented boyfriend, the baseball bat in one hand, the knife in the other.

"Don't hurt him, please." She needed the toilet so badly.

"I wouldn't dream of hurting him. Not our lovely Oli. The prankster, the joker."

Oliver's eyes rolled.

Isla continued pleading. "He didn't mean anything by it. He's an idiot, but–" She jumped when Elf Man hit Oliver on the head with the bat, not hard, but enough to cause pain.

"Is that right, Oli? You didn't mean to hurt my feelings?"

Muffled, gibberish, her boyfriend's response sounded a lot like, "Fuck you!"

She tried to grab the pom's attention. "He didn't mean that. He's concussed."

Isla screamed when Elf Man used all the power he could muster to crack the top of Oliver's head with the bat, the sound of cracking skull enough to make her puke.

Blood dripped from the bat before he brought it crashing down a second time.

Listening to Elf Man swear at his victim, she cried, "You're killing him!"

Watching the pom beat her boyfriend to death, she sobbed.

Oliver coughed and spluttered after the third and fourth batting.

Elf Man kicked Oliver's chest, tipping the chair on its back.

She gasped when Elf Man continued to batter her boyfriend's beautiful face with the blood-soaked bat, each time spraying the walls a darker crimson.

Scared for her life, she struggled with her restraints. They were tied so tight, she held little hope of freedom.

Out of breath, Elf man pointed the bat at her. "He deserved that," he said, surveying his handiwork. "And you deserve better than him, let me tell you."

Isla couldn't stop crying; she kept staring at the bloody mess that was once Oliver. His legs twitched. "You bastard! I'm gonna fucking kill you!"

"You're not crying over this cheating piece of shit, are you?" Elf Man asked, showing her a video of Oliver sat behind a table in a nightclub.

Spotting blonde hair going up and down, and noting Oliver's happy face, her life dropped away from her in a single moment. Not for one minute did she think of him as the unfaithful type. "Fuck you!" she hissed, unable to stop watching some bimbo pleasure her man.

When she flew into a fit of rage, contorting and twisting in her chair, Elf Man tutted and walked away with the bat and knife. Possessed by anger, she struggled so much the plastic ties drew blood around her wrists and ankles.

The sight of the psycho carrying a funnel in one hand and a bottle of bleach in the other made her stop fighting.

Instead she begged and pleaded with him to let her go, that she would behave.

She would give him whatever he wanted; she would fuck him.

Nothing worked.

Elf Man grabbed her chin and stuffed the funnel in her mouth.

Isla cried, desperate for him to stop, watching him raise and turn the bottle.

She screamed through the nozzle until bleach trickled down her throat.

Coughing, trying not to swallow the corrosive liquid, the cleaning fluid continued to run down her throat, until her stomach burned, and the pain led up her chest and into her mouth. Her saliva turned dark red.

After Elf Man whipped the funnel out, he stood back and watched her.

Isla screamed until blood gargled. Stuck in her chair, she writhed in agony.

"Enough." Elf Man picked up his bat.

She wanted to die.

The pain too much, she longed for death when her killer swung the baton at her head.

37

"Shane, it's ready!" Georgina shouted, using tongs to take the snags off the barbecue. With a separate set of tongs, she turned over her veggie burger.

Sunday evening and she'd arrived home an hour earlier. Salty and sandy after her day on the beach, she didn't mind; she would be taking a shower after dinner. Picking up her stubby, she took a swig. "Shane, did you hear me? Yours is ready."

"All right, keep your knickers on, I'm here." He stepped out in a pair of shorts and vest. She liked him in vests; she loved his arms and legs, the muscle definition that other guys lacked.

Settling down at the garden table, Georgina helped herself to some salad he'd prepared for them, knowing she wouldn't be home on time. Always late, especially when she went surfing with Mingzhu, she rang ahead to let him know. In fairness, he didn't need to be psychic. It happened every time without fail. She wedged her veggie burger inside a bun and took her first bite. Delicious.

She and Mingzhu had spent the afternoon keeping an eye out for Elf Man, which wasn't surprising after their last outing when Georgina's Jeep was stolen and promptly returned. Elf Man being out there gave her the jitters, but she'd not heard from him all weekend. Why he decided not to take the money had baffled her and Shane.

He worried her with how quiet he was being. They weren't the kind of couple who didn't talk, yet this past week or so he'd gone silent, and every time she brought up his behaviour, he told her not to worry. Not being stupid, or shallow, she knew when something was wrong. And even now, watching him eat his hotdogs, he did so in silence. No, "how was your day?" Nothing like that. "I had a good set today," she said, trying to make conversation.

"Hmm? Oh, good."

"I met a great guy," she said with a grin. "He bought me drinks, we went back to his house for amazing sex." Tutting, she waved her hand in front of his face. "Hello? Earth to Shane. Wake up, babe." When he focused, she said, "Jesus, what's the matter with you? This is getting beyond a joke now, baby. Talk to me, please?"

"What? Nothing's wrong, all right? Having a go at me isn't going to make me talk more."

Speechless, she pushed her plate away and stood, her shower calling her. "Fine! You stay down here by yourself!" And as she strutted inside, he called after her, apologetic. He could do one for all she cared, she told herself, climbing the stairs.

In the bathroom, she stripped off and stepped under the warm water. The sand and salt washed away, leaving her skin supple and refreshed. While washing off the gel, the door creaked open. She turned to find a sorry Shane holding a couple of her flowers out of the garden. Beckoning him in with her finger, he dropped his shorts and joined her.

. . .

After the longest shower of her life, and the most passionate kissing in a while, she stepped out and dried them both with the same large towel. In the bedroom he made love to her more slowly than he had in a long time.

Shane pried himself away from her long enough to brew them a cup of tea each.

While lying there, she thought about Isla.

When they'd left their friends' house on Friday, Isla was in the tub. Smiling, Georgina thought about asking her what happened.

And when she thought back, she had not spoken to Isla since that night.

Scrolling through her messages, she noted the dates. Every day she received communication of some sort from Isla. It had been almost two days. Lying beneath the sheets, with Shane making noise downstairs, she typed, "*Long time no speak. How you doing after Friday? xxXxx*" They had a specific format for their kisses.

"Here," he said, placing her mug of tea on her bedside cabinet.

He climbed in beside her and spooned. "Mmm, this is more like it," she said, his arms wrapped around her. She groaned when her phone bleeped. "Sorry! Isla," she said unwrapping him and picking up her mobile.

"*Bit busy now, George. Had to leave. Scared. You should do the same X*"

Not believing her eyes, she sat up and reread the text. Everything was wrong with the message, from the writing itself, to the format of the kisses. Isla sent one capital X. She never sent only one kiss, ever. Isla's kisses were identical with every text: xxXxx. There were always five, and the middle kiss always, always a capital.

"What is it?" Shane asked, sitting up.

She handed him her mobile. "I think something's happened to Amelia and Isla," she started, noticing his expression change from concern to "not this again". "Hear me out, please. You think Amelia and Kereama are up north somewhere, that they ran off to get away from all this, but Isla's different, she's a fighter; she and Oli wouldn't run away, would they?"

Shane conceded that they were both fighters.

"And now we're supposed to believe that they packed up their ute and skipped town?" He was coming around to her way of thinking. "Look at how she's written it. Isla can't spell. She doesn't type out words like this. And neither does Amelia." He nodded. When he reached for her mobile, she handed it to him. "And what about Isla's kisses? She doesn't give one big kiss, ever. She gives two small kisses, then a big one, followed by two small. I swear, whoever wrote that message, it's not Isla."

"All right, you may have a point, but what do you want me to do? We can call the police again, but they won't be much help. They weren't last time, and we had evidence of him being inside our house. With this, we'll be giving them what? Our friends telling us they've gone away for a few days. They won't take it seriously, baby. What do you think we should do?"

"Let's go over there. Amelia's is all locked up. Please, Shane, I want to go and check for myself."

"What, now?" He handed back her phone.

"Absolutely," she said, pleading with him.

When he took his time, she said, "I'm going over there, with or without you. So, either come, or don't, I don't care. This is important." She whipped off the covers and started to dress, pulling her knickers on and a T-shirt over her head. She felt his arms around her waist and his lips on her neck.

"You win. Let's go!"

Having thrown on some clothes, Shane met her in the kitchen, where she picked up her keys from the counter. "Ready?" she asked. After picking up an apple, he followed her downstairs and out onto the driveway. In her Jeep, she turned on the engine and opened the gates with the remote control.

Pulling up outside Isla and Oliver's house, Georgina noted it was all locked up and the drive deserted. None of their cars were there. "The ute's gone." With apprehension, she stepped out of her Jeep and walked up to the front door with Shane by her side.

When no one answered, she peered through their window. Dark out, the street lamps were her only light. It was no use, she couldn't see anything through the glass. One thing she did notice: "When Isla goes away, she puts the lights and curtains on a timer."

"Yeah? Maybe she forgot this time?" Shane shrugged.

"Why are you so determined to not believe me?" Georgina turned to him. Her boyfriend took a step back and gave her a "who, me?" glance. And then she remembered meeting one of Isla's neighbours before. She walked back down the drive.

"Where are you going now?"

Georgina walked along the pavement and up the neighbour's front path. She knocked. "If Kylie doesn't know anything about Isla going away, then she hasn't gone anywhere." She prayed Kylie had a key.

"Have you met these people before? You can't go knocking—"

"Oh, hi George," Isla's friend and neighbour said, opening the door and leaning against it. "Been a long time." Her smile faded. "Are you all right? Is something wrong?" She put her hand on Georgina's shoulder.

When Kylie shook her head to Georgina's question, Georgina glanced at her boyfriend. "She wouldn't leave her house in the dark, Shane," was all she needed to say as Shane pulled her back down the path, thanking Kylie for her time.

"You've convinced me," Shane said, his voice quiet and deliberate. "I'll phone Sergeant Kennedy first thing in the morning."

38

"You'll be here in an hour? Thank you so much, sergeant." Shane hung up his mobile and stared at the ceiling. Georgina showered next door. Half past eight on a Wednesday morning and ordinarily he would be on his way to the cricket ground. Instead, he had an interview planned; he would be answering police questions. "Damn!" He sat on the edge of the bed.

Sleep. Even before the Elf Man troubles sleep had eluded him, the thought of losing another season high on his list of worries. What if he failed to win the Swans any trophies? He would go down in history as the biggest sporting failure of all time. Every Swans captain had won at least one trophy.

Pulling on his boxers, he got down on his toes and hands. A hundred push-ups and fifty sit-ups were his staple. The best way to start his day. Some people preferred a shower and a fruit juice; some liked a cigarette and a hot cup of coffee; he made himself perform push-ups and sit-ups before he did anything else.

He was such a coward, he told himself, as sweat dripped onto the carpet. If he were any kind of man, he would have sat her down and spelled it out to her: I'm a cheat, and Elf Man's using photos to blackmail me.

Breathless, he paused before commencing his sit-ups. Why had the pom gone quiet over the weekend? Shane didn't like the silence. At least when Elf Man contacted him, he knew roughly what he intended. Not knowing when he would strike was worse.

Feeling his stomach muscles tense, he pulled himself up, and back down again. What did Elf Man want? Why wait? What was his endgame? He had gone after Kereama, Oliver, Isla, and Georgina so far. So, what did he want? If Shane could figure that out, he would be halfway to resolving the conflict.

She walked in drying herself with a towel. "When are they coming?"

"Soon. Within the hour. Please don't get your hopes up. If they didn't take the video seriously, what do you think they'll do about this? You're giving them proof Amelia and Isla are still answering their messages." He wouldn't tell Georgina, but he believed her. Something had happened to his friends. Isla and Oliver prided themselves on being tough. They wouldn't run and hide from some pommie psychopath; they'd stay and fight.

A long, warm shower later, he dressed himself and met Georgina in the garden, where she sat eating her breakfast. While he cried off work for the day, she postponed a photoshoot for Ripped Energy Drink. After the interview, he was taking her shopping, to try to take her mind off Elf Man.

Conversation sparse between them, Shane ate his bowl of cereal wanting to talk to her. Hell, he wanted to apologise, to beg for forgiveness. He didn't want to lose her, and if she found out he so much as kissed another woman, she would leave him.

"I'll let them in," Georgina said, hearing the doorbell.

Two minutes later, Senior Sergeant Scott Kennedy and Incremental Sergeant Janae Willis stepped out into the garden.

Shane invited them to join him at the table. "You had any luck with Chatter?" He noted the police officers' nonchalant expressions.

"Our cyber unit are trying to contact Chatter's CEO," Kennedy replied. "As I'm sure you'll appreciate, dealing with corporate companies like this is problematic. But we've been looking into Elf Man's life back in the UK."

"And?" Georgina leaned forwards, listening.

"Our sources over there tell us he's popped up recently," Willis said.

Confused, Shane scratched his head. "And? What does that mean?"

"He has no history. They say there's a home and work address for him for the last eighteen months, but nothing prior to that."

"I don't understand, how can someone have no history?" Georgina looked to Shane and the officers for answers. "Everyone has a past. Don't they?"

"We've asked the UK police to look into him for us," Kennedy said, his voice reassuring. "In the meantime, we're following up on Mr Tua's assailant. This is him, isn't it? This is Elf Man here." The officer gave Shane the picture.

"This is him?" He couldn't see his face. "What a shit photo. The cap's covering his face. But if you say this is him, we think he stabbed Kerry." He handed the picture to Georgina. "Didn't the station have more cameras?"

"This was the best we could get," Willis explained. "He knew how to disguise himself. He uses the cap to his advantage. We know how frustrating this must be for you, Mr Daley. Please be patient with us. We'll catch this guy."

"And in the meantime, we're being terrorised," Shane said. "What about putting a patrol outside our house? Where are we with that?" He didn't like the shared glance.

"Our super won't go for that, I'm afraid. He says we can't waste man hours." Kennedy gave him an apologetic look. "The best we can do is give you an alarm to keep in your home. The line goes through to our HQ in Parramatta, but the first responders will be local to you. They can be here inside two minutes."

"That's what I'm talking about," Shane said. "Set us up with one of those bad boys." An alarm would work. Having police parked outside the house would have given the neighbours something to talk about.

"I'll request one now," Willis said, taking her phone out of her shorts pocket. "It'll take a couple of days."

"You're kidding me! How long?"

"We need to arrange installation. This is linked directly to your phone line. It's not something I can hand to you that you keep on you. Think of it as your wired Bat Phone." She continued typing on her mobile.

Still better than a patrol car outside the house, he thought.

Georgina squeezed his knee. "Tell them." She caught Kennedy's attention. "Say, have you seen Kereama lately?"

"Mr Tua? No, not since giving him an update, why?"

"He's missing," Georgina blurted. "They're all missing. Kerry, Amelia, Oliver and Isla; they're all gone. Please help us find them."

"Just hear us out," Shane added, knowing how dramatic his girlfriend sounded. "We went over to Isla and Oliver's last night. Their house is all locked up, left dark. George says Isla always puts the lights and curtains on timer, which they weren't." He noticed their expressions as he told them about Isla's neighbour not seeing her.

He also informed them of the text messages from both Amelia and Isla, and how their very makeup had changed.

Georgina showed them the texts in question. There was no way they were going for their story.

"Honestly, Mr Daley, there's not a lot we can do for you on this. By your own admission they're replying to you. If we can't file a missing persons form, we can't launch an investigation. I'm sorry!"

"But what about the text messages?" Georgina said to Willis. "You must have mates you know almost as well as yourself, right? There must be little details you know about them. With Amelia and Isla, I know their texts. Please, won't you look into it for us?"

"I'm sorry, Miss Shaw, but the sarge is right. If we can't file a report, we can't create a case number. Without that, we can't start an investigation."

Shane didn't argue; he left Georgina at the table, thanked the police officers for their time and walked them out to their car. Upstairs in the kitchen, he stood by the sink and observed Georgina below. She wanted a better answer and he didn't blame her. Useless! They were useless.

39

The Westfield Shopping Centre on Market Street wasn't especially busy. Visitors were sparse, which Georgina preferred when in stores looking for clothes, not that she needed more. Her wardrobes were chokka already. Picking up a pair of trainers, she checked the Nike store for Elf Man. Wherever she went, she felt his eyes on her.

No use. Even shopping couldn't take her mind off her friends being missing. Despite the police's refusal to investigate, she knew something had happened to them. Those texts were not from Amelia or Isla. Putting the trainer back on the wall display, Georgina moved further down and spied a pair of white trainers with a touch of pink.

"Um, hi! I'm so sorry to disturb you while you're shopping, but can I ask you for your autograph, please? My daughter's such a huge fan of yours," a woman in her fifties asked. "When I saw you in here, I just had to come in."

Georgina told her it was fine. She asked for the teenager's name, took the pad of paper and scribbled her signature, adding a little note that said, "Keep Surfing!". According to the mum, the daughter was bullied a few years ago, until she took up shortboarding, and met a new group of friends who helped her with her tormentors. The girl had flourished since, and Georgina had inspired her to take up the sport, apparently. The woman thanked her, shook her hand, and walked out of the shop beaming.

"Wow! What a great story," a store clerk said, who had overheard everything. "How you can inspire people like that. Doesn't it just make you go all gooey inside?"

Every time, Georgina thought, watching the woman walk out of the shop. Georgina got talking to the shop assistant, which took her mind off Elf Man and everything else. The clerk, a tiny brunette girl, maybe twenty, twenty-one tops, had no interest in surfing, but judging by the healthy tan, loved beaches. Amelia would get on well with her, Georgina thought with a pang of sorrow.

The assistant apologised for gabbing and let Georgina continue shopping. While studying the many styles of Nike trainers, she sensed the clerk staring from afar. She didn't mind, the girl was star-struck; she experienced it wherever she went. All perfectly normal with two and a half million followers. And a large proportion of those fans were Australian, and more specifically from Sydney. Over the years, Georgina had grown used to living in the public eye. She wouldn't admit to loving fame outside of her own mind.

Picking up the white with pink trim pair for a second time, she walked them over to the counter, noting the clerk barge past a fellow cashier to serve her. Georgina ignored it, smiled, and paid for the footwear. The cashier said "goodbye" a touch louder than she should have, and with a smattering of desperation. Georgina waved and strolled out, letting out a lungful of relief air. Desperate people scared her.

Approaching midday, she was supposed to meet Shane by the escalators at noon. He'd acted suspiciously when he'd left her an hour earlier. Approaching the escalator, she couldn't see him. At the foot of the moving staircase, she stepped to the side and turned round, taking her phone out of her bag.

There had to be a way to get inside Amelia or Isla's houses. Then she remembered Amelia had given a spare key to her mum. Having grown up with her from a young age, Georgina was almost a member of the Thomas family, and vice versa. She had to be careful: she didn't want to scare Amelia's mum.

Fortunately, she had the number stored in her phone. "Hi!" She was glad to hear the voice. After the initial niceties, she asked Amelia's mum if she still had the spare key. It turned out that Amelia had sent her a text telling her she was up north with Kereama for a break.

Amelia's mum replied in the affirmative. The only problem: she lived in Adelaide, a good fourteen-hour journey away. Georgina offered to drive over there to pick the key up. She was cut short when her second mum said she would drive to Amelia's; she wanted to water the garden and clean up for her daughter's return. The downside, she wouldn't be arriving until Thursday night.

Trying to hide her disappointment, Georgina offered to put Amelia's mum up for the night, but she refused, saying she would sleep in one of Amelia's spare bedrooms. Georgina hung up, replacing her phone. On Thursday night, she would know more about what happened to Amelia and Kereama.

Turning round, she saw Shane walking towards the escalator on the second floor, a guy with a baseball cap on close behind him. Georgina smiled up at him, as he got to the top of the moving stairs. For some reason, she zoned in on the bloke behind him wearing the cap. There was something off about him.

The descending escalator clear of shoppers, she panicked

when she realised who the cap-wearer was. "Shane! Behind you!" she shouted, as her boyfriend stepped on the top stair.

Georgina saw Elf Man's foot hook Shane's around his right leg.

Shane's eyes widened and he yelled out as he tripped and fell onto the metal stairs.

She winced at the sight of her boyfriend landing on his left arm, before rolling down the rest of the steps. "Shane!" she cried, crouching to aid him.

Fully conscious and in pain, sweat formed on his brow. He'd adopted a pallid hue.

Georgina heard a whistle from up on the second level.

Elf Man stared down at her, a satisfied grin splattered across his face.

Even from a distance he was ugly.

She glared up at him until he disappeared from view.

"It's broken, babe."

She looked down at Shane's misshapen arm; bone stuck out, but not through the skin. The metal stair had broken it cleanly. When she glanced back up, Elf Man was nowhere to be seen. Instead of going after him, she accepted help from the crowd who'd gathered after hearing the commotion.

Scanning the upper walkway for him, nothing. They were in trouble.

40

D I Coates picked up his mobile.

"It took some finagling in the probation service, but Mr Luckland came through with the name you're after."

Excited, he waved at Sergeant Packard to join him. "Go on! Who is it?" He had the PNC open, wanting to insert the name in the search bar, his fingers poised.

"Really? Is that all you're going to say?" Bennett said, clearly hurt.

"Bennett, please can I have the name? I've been waiting on this for days now." Coates didn't want to massage his ego; he had a rapist and murderer out there, more than likely going to strike again, and he had no clue where. "I appreciate everything you and the justice secretary have done, and I'll send you both a basket each, all right? With a cherry on top. But please, please, please give me the sodding name."

"Danny Elfman."

"Daniel Elfman." Coates typed the name into the search bar.

"Did I just say Daniel? No, I said Danny Elfman."

Coates glanced up at Packard, who looked confused. "You mean, as in the film composer?" He deleted "iel" and typed "ny" instead. He found the correct entry and studied the screen. The photo of Elfman was a spot-on match for Arthur Peebles.

His partner scribbled the name on a piece of paper and returned to his desk.

"Before I go, detective, the justice secretary asked me to convey his wishes for this to be handled discreetly. We don't want the press getting wind of it until he's in custody, is that understood? Now, go do your thing."

"Yes, sir." Coates hung up.

"We have a home and work address listed for him," Packard said.

There was little he could glean from Elfman's file. This Danny Elfman had no history. The addresses were about the only details on screen. "Let's go find this guy." He wrote them on a piece of paper, picked up his jacket and walked with Packard through the office, into the corridor and up to the lift.

"How do you want to play this?"

Coates checked his watch: 15:35. "How about you take his home and I'll take his work? Take a couple of uniforms with you." He read the name of the company Elfman worked for: McGiven, Niall and Sanders, which sounded more like a solicitors' firm than an insurance company. Located in Brighton, in Regency Square, he wondered if the building would be as lavishly decorated as most solicitors. Elfman's home was situated in the Seven Dials area.

Out in the car park, Coates said farewell to Packard, got into the driver's seat of his requisitioned Peugeot and set off on the half-hour drive to Brighton.

Traffic was light to start with and became heavier the closer Coates came to his destination. While driving in silence – he never listened to the radio – he wondered why Peebles had chosen Danny Elfman? What an unusual choice! Coates shrugged it off; he would find out when he apprehended him.

After parking nearby, Coates entered the office to find two uniforms had already sealed off the basement where Danny Elfman a.k.a. Arthur Peebles worked. Elfman's colleagues had all been ordered out of the office. They stood in small groups in reception, gossiping. He noticed how scruffy the area was, which didn't bode well for the kind of ethos the company had. "Where're we at?" Coates asked one uniform. "Is Danny Elfman in custody?"

"When we arrived we asked for Elfman, but the receptionist said he left over a week ago, sir. The basement's sealed off, as requested. The CEO and the suspect's line manager are waiting on you upstairs on the second floor for an interview."

As usual, Coates felt the accusatory stares from the staff, who were all murmuring. "Good work, sergeant." He thanked him and took the lift up. Stepping out of the elevator, he was greeted by a man in his mid-fifties with greying hair. He stood a couple of stones overweight, if his paunch told Coates anything.

"Detective?" The man held his hand out and wore his smile like a professional salesman. "I must thank you for meeting with me finally. It was just awful what happened to Carl."

Coates, confused, asked, "I'm sorry! Who's Carl?"

"Isn't that why you're here? To ask me questions about Carl Hannigan's murder?"

He shook his head. "Um, no, I'm afraid that has nothing to do with me, Mr...?" The man took a couple of seconds to identify himself as Mr McGiven, one of the three owners. "I'm not here to discuss that. I'm here to talk to you about Danny Elfman."

"Oh! Shame," said the CEO. "Carl was one of my best salesmen. And to die in such horrific circumstances."

"All right, Mr McGiven, I'm going to bite. How did he die?"

"The officer I spoke to said they found him by the front door of his home," the owner said, his eyes sad, "with over fifty stab wounds to his face and neck."

Too similar to the murder Peebles had committed inside, it had to be him. "That's terrible. I'll tell you what I'll do. Give me the detective's name and I'll confer with him on the case, is that all right with you? I believe Elfman might be responsible."

"Danny? I don't think so, detective," McGiven argued. "If you'd met him, you wouldn't believe it either. Whoever murdered Carl... He's a mad man. And Danny Elfman's far too meek and mild mannered for that. Come! Let's discuss this in my office."

A short walk later, Coates sat opposite the CEO in a plush, well-decorated and spacious office, the room unlike the rest of the building, with new carpets, which contrasted with the threadbare ones laid throughout. "Nice room," he commented.

McGiven ignored him. "You see, the probation service contacted me regarding Danny Elfman about eighteen months ago. They told me that they were relocating him and needed to find him gainful employment. They paid me to take him on at first, until we were certain he would stay the course, at which time we made him a permanent offer."

"So, would you say he was a decent employee?"

"He was perfect for the job. What you must understand is, the customer service team are responsible for all incoming traffic from clients, and sometimes they take calls from customers wishing to cancel their first premium payments. They might be within their twenty-eight-day cooling off period, for example, and it's up to the CS representatives to carry out their wishes, which in turn affects the sales team's bonuses. There can be some animosity between the teams in the basement."

"Right, and you think Elfman's perfect for the role because?"

"He takes the abuse. As much as I respected Carl, he could be, how should I put this?" McGiven looked to the ceiling, drumming his fingers on his chin.

"An arsehole? You can say it. I can imagine he gave Elfman

some aggro, am I right?" The guy sounded like an arsehole; Coates had met people like Carl before.

"You could say that. But Danny took everything in his stride. Carl made everyone on the customer service team cry at one time or another. All except Danny. He was made for the job, I tell you. And he wouldn't backchat, or moan. I had a lot of respect for him because of that. The whole sales team seemed to dislike him, detective, not just Carl, but he wouldn't hurt anyone."

"That's all very well, Mr McGiven, but the fact remains we have his DNA all over a dead body in Lewes. We found the poor woman in an industrial bin. She was raped, murdered, and then dumped there. We have enough evidence to convict him. All we need is to apprehend him."

The CEO, shocked, picked up his landline phone and spoke to someone. He hung up and explained that Patrick Jacobs was the best person to speak to: Danny Elfman's line manager. "He's downstairs, detective."

With a handshake, Coates thanked the owner and walked out of the office, along the corridor to the elevator.

41

The room small, inside DI Coates sat opposite Patrick Jacobs, Elfman's direct line manager, a well-dressed man in a close-fitting suit. "This might come as a shock, but I believe he has murdered a young woman in Lewes. Anything you can tell me about Elfman is appreciated."

"Really?" Jacobs scratched his head. "Danny?"

"I appreciate that you think he's this, how did McGiven put it? Oh yeah, 'meek and mild' pushover, but I promise you, he's not. The woman we found dumped in a bin was raped and murdered, Mr Jacobs. And there's no doubt who's responsible. He didn't try all that hard to hide the fact, which means either he's sloppy, stupid, or he doesn't care. And the latter bothers me. He made himself a cosy existence in prison."

"Wait! Danny was in the nick? Before he started here, you mean?"

"Oh yes, you wouldn't think it to look at the guy, but he's tough as old boots this one. Which is why I need to find him before he chooses his next victim."

Jacobs stared into nothing. "He used to sit on his phone looking at pictures of girls on Chatter. He was no harm, really."

"I assure you, he's anything but harmless."

"And you think he might be responsible for Carl as well?"

"Mr McGiven tells me Carl was stabbed multiple times in the face and neck. While in prison, an inmate was found with stab wounds over his face too. And according to the governor, Elfman lived very comfortably thereafter."

"This is a total head spin. He wouldn't say or do anything to draw attention to himself. He never spoke unless spoken to. What you're describing can't be Danny. He was just a sad and lonely bloke."

"I heard he had some dealings with Carl?"

"Well, yeah, Carl had a problem with everyone. He was the alpha, in among a group of alphas, do you understand? There are twelve hungry members on the sales team, and they all work hard and play hard. But they looked to him as a leader. They always followed him, and for some reason, Carl took an instant disliking to Danny... I mean, now we're talking about it, Danny might've secretly wanted to hurt him. But Carl wouldn't be the only one; the whole team bullied him."

"Bullied him, how?"

"It was all verbal, never physical," Jacobs explained. "The customer service team sometimes take calls to cancel sales, which affects the team's bottom-line. The problem is, they're all bullshitters. You know the type, they'll say and do anything to get a sale on the board. Unfortunately Carl couldn't build rapport with his customers to save his life; he loved to tell stories, to bullshit. And that meant he got lots of sales wiped off the board."

"And that meant aggro for Elfman, right?"

"Right! Anyway, the pods work on an automated dialler, so between calls the sales team amuse themselves."

"Or give Elfman shit."

"Right!" Jacobs' brow furrowed. "I still can't believe... Danny didn't react, ever. If I thought the verbal affected him in any way, I might... And now you tell me he's murdered a girl in Lewes, and possibly butchered Carl?"

"Do you have any idea where he might be?"

Jacobs shook his head. "No! I mean, we talked a bit during our cigarette breaks, but he never spoke about anything personal. The only thing I can think of is he loved Chatter. He used to hide his phone between calls. He thought I couldn't see him, with his head down."

"Yes, you mentioned Chatter? What *is* that?"

"Really? Chatter's a social media app, along the same lines as Facebook, Twitter and Instagram. Danny used it constantly. When he did speak, he would always talk about Georgina Shaw."

"I'm sorry! Who?" By the incredulous expression on Jacobs' face, Coates knew he should have had an idea who she was.

"What rock have you been hiding under?" Jacobs almost laughed. "She's a famous Aussie surfer and model. Going out with Shane Daley?"

"Nope, sorry!"

"Shane Daley's the captain of the Sydney Swans, the Aussie Rules team. Between the two of them, they're mega celebrities. Georgina Shaw has a couple of million followers on Chatter, and she takes part in the WSL Championships every year. Danny's obsessed with her, always scrolling through her photos."

All very interesting, except it didn't help. "If you can think of anything that might help me find him, I would appreciate any input. Anything else at all?"

"I'm sorry! I spoke to him more than anyone else here, but I can't. He lives nearby, the Seven Dials area, I think. Apart from that, I don't think he had a busy social life. Like I said, he was a pretty sad, lonely guy."

Coates thought he had achieved all he could with Jacobs.

"Thank you for your time." He asked his interviewee to send in the next member of the sales team. The manager left the room. While waiting, he picked up his mobile and dialled Packard's number. "Yeah, how're you getting on?"

"We're in," his partner replied. "Everything's in its place. He left a load of clothes behind, his laptop, passport, everything. He's done a bunk, although you would be forgiven for thinking otherwise."

"How do you know he isn't still there?"

"His post is building up. It seems he took off in a hurry. But he's not going to get far without his passport, is he?"

Elfman's departure didn't make much sense to Coates. Why leave most of your belongings behind? And where would he go without his passport? "Are you talking about his Peebles or Elfman paperwork?" He guessed the ex-convict wouldn't own one under his old name now.

"Danny Elfman," Packard confirmed. "I'm looking at it now. It's still in date; in fact, it was only issued a year ago. Why would he make a run for it without this?"

"Because he can be traced with it. And he might have a fake passport, who knows? I would use a fake one, if I had to leave the country fast, wouldn't you?" He had a thought. "Do me a favour? Open his laptop and check his browse history. I'm going to ask Cyber to do the same with his work computer. Let's find out what secrets they hold."

"Sure thing," Packard affirmed.

Coates hung up and waited for a member of the sales team to enter. Coates thought apprehending Elfman might be hard going. He could be anywhere by now. His charge might not be in the UK anymore.

Using his mobile, he looked up the name Georgina Shaw on Google. A list of options came up. He had the choice to view her on Twitter, Facebook, through the World Surf League website, or via YouTube. Coates chose Chatter, and because the app wasn't installed on his phone, Google Play gave him the chance to download it. "When in Rome," he mumbled.

After joining up, which took thirty seconds, he was officially a Chatter member. He never liked social media. But looking at photos of Georgina Shaw, he understood why Elfman enjoyed her so. A talented surfer, she appeared to be far more than that, even to his old eyes. Stunning didn't do her justice, he thought, scrolling through pictures of her in various poses, and varying degrees of undress, although never less than in skimpy swimwear. If truth be told, he enjoyed her in a bikini the most. "My word," he said, stopping at a photo of Shaw with a gorgeous girl either side of her, all three in bikinis.

"Ah-hem." Coates looked up to see a guy in a navy suit cough a second time.

Coates switched his phone off and asked the sales team member to join him at his table, the bloke in his early twenties and dressed to impress in a tailor-made suit.

42

Wednesday morning was hectic for Coates. Instead of driving to police headquarters in Lewes, he drove straight to the offices of McGiven, Niall and Sanders to complete his interviews with the sales and customer service teams. Having arrived late afternoon the day before, he'd only managed to speak to two team members and Patrick Jacobs, the floor manager.

Fiona Wilton, his first interview of the day, knocked on the door. He called for her to enter, and a lovely-looking brunette girl poked her head around the door. "Please, come in, Miss Wilton." Coates invited her to sit down opposite him. Like her other teammates, Fiona dressed to impress. She wore a light grey two-piece suit and white blouse. "Thank you for coming."

Before he'd left the offices the previous night, he wrapped Elfman's work laptop up in cellophane and drove back to HQ on Church Lane. He then carried the computer to the Cyber department, where he asked for them to check its search history.

As he left for home, Packard arrived in the station car park. Coates checked with his partner what he'd found in the flat. According to Packard, Elfman had an interest in everything

Australian. The online history showed Elfman used Chatter, and Google Maps the most.

"I thought Patrick was having a laugh when he said you want to talk to us about Adrian Mole," Fiona said, jump starting proceedings. "I thought you were going to ask me about Carl."

"Excuse me, Adrian Mole?"

"Our nickname for Elf Man. He's so ordinary, Elf Man actually looks a bit like him."

Impressed, he raised an eyebrow. "I'm surprised you know who Adrian Mole is. Aren't you a bit young to remember that? And what's this Elf Man business?"

"Another name he hated," Fiona confessed. "It sounds horrible, but no one liked him. I mean no one, not even Patrick, who spoke to him more than anyone else. I caught Elf Man trying to sneak a peek at me from behind his screen so many times. The thought of him eyeing me up makes my skin crawl."

"So, it's safe to say you and he never talked about his social life at all?" He didn't need to ask the question. Her expression, the turned up nose and look of contempt gave him everything he needed.

"What social life? He didn't have any friends inside, or outside work. The way I understood it, Elf Man lived on Chatter. If you want to know more about him, look into that. He was obsessed with Georgina Shaw. I bet he's even got little photos of her on his walls, the ugly, sad perv."

A brief silence fell over them, then Fiona chuckled to herself.

"Do you want to hear something funny? He went around telling people that he was flying out to Sydney to meet her. You couldn't make this shit up. How deranged can you get?"

Coates smiled, making out he was laughing at Elfman.

"He even cheeped his plane ticket as proof. The guy's an

absolute arsehole, and I hope you catch him. Carl was lovely; he didn't deserve to die like that, no one does."

"Show me that plane ticket, would you?" Coates asked her, sliding his mobile across the table. He waited for Fiona to open the Chatter app. Once she had, she scrolled down for the right picture. "Thanks." He took the phone back and studied the photo. It showed the date and time of the flight, but not the name of the owner.

A line of enquiry, if nothing else. Fiona's scoffing made him apprehensive of believing her story. "And how long ago did he disappear?"

Her face changed, more serious. "Well, he never came back after that Friday, and we know why now, don't we? He put the picture of his ticket to Sydney up in the afternoon, and your lot say he stabbed Carl that same Friday night. So, he obviously murdered Carl and did a runner."

Unable to argue, Coates continued discussing Elfman with her for a further ten minutes. Dismissing her, he walked her to the door and asked her to send in the next sales team member. There were twelve people to interview on that team, and eight on the customer service side. He would be there all morning, and part of the afternoon. While he waited, he logged on to Chatter and Elfman's page.

At the top of his page: Elf Man. It was written how Fiona had said: Elf Man. Why would he want his username written like that? One of his last cheeps showed a picture of the plane ticket to Kingsford Smith Airport, Sydney.

With the name on the ticket omitted, Coates couldn't find out if Elfman flew to Sydney, or not. Four thousand pounds he had spent. Without a name to search, he couldn't go to Qatar Airlines and ask if he'd flown on the date shown on the picture. Or could he? If Elfman had used a fake passport, his photo would be on their system. Coates exited Chatter and phoned

Packard. "Yeah, I need you to do me a favour," he said, hearing a knock on the door. "Contact Qatar Airways and ask for a passenger manifest for..." He reeled the date off and hung up.

Now that he had his partner working the airlines angle and Cyber scouring Elfman's digital fingerprint, he hoped they would find him soon. But what if Elfman was over in Sydney? What could Coates do then? He had no desire to fly over to Australia; he hated flying at the best of times.

43

Shane stared up at the dark clouds through the living room window. Outside in the garden, the wind had dropped. Eerie and still, the promised storm edged closer. Predicted to be the biggest thunderstorm of the summer so far, he loved freaky weather, the more violent the thunder and lightning the better. He winced at the pain in his arm.

"Here, take these," Georgina said, handing him painkillers and a glass of water. "I'm going to lock up downstairs."

She hadn't spoken to him all afternoon, not after he'd snapped at her during lunch. That was the most she had said to him in hours. He regretted snapping, but she didn't understand how he felt. The embarrassment and humiliation ate away at him. He remembered a crowd gathered around him, and a couple of people taking photos, which would end up in the newspapers.

Being in the public eye had its merits, and huge pitfalls. Every time he made a mistake it ended up on page one or two of the daily rags. Fortunately, Elf Man had yet to use his incriminating photos. The "yet" bothered him the most. What was this freak waiting for? Elf Man could have caused him great distress. He could have broken Georgina's heart by now, split them up and caused mass devastation.

With his arm in a cast, Shane walked over to the table and picked up his sling. His sling on, he rested on the sofa, wanting to hear the approaching storm, so he kept the volume low on the TV. It excited him, hearing the thunder rolling towards the house. Rain gently pattered against the windows. "George, I'm sorry about earlier!" he shouted, as she walked away. "I'll make it up to you, I promise."

"Whatever! I'm going up."

"Night," he said, watching her disappear. Anger made him throw the remote at the armchair, not stupid enough to smash it against the wall. The rain increased in intensity, the patter becoming more sustained, more like a hiss. "Here we go," he told himself, getting up from the sofa and walking to the window overlooking the garden.

Staring out at the dark, he watched the drips roll down the glass. The first clap of thunder, quiet and far away, made him shiver with excitement. He swore that one day he would move to the States and chase storms, for fun.

The first flash of lightning lit the garden. In darkness, his own reflection stared back at him. Thinking it might be a good idea, he hobbled over to the wall and turned the lights off. "That's better."

In his shorts pocket, his mobile vibrated. He used his fingerprint to open it, and a text from Elf Man sat there. Stood in front of the window, he opened the message to find a photo of himself looking through the glass, taken from behind the perimeter wall. He wore the same clothes. *Tonight's the night*, the writing below the picture read.

Not liking the sound of that, he dropped his phone and hobbled through the living room to the stairs, where he tried his best to climb them with his injured knee. The fall had broken his arm and sprained his left patella. "George!" he yelled. "I need your help, babe. I'm sorry about earlier."

In her bed garb – knickers and long T-shirt – she joined him at the bottom stair and aided his ascent, allowing him to use her as a crutch. "I'm sorry," he repeated halfway up. Georgina said she forgave him, although words were cheap; he knew she didn't mean it, and when on the landing, she sped ahead to the bedroom.

Instead of trying in vain to beg for her forgiveness, he ignored her when he walked into their bedroom and stumbled over to the wall safe hidden behind a painting Georgina loved. He took the picture down, entered the code and opened the safe.

"What do you need in there?"

"Now it speaks." He took out his Beretta and full clip. "Just as a precaution," he added, turning to her. He slid the magazine in and chambered a round. "I'll be downstairs, if you fancy joining me later?"

On his way out, Georgina said, "He's here, isn't he?"

Stopping with his back to her, he tucked the pistol into his shorts and turned to her. Shane didn't want to scare her. "You locked the back door, right?"

"Of course. But that doesn't answer my question."

"No, he's not here," he lied. "Would you want to be outside tonight? Nah, this is just a precaution. Better to have it–"

"And not need it, than to need it and not have it," she finished.

Shane chuckled. "I've said that a few times, huh? Doesn't mean it's not true." He was happy seeing a smile on her face, if only fleetingly. "Come down and join me."

"Maybe later, when the storm gets here."

Taking his leave, he hobbled back downstairs and stood in front of the window, his pistol handle sticking out of his shorts. "Come on, you bastard," he muttered, holding the handle. With the doors locked, Elf Man couldn't get inside. And if he did, Shane would pump him full of bullets, prison or not; he would protect his castle, his love. Georgina was his guiding light, his North Star, and he would fight for her, even banged up. "I'm ready for you."

She screamed upstairs.

"George!" He leapt towards the stairs, ignoring the stabbing pain in his knee and arm. Up each stair with a wince he went, until he flew across the landing, the gun in his hand. With a kick, he almost took the door off its hinges to find her crying, her mobile on her lap. "What is it?"

Georgina held out her phone, her hand shaking. "She's dead."

Not really wanting to find out, he glanced at the bloody picture of Amelia with her throat sliced open, lying on the floor, her dead eyes staring into the camera. Ready to throw up, he dropped the mobile on the bed and sat next to his girlfriend. "I'm so sorry," he said, pulling her into him, stroking her hair on his lap. "This shouldn't be happening. We're supposed to be out there enjoying ourselves. I'll phone the police."

Georgina screamed again when the lights went out.

Shane helped her upright and picked up his mobile. No bars. Reaching for the landline phone on his chest of drawers, he put it to his ear: nothing. No dialling tone. Dead. Without scaring her, he got up and told her to stay in the bedroom, while he went to check on the fuse box. "It's probably nothing, baby," he said, not convincing himself, much less her. "I'll be right back."

On the ground floor he found the box by the front door. The fuses had been tripped by something. Reaching up, he pulled every switch up at once, to no effect. The house remained in darkness, only occasionally lit by the approaching lightning. He gulped. He would have to go outside to check the wiring. "Shit!"

Georgina shouted at him from upstairs. With gun in hand, he hobbled up to the bedroom, groaning in pain with each step, to find her staring at her phone. "What is it? What's wrong?" He took the mobile away from her for the second time. Tears coursed down her cheeks.

And there it was! The photo of him with Valerie on his lap at Fever nightclub. A damning picture of her kissing his neck. How could he respond? "It's not what you think."

Beyond words, Georgina fell onto the bed and buried her face in her pillow. Sitting down next to her, he reached out and tried to comfort her, rubbing her back. "I'm sor–"

"Get out!" she snapped.

"Please, baby."

Pulling herself up, her face red and puffy from crying, she stared at him. "I said, get out! Go on! Go downstairs. Go into the rain. Go anywhere, I don't care, you bastard!" And she fell back down and buried her face in her pillow.

Shane didn't want to leave her in such a state.

His secret was out there.

He would make it up to her; he had to. He couldn't lose her.

44

With Georgina upstairs in the bedroom, Shane went back to watching the storm in the distance. Every thirty seconds or so the room lit up in a fleeting display of Mother Nature's wrath. Elf Man was out there, Shane thought, the pistol back in his shorts. Quiet in the garden, no sign of their tormentor, he watched out for him. "Where are you, Elf Man?"

No sooner had he asked, than the pom appeared in a series of flashes, stood in front of the pool, staring up at him, his arms outstretched, and fingers gesturing for him to come outside and face him. Elf Man was drenched through, not carrying anything.

Another scream came from upstairs. "He's here, Shane."

He walked towards the stairs. "Not for long. Stay where you are, baby. Don't come down here until I tell you."

"Wait! You're not going out there?"

Her voice faded away. He found himself at the sliding patio door. He paused for a moment, thinking, go out and kill the mongrel, or stay in and play it safe? An inner rage made him flick the lock and slide the glass door across, the hiss of the rain slamming against the paving slabs. A rumble of thunder reverberated through the concrete as he took his first step outside.

"Where are you, you piece of shit, huh?" He held the pistol out. "Where are you? I'm going to fucking bury you."

Out in the pouring rain, Shane did a panoramic scan of the garden, twisting, left, then right, behind him, in front.

Visions of Amelia's slashed throat flashed before him.

Further into the garden he went, spinning around with the pistol, ready to fire if he saw the slightest movement. Rain pummelled him, dripping into his eyes.

Out by the swimming pool, where the pom had stood only a couple of minutes earlier, his itchy finger on the trigger, Shane stared up at the house, where Georgina stood looking out of the living room window.

"You want me, Elf Man? I'm right here," he bellowed, trying to shout louder than the thunderous roars above him. "Let's finish this, you and me. I'll even put the gun down, how about that?"

Nothing.

Elf Man didn't appear.

Shane stood holding the pistol out, waiting for the pom to show himself.

Georgina beckoned him from the bedroom window.

"Fucking coward!" Shane shouted before turning. As he walked towards the house, Shane felt eyes on him.

Reaching the patio door, he quickly jumped inside and slid the door closed so fast, he thought Elf Man would appear.

Shane locked it. "We're safe," he yelled up to her.

With his clothes dripping, he picked up a towel Georgina had left by the patio door and dried his hair.

In the living room, he found her stood by the window, her arms crossed. "He's fucking with us, honey." He placed the gun down on the coffee table before stepping behind her and putting his hand on her shoulder. When she shrugged him off, he let his arm drop by his side. "I'm sorry! I'm going to make it up to you, I swear." He tried holding her waist.

"Don't touch me!" she hissed. "The only reason I haven't thrown you out's because he's out there, and I don't want you to end up like..." Her voice trailed off. Georgina bowed her head and let out a sob.

Shane was speechless for once. On any normal day, he would know what to say to appease her, his special ability, not that he had ever been caught cheating on her before. "All right, I won't touch you. It might not be any consolation, but I didn't do anything with her. We kissed, that's all."

"And that's supposed to make me feel better?"

"A bit, maybe. I love you, and I don't want to lose you, George." He tried holding her again, but she bucked him off. "I'm going to get changed, give you some time. Then I'll pop next door, see if they have power. I'll phone the police from there."

Upstairs in the bedroom, he stripped off, used a towel to dry his soaked skin and found a newly washed pair of khaki shorts and freshly ironed vest.

Refreshed, he looked down at the garden.

Amelia's dead eyes flashed before him. Shane wondered what had happened to Kereama. And what of Isla and Oliver? Had they suffered the same fate? He felt guilty for not listening to Georgina earlier. Those texts had changed, far too well-written for Amelia and Isla; they wrote in text format. He should have listened to Georgina, he thought, kicking himself.

After a good half hour of torturing himself, he wandered back downstairs to find her still staring out of the window. "I'm sorry I didn't listen to you about the girls." Nothing. "I should've been more supportive. You were right about their texts."

Georgina whizzed round. "And it only took a photo of Amelia to..." She turned back round and sobbed. "It's not fair!

Ames didn't do anything to him. Why? Why her? What did she ever do to that... That bastard?"

Stood behind his girlfriend, Shane went to touch her, but thought again. "We'll be all right, baby, I promise," he said, attempting to reassure her. He wanted to hold her, to cradle her in his arms and tell her everything would work out.

"And when we do, we'll talk about us."

He was encouraged that she still talked about them in terms of us. Shane didn't want to hex the situation by saying something stupid. "I'll do anything you want to make it up to you," he said, the hiss of the rain against the window competing with him. "If you need some space, I can go stay with some mates. Literally anything you want me to do, I'll do my best. Only, please, don't throw us away."

"Throw us away?" She turned to him. "You did that the minute you kissed that girl. What is it, Shane, huh? Am I not enough for you? You guys think unless you're fucking girls left, right and centre, you're missing out? You make me sick. I can't even look at you."

The way she said she couldn't look at him cut deep. Georgina meant every word. But of course she did, he told himself, she'd only just found out he had cheated on her. Trusting him again would take time. He would do everything in his power to win her back. "I'll leave you alone." His voice was dejected, small. "I *am* sorry!"

Shane went to walk away, reached the staircase and turned back. He couldn't leave her now, not with the psycho Brit out there. If he left her to mull it over, she might see sense and ditch him. Georgina deserved a decent, honest guy. But he couldn't let her go; he didn't want to. "I'll be right here," he said, going to sit on the sofa.

"I thought you said... Look out!" Her eyes grew large, fearful.

Without hesitation, he turned to find the pom in front of

him, those thin, ugly lips enjoying themselves. The shock of seeing him close up made Shane freeze for a moment. Elf Man was in his house. How? His brain fired questions at him.

Something kicked him in the belly, knocking the wind out of him.

Georgina screamed.

"You thought you were lucky last time, didn't you?" Elf Man growled. "Not so lucky now, huh, tough guy?" His grin widened.

Shane glanced down, a handle sticking out of his stomach. His blood trickled over the Brit's fingers.

The dull pain turned into a searing stabbing pain, as the pom yanked the blade up, tearing through his flesh and intestines until it couldn't go any further.

Shane couldn't scream; he couldn't make a sound, other than to groan.

Feeling his life drifting away, an inner rage made him grab his attacker by his throat with his good hand and force him backwards until his quarry hit a wall with a deep thud.

Shane put everything he had into strangling the Brit, before he attacked Georgina.

He dug his thumbs into Elf Man's larynx as hard as his dying hands could muster. "Die, you fucking bastard." The room spun.

Another surge of pain racked his body, as the pom yanked the blade out.

Bleeding, Shane's life force soaking into the carpet, with each passing second he came closer to death.

The Brit's face turned purple, but not purple enough. Shane wanted, needed, to stare into the pom's dead eyes before he left Georgina alone. With all the energy he could muster, he clung to Elf Man's throat, squeezing the life from him... Until his hands started shaking.

Another stabbing pain enveloped him.

"Please, no!" Georgina shouted. "Stop! You're killing him."

Three more stabs from Elf Man forced Shane to give up, his hands not strong enough to continue. His legs buckled beneath him.

Lying on his back, blood pouring out of his once-toned abdomen, Shane stared up at Elf Man's recovering face. Shane was cold, shivering. He tried to call out to Georgina, who stood with tears cascading down her cheeks.

Catching his breath, Elf Man sat on him.

Shane tried to shy away from the serrated blade against his throat. Then, Elf Man smiled down at him and yanked the knife to his right, the teeth of the knife tearing through Shane's flesh. He glanced over at Georgina, his love, one last time, clutching his neck, attempting in vain to stem the bleeding.

So beautiful. Georgina was his greatest victory. Forget football, forget all sporting competitions, skydiving, everything. She was his life. He took one arm away from his neck and reached out for her. "I love you." The blood in his mouth gargled his words.

45

Fear paralysing her, Georgina reached out for Shane's hand, wanting to speak to him, wanting to tell him she loved him. His white vest red, blood pooled around him.

She couldn't take her eyes away from him. He stared up at her, his arm outstretched, until it went limp. His whole body relaxed, his eyes motionless. "Shane!" she said, her voice tiny. "Speak to me, baby."

With no time to mourn, her attention moved to Elf Man, who looked up at her with such evil intent, she knew she was in this for her life. "No, get away from me." Her feet were able to move again.

The Brit rose from Shane's dead body holding the blood-soaked knife, his clothes sodden. He took a step forward, which she matched back. "This is all for you, my love. Everything I've done is for you."

Between her and Elf Man sat the coffee table. Shane's pistol perched on top piqued her attention. Georgina tried not to give its existence away. The Brit hadn't seen it. Every part of her wanted to lunge.

"Don't get any ideas," he said, holding out the knife.

"Why are you doing this?" she asked, instead of acting on her impulses.

"I love you, George. Don't you see that? Out of all your friends and family, I'm the one who really loves you. Shane didn't; I caught him cheating on you, and I've only been here for a week or so. Imagine how many bitches he's slept with while you were together."

Georgina swallowed. "Shut up! Don't you talk about him!"

"And that bitch, Amelia." He took another step closer. "She was never your friend. She wanted you to fail. She never supported your surfing, not like I did. Oh, yeah, I watch you every chance I get. When you wiped out mid-tournament, I watched you getting resuscitated, and it was the most intense experience of my life, and most joyous when you coughed and spluttered your way back to me. But Amelia didn't feel that. To her, you were her competition. She didn't love you."

Georgina took another step back.

"Aren't you going to thank me?" He switched hands with the blade.

Not wanting to dignify his question, she glared down at the gun and made a move, lunging at the table.

"I don't think so." Elf Man struck her cheek with the handle of the knife, making her fall. "I told you not to go for it, didn't I? Didn't I warn you?"

Lying on her back, Georgina rubbed her cheek. "Ow, that really hurt."

She felt exposed, wearing only a pair of knickers and a long T-shirt.

The way he appraised her made her skin crawl. And the video he took of her sleeping, the way he groaned while the camera shook in his hand.

The panic in his eyes surprised her. When Elf Man went down on all fours and reached for her cheek, he apologised to her, begging for her forgiveness. "I'm so sorry! I didn't mean to. I'll never hurt you."

Georgina flinched at his touch; she didn't want him anywhere near her. He was insistent, leaning over her and cupping his palm over her cheek. "Leave me alone!" She crawled back as far as she could, until she leaned against an armchair. "Don't touch me!" Panic set in when he ignored her pleas.

"I'm so sorry! I didn't mean to hit you," he said, his eyes sorrowful. "Forgive me? It won't happen again, look." He picked up the pistol. "I'll hold on to it for you. How about that?" He stuffed the gun in his shorts, in the small of his back. "Gone. I hate guns, don't you?"

Thinking she had to be smart, Georgina looked up at him. "I was going to ask you to destroy it." Mad at herself for being too slow, she couldn't think of anything else to say. "I hate them too."

On his knees, Elf Man crawled towards her. "Oh, you don't know how long I've waited for this," he said, sitting down in front of her, the knife in his hand still dripping Shane's blood over the carpet. "I've loved you since the moment I saw you on Chatter, can you believe that? I knew we were destined to meet, destined to be together."

Georgina realised he meant every word. The Brit wouldn't hurt her; he worshipped her. The knife close, too close for her liking, she had to lead him away from it. "I believe you, Elf Man."

"Danny," he corrected. "Please, call me Danny."

"All right, Danny. I believe you. I didn't see it before, but I see it so clearly now." She reached out for his blade. "Why don't you put that knife down? You don't need it, it's just you and me here."

Feeling nauseous, the thought of touching him repellent, she reached out a little further, hoping he would hand the blade over to her. "Please? For me? Put the knife down and we'll talk.

You can tell me all about yourself, and I'll tell you things about me that you didn't know."

Elf Man relaxed, the blade in his hand dropping to the floor. "You're right. I don't need this."

Instead of handing her the knife, he placed it behind him. Georgina's hope dashed, she kept the forced smile on, even when Shane's bloody body made her want to cry. She couldn't; she had to be strong. "That's better." She held eye contact with her captor, keeping him calm. "I'm thirsty, Danny, are you?"

"Yeah, I could use a drink."

"I'll go and make us one." Georgina went to stand, until Elf Man put his hand on her shoulder and pushed down hard, helping himself up.

"I'll make them." He smiled at her with those horrible lips. "I need to practise making my queen drinks. What would you like, my love?"

Not listening, Georgina kept her eye on the knife behind his foot. When he asked for a second time, she said she would love a glass of wine. In the fridge, she told him, as he stepped away.

The knife sat between them.

"Going now," said Elf Man, making to move.

Seizing her moment, Georgina lunged for the blade. It was within her reach, when Elf Man's trainer came crashing down on it. With her hand pinned to the carpet, she looked up and saw the fury in his eyes. "You bastard, you killed him. You killed my Shane." The pain in her hand grew.

Elf Man grabbed her hair, pulled her up and slapped her face so hard her lip bled.

"No! You mustn't do that, my queen. He's dead because he didn't love you, not the way I do. He had no honour. A queen like you deserves the most honourable man."

"You're fucking crazy," she screamed, trying to free her hand.

Elf Man released it and took a step back, reaching behind

him and pulling out the pistol. He pointed it at her head, leaving the knife between them. "Now that wasn't very nice. I never played the insanity card in court, not once, even though my lawyer suggested I should. I could've been sent to a hospital, instead of prison, but I chose to be honourable. I took my punishment, and now I'm a free man. Do you understand? I'm the most honourable man you'll ever meet. Shane didn't deserve you, but I do."

Georgina, angry at the sight of Shane's bloody corpse, went for the knife and grabbed it when Elf Man swung the pistol at her, smashing the butt of the handle on the top of her head.

A foot on her back pinned her to the floor. "That was stupid, my love."

His hand grabbed her hair, as he yanked and pulled her into the middle of the living room, away from the knife, her lifeline. She screamed in pain, using her legs to keep him from tugging out a clump of her hair. "You're hurting me!"

Before she knew it, she lay on her belly again, her hands behind her back. He grabbed them and she realised he was tying her up with cable ties. "No, please, I'll be good, I promise."

"I wanted this to be simple." He helped her to her feet. "I wanted you to fall in love with me on first sight, like you see in the movies. Like how I fell in love with you, from the second I saw your photo." He pushed her towards the stairs. "But I was naïve to think your love would be instant. It will take time and I have to earn yours, and prove my own to you."

He held her all the way downstairs, never letting go. Tied up, there was nothing she could do except run. At the patio door, she waited for Elf Man to slide it across before she shook him off and ran into the pouring rain.

"Come back, my queen!" Elf Man shouted. "Where do you think you can go?"

Georgina sprinted towards the swimming pool, her bare feet

splashing the surface water on the lawn. If she could run to the back fence... Then what?

Running along the pool, she heard a gunshot from behind her, slipped and fell in the water. Thunder boomed above her. She hoped one of her neighbours noticed the shot, then realised the hiss of the rain would have drowned the noise out.

Elf Man grabbed her and pulled her out of the water inside thirty seconds.

Stood in front of him, she braced for her punishment, which came in the form of a backhander. With her split lip and swollen cheek, she walked with him towards the garage. "Where are we going?"

"Somewhere no one will find us." He opened the garage door and waited for her to step inside. "Oh, and you're driving. If you get any funny ideas, I'll have this here gun trained on you, my queen. I don't want to hurt you, right? So, please don't force my hand."

Soaked, she jumped into the driver's seat of her Jeep and told him she didn't have the keys, that she would go back inside and fetch them.

Elf Man pulled them out of his shorts. "Always be prepared," he said, handing them to her, his pistol aimed at her side.

46

"The passenger manifest's come through," Packard said, over the partition separating them.

Coates walked around to his partner's desk and stood behind him. "And they come with passport photo ID?" He waited for Packard to bring up the first passenger on board the flight shown in Elfman's picture on Chatter. Packard didn't answer.

"Absolutely." A picture of the passport appeared on the screen. "Qatar Airways uses a mixture of Airbus A350-1000 and Boeing 777s to Australia. The most passengers they can carry is four hundred and ten, so it shouldn't take too long to find Peebles, or Elfman, or whatever the hell his name is on here."

"Well, we know he's not going by either, don't we!" Coates knew the passport in Danny Elfman's name was safely stored in a plastic bag in evidence. "At least if we find out his fake passport name we'll have something to give the New South Wales police."

"Shoot! This is taking ages to switch between passports," Packard said, clicking on his mouse. "You might as well take a seat, sir. This is going to take a while. I have four hundred and nine left to go, and I'll bet you he won't appear until the end, if he appears at all."

"Oh, he's on the list." Coates walked back to his own desk. "I'll put money on it. He paid four grand for a first class ticket. And I don't think he'll miss his chance to meet Miss Shaw, do you?" At his desk, he went back to his own monitor.

"I wouldn't miss an opportunity to meet Georgina Shaw." Packard's voice had a tone. "She's stunning."

Having to agree with his junior partner, Coates had Shaw's Chatter account up on the screen. Even off duty, he would pull her photos up and scroll through them. She was beautiful, very easy on the eye, as his dad would have said if he were alive. And a talented surfer. "Right, time to speak to Chatter's CEO."

"Good luck with that, sir. He's tougher to contact than Mark Zuckerberg. I can do that for you, if you want? I know you're not keen on social media."

"I'm learning, thanks. No, you carry on with the manifest." Now Coates had the Chatter app on his phone, he could appreciate what the fuss was about.

Aimed at young, beautiful people predominantly, or artists, authors, actors and such, Coates considered Chatter a marketing tool, a way of presenting the account holder in a more human way. And it worked. Glancing at one photo of Shaw, he noted that she mentioned three companies on one entry alone: a surfboard manufacturer, a clothing label, and a photographer.

That picture had half a million likes, and two thousand comments, most of which were followers telling her how beautiful she was. According to one source he read, influencers with a huge following could charge vast amounts of money just for mentioning a company name. What a different world he lived in now.

Finding the contact tab on the app, he scrolled through the options. There was an address in Los Angeles, a phone number included. With a big sigh, he picked up his desk phone and dialled. "Yes, I'm Detective Inspector David Coates of the Sussex

Police, England, and I'm investigating a possible double murder."

Over the next fifteen minutes, he explained his reason for calling to at least four different members of staff at Chatter HQ, then had to argue why he should be allowed access to user data. "If you're not in a position to help me, find someone who can. I need to read those files. Danny Elfman, or as he appears on here as Elf Man, is the prime suspect in two murders, do you understand?"

He listened to an American female tell him why they couldn't give him access to their data. "And if it were your husband's murder, your daughter's or sister's I was investigating, would you be so reticent to give me those files? Please, this guy has raped and murdered one woman for certain. I beg you, please, I just need to see what messages he's been sending and to who."

The woman said nothing, which Coates took as a good sign. He pumped his fist when she agreed to discuss it with her line manager. Asking him to hold, the line went quiet. "How're you getting on?"

Packard gave him a thumbs up over the partition.

"My manager's allowing you access to Elf Man's account. I'm going to give you the username and password. This will let you view it, cheep as the user, everything. We strongly urge you not to participate in any way on the account."

"Thank you so much," he said, pen poised. "I promise I'll only look at the messages. I won't touch anything else." The lovely Southern accent gave him Elf Man's username and password, which was case-sensitive. Once inside, he thanked the woman again and hung up. "He's definitely over there."

"I don't believe it! How'd you wangle that?"

Coates ignored his partner and showed him the photo message on Elfman's account of the Qatar Airways first class cabin seat. Then one taken through the window of clouds below. "He's in Sydney." Coates glanced at a picture outside a pub called The Starfish.

"That's on Bondi Beach, sir," Packard explained, having been to Australia a few times. "Now we know where he is, do we need to go through the manifest?"

"Of course. We need to know what name he's registered under. He might've booked a hotel room, hired a car, you name it. Sorry! I appreciate it's a chore."

Watching Packard with a modicum of pity, he scanned the office for DCI Morgan. "Sir? Can I have a moment?" His superior strolled over to his desk and leaned on the back of his chair, kind of like a teacher might do to a child, which he found condescending. "Peebles – or Elfman or whoever – is over in Sydney as we speak. It seems he's become obsessed with Miss Georgina Shaw."

DCI Morgan shrugged.

"Local celebrity, a Chatter influencer. It doesn't matter. The point is, he's over in Australia, which means he's out of our jurisdiction. We have to confer with the New South Wales police now, don't we?" He didn't like the way his chief folded his arms.

"I was afraid this might happen," Morgan said. "Chief Constable Gately sent me a memo earlier from the Home Secretary via Justice Secretary Richard Luckland. It says that if Peebles has left the country, a representative of the UK must assist in his apprehension. This is a sensitive matter, David, I'm sure you appreciate that."

"What does that mean?"

"You're going to Sydney. And before you try suggesting Sergeant Packard takes your place, I need someone more senior. I'm going to request Gately partners you up with a sergeant over there. We want you to have seniority."

"But sir–"

"But sir nothing, Inspector Coates," Morgan interrupted. "We need this done quietly, do you understand? I'll make sure you're met at the airport. Now, go home and get ready. You'll be booked on the next flight out."

Not being given time to argue, he swore under his breath. He didn't want to go to Sydney. "The local police can handle this, surely? Sir?"

"What are you still doing here, David? Move it!"

Grabbing his jacket, Coates walked up to Packard. "Keep on it for me, yes? When you find out what name he's using, get me a list of hotels and car rental places to contact, would you? If we're lucky, he's used his passport for that at least."

"I'll do you one better than that, sir. I'll phone them for you, how about that? The next time I speak to you, you'll have the make, model and registration of the car he's hired, and the name of the hotel or bed and breakfast he's staying at."

"Thanks, Gary, I appreciate it." Coates patted his partner on his shoulder. On his way out of the office, he stepped in the elevator and waited until the doors closed before kicking the walls to let off steam. Not one part of him wanted to fly to Australia.

47

With visibility through her Jeep's windscreen near zero, and with her headlights on full beam, the hour-long journey was intense because she couldn't tell where they were heading. Elf Man wouldn't let her in; he kept the gun trained on her. "I might be able to help you if you said where we're going," she suggested, spotting a sign for what she thought said "Heathcote".

"I think we both know you're not going to help me... Yet. But I'm certain you'll grow to love me, my queen. I've still got to prove myself to you. And I will, and then you'll have me as your king."

With her hands tied to the steering wheel with cable ties, she slowed down for a steep turn. Driving in torrential rain scared her. She enjoyed high octane thrills, but not steering in this, with a psychopath sat next to her. "We can't just keep on going! Please tell me where we're heading."

"All right, your wish is my command," he said, his hands up in mock surrender. "Further up here you'll find an abandoned hospital–"

"Waterfall Sanatorium? We're going to Waterfall?"

"Yeah, you know it?" Elf Man asked, surprised.

"Of course! Everyone knows it. Urban explorers used to upload their photos inside the hospital, until it became too overgrown and dangerous. It's just crumbling bricks, trees and brambles now. Why are we going there?"

"That's what you and the Urbex community think." Elf Man trained the gun back on her. "I found a way in. Instead of booking a fancy hotel, I studied this place on Google Maps. It's amazing how much you can learn from it. I found out where you live in Point Piper from your cheeps and then checked it on Maps. I guess you should be more careful how much detail you include in your posts in future, huh?"

She continued driving the Jeep along the Princes Highway, the A1, through Heathcote until Elf Man ordered her to slow down. When he told her to pull over, she obliged, parking at the side of the road. "I can't leave her here; someone will steal her," she complained.

Elf Man got out, switched a torch on and directed her to a hollow bush tucked inside the woods suitable for hiding her Jeep, which she and Elf Man disguised using branches broken from the trees above. With her car hidden, Georgina walked barefoot in front of him in the rain. Thunder roared and lightning threatened to strike overhead. "We won't get through," she said, having to navigate a muddy path, climbing over downed logs. "We need to turn back." Her captor didn't listen; he kept nudging her with the gun.

"Don't be so defeatist, my love," Elf Man retorted. "We're nearly there."

Georgina had to endure the rain, mud and scratches associated with hiking through thick undergrowth. By the time they breached the sanatorium's perimeter defences, she needed a rest.

Looking up at the broken walls of Waterfall Sanatorium, she

remembered the tales told to her as a kid. Haunted, they said. Spirits of over two thousand dead tuberculosis patients walked these woods, they said. Friends in her class at school told her and Amelia of this place. The hospital where lost souls went to die in silence, their families having packed them off. Georgina felt the muzzle of the gun in her back through her drenched T-shirt.

"Come on, I'll show you a way in." Elf Man prodded her the way to walk. "Remember, any funny stuff and this will go off. Go steady."

She couldn't run anywhere. Eventually, he overtook her, and she followed him, brambles flicking back, scratching her face, occasionally catching her bare legs. Georgina wanted to jump on his back and punish him. Instead she walked behind him, dreaming of blowing his brains out, or sticking him in his throat with the knife he carried.

"Here we are." He crouched and climbed over a crumbling hole in the wall that had once housed a window.

Georgina followed him inside. The east building had far more structure left to it, including a roof. Before she climbed inside, she noted the derelict structure had four storeys. "Where to now?" she whispered.

Actually, she didn't want to reach their destination. When they arrived, it would be her and Elf Man alone together, until either she managed to flee, they were found by someone, or until he killed her. Elf Man was unhinged, disturbed.

This building, unlike the first couple they had walked past, looked in pretty good shape considering it had not been lived in for thirty-four years. Windows were shattered, certainly, and the walls were cracked everywhere, but the structure stood on its own. She only saw what the flashlight wanted her to see. In daylight it would be worse, she thought.

"It's just up here."

To her left was what appeared to be a small room. Through the darkness, watching the torchlight, she saw a doorway. Elf Man led her inside. On the debris-covered floor, her captor shone the light on an old battered mattress. Holes in the ceiling leaked puddles of rain. "Here? You want me to stay here?" She stood, her hands in front of her, bound. "I thought I was your queen? Would a queen settle for such rank accommodation?"

"Oh, now you want to be my queen, do you?" he said, pointing the gun at her chest. "Funny. Only an hour or so ago you wanted to stick me with this knife." He took the blade out and pointed it at her. Then he slid the pistol in his shorts. "I tell you what, convince me that you want to be my love, and I'll consider upgrading our living quarters. How about that? And I'll prove to you I'm worthy of your love."

Was he for real? The scary truth: she believed he meant every word, every syllable even. He shone the light on the mattress, then on a metal bar next to it that she could see was bolted to the concrete floor. "What the hell's that doing there?" The strangest place to find what looked like a bike rack.

"No idea, but it's going to be useful."

She took a couple of steps back when he approached her with the knife. When he cut her ties and freed her wrists, she understood what he was doing. Her freedom short-lived, he grabbed her left wrist and yanked her over to the metal bar.

Taking out two more cable ties, he secured her to the bar. "Sorted," he said, shining the torch in her eyes. "You sit and relax. We've got a long night ahead of us. This storm's supposed to last until late morning."

Elf Man sat in front of her, the flashlight lying on the ground next to him giving them the only light, and stared. "We're all alone now."

What did he want from her? One answer was obvious from the way he gazed at, first her legs, then up to her waist, then her wet T-shirt, which clung to her breasts. Georgina dared not talk, in case it made him move towards her. She tried to avert her eyes.

"You are lovely," he said, playing with the knife, scraping the metal against the hard ground. "And what I love about you the most is you don't realise how stunning you are. You're above the vanity that your friends suffered."

Staring at him, she growled, "Don't you talk about them! They were my mates. You have no right. And you don't know me as well as you think. I love the fame. I'm always taking selfies."

Her words seemed to trouble her captor, who grew agitated. "Nah, you're better than that. You're just being difficult because I haven't proved myself to you yet. But you'll see sense. Before we leave here, you'll believe I'm your soulmate."

"Ha! Buckley's chance of that happening." She laughed. "You're a psychopath. I could never love someone like you."

Georgina realised her defiance had gone too far when he launched himself at her with the knife. She gulped as he grabbed her hair and pulled her head back, exposing her throat, which he stuck the blade on. "No! Please, I didn't mean it." She squeaked, afraid to move in case the blade sliced her flesh.

"That was nasty, my love," he said, his mouth an inch from hers. He sat so close, she could smell his foul breath. "And you're not a nasty person, are you?"

She closed her eyes when he licked his lips. "No!"

"Good. I would hate to think I'm wasting my love on the wrong queen." Elf Man made a sort of chuckle in his throat. "No, you're the one for me."

48

David Coates' plane touched down at 16:08 on Friday afternoon at Kingsford Smith Airport. DCI Morgan had booked him on the earliest and fastest flight he could find, which flew from Gatwick and took twenty-three hours, including a two-hour-and-twenty-minute layover in Dubai.

Not expecting to be in Sydney for any length of time, Coates had packed the bare necessities for his trip, managing to cram everything into one holdall. He felt smug avoiding baggage claim, sailing through customs, and walking into the Arrivals lounge. With his ID in his trouser pocket, ready to pull out at a moment's notice, a police officer in a light blue short-sleeved shirt and black trousers waved him over. The female cop stood next to him carried a placard with Coates' surname written on it. "Sergeant Kennedy?" Coates held out his hand.

Kennedy shook it, but didn't say anything.

"Incremental Sergeant Janae Willis," said the ginger officer with the ponytail. "If you'd like to come with us inspector, we'll get you squared away and fill you in on where we're at. I understand you're booked into the Sydney Boutique Hotel?"

"So it says on my itinerary." He looked at the piece of paper

Morgan had given him. He liked Willis on sight; she had a genuine way about her. Affable and professional. Coates thought he might have trouble with Kennedy. "If I can drop my stuff off, I would love to make a start on finding Peebles."

Still no word from Kennedy. He followed the two armed officers out of the main doors to their car, which was parked directly outside. Willis went to open the boot, but Coates said not to bother, that he only had hand luggage. Kennedy sat in the driver's seat, while Willis took the passenger side.

The first thing Coates noticed: the heat. According to his phone, the temperature stood at twenty-eight degrees, full sun and zero chance of rain. Kennedy started the engine and the air conditioning came on. Coates wanted to talk about the case. Instead, he watched the world go by as they drove from the airport to the hotel.

Willis asked him, "How was your flight?"

Kennedy kept staring at him in the rear-view mirror.

"Fine," he replied. "A bit long for my liking, but hey, I'm here now."

When they reached the hotel, he checked in, grabbed the key to his room, dropped his bag off and went back to join his colleagues. Within ten minutes, he sat in the back of their car again. "Right, where are we up to?"

"Fill him in, Janae," Kennedy said, pulling away from the kerb.

"We're taking you to the crime scene first," Willis said.

Coates leaned forward. "Crime scene?"

Kennedy snorted, while Willis turned in her seat to face him. "I know you're tired, having been on a plane for the last twenty-four hours, inspector, but there've been some major developments in this case. We're taking you to Miss Shaw's house, where we found her boyfriend, Shane Daley, dead at the scene."

"Dead, how?" Coates noted Kennedy's attitude.

"From what the coroner can gather, he was stabbed in the abdomen. The suspect then sliced him open. He had several stab wounds on his stomach, so the medical examiner believes Daley fought with the suspect, before he slit Daley's throat. A bloody mess, is what it is. No sign of Miss Shaw, so we assume she's been abducted."

Sitting back in his seat, Coates cursed under his breath.

"Shane Daley's a celebrity in this city, inspector, the captain of the Sydney Swans, with a huge following on all the major social media apps, so you can imagine keeping this away from the news has been a nightmare."

"And this is why he's here," Kennedy chirped, staring at Coates in the mirror still. "Isn't that right, inspector? You're here as a public relations exercise. The way I hear it, this guy, Peebles, your lot released him early, and your ministers want to save themselves embarrassment. So, instead of handing this case over to one of our guys, your government talks ours into calling you in. I tell you, what a load of crap!"

"Is that right, inspector? Are you here to brush all this under the carpet?"

"Hey, I don't care what you've heard," he snapped. "I'm here to bring Peebles in, to stop him hurting anyone else, and I will, with or without your attitude. If you have a problem with me being British, then you need to sort it. Your super's instructed you to help me apprehend him, so either help me, or drop me off here and I'll make my own way. Is that all right with you, *sergeant*?"

Kennedy tutted. "Well, go on, tell him the rest," he ordered Willis.

"Wait! There's more?"

"You could say that," Kennedy replied. "Peebles, or Elfman,

or whatever the hell his name is, he's been busy while you've been up there."

Waiting on Willis to elaborate, Kennedy pulled up outside a gated house.

"Are we here?" Coates stared at the gates. From what he gleaned from Shaw's Chatter account, she and Daley lived in luxury. He'd read up on Point Piper, the most affluent suburb of Sydney. The house behind the walls consisted of mainly glass.

The gates opened and Kennedy drove them inside, where Coates saw two more police cars and an unmarked car parked up in front of the building. "We have company?"

"Nothing to worry about, inspector." Kennedy switched off the engine and turned in his seat to face him. "Our chief superintendent's here."

His colleague's remark, and smug grin told him the opposite. Coates ignored him and opened his door. "Sorry, sergeant, what were you going to tell me?" He waited for her to shake her head, telling him she would catch him up after they'd been to the crime scene. He nodded and stepped into the hot sun, putting his shades on. He whistled, impressed. "Surfing bought all this?"

"Uh-huh, surfing, footy and modelling."

Following Kennedy's lead inside the house, Coates walked upstairs to the first floor, which he assumed was the living room. It had to be, given the huge television mounted on the wall, the sofas, armchairs, and coffee table. Expensive-looking paintings adorned the walls. He didn't need to ask where the crime took place; there was blood everywhere.

Willis pulled out her mobile and handed it to him. "We found the body here, on his back, laid out like this, his arm outstretched."

"Like he was reaching out for Shaw?" The photo showed Daley's eyes were open. His once-white vest red in the picture, Coates flicked through them. He studied close-ups of the wounds. Overkill. Why carry on stabbing someone after an injury so severe? And as for slitting the footballer's throat, again overkill. "He's enjoying himself," Coates said to Willis and Kennedy. "He didn't need to continue with the assault."

"If your guy's obsessed with Miss Shaw, Daley's a threat, wouldn't you say?" Kennedy folded his arms. "Killing her boyfriend would have been satisfying to him."

Coates agreed. "What else did you find?"

"Daley's a licensed firearm owner, with two pistols registered under his name," Willis explained. "We found this Beretta Bobcat in Miss Shaw's handbag."

He glanced at the photo of the small handgun.

"But we can't find the Beretta M9 anywhere. Daley has a safe in the master bedroom hidden behind a picture. The locksmith's been, we've looked inside, and we found shells but no pistol, which is why we believe Peebles now possesses a firearm."

Gun control was what he loved about the UK. Arming police officers only incited criminals to arm themselves, in his opinion. "Great!" He heard voices approaching from the stairs.

"Here he is," a man in a dark-blue police uniform, complete with stripes on his arms, a sturdy hat and polished-to-a-mirror-shine shoes said. "Detective Inspector Coates, am I right?" He neither smiled nor held his hand out. "Here to show us how you do it over the pond, I hear. My detectives aren't good enough for this case apparently. Oh no, we need training from a real detective, a pommie detective."

Coates groaned inside. "Nope, just here to apprehend Peebles and I'll be on my way, sir." The look of utter contempt made him angry.

"Ah yes, Arthur Peebles," the uniform said. "Your government's embarrassment. If I had my way, I would let the press in here now. But, my boss read me the rule book and ordered me to extend you my every courtesy. Welcome! That being said, trying to hide five murders isn't going to be easy, is it, Detective Coates?"

"Excuse me, sir, five?" He glanced at Willis, who shrugged.

"Sorry! I didn't get around to telling you before we arrived," she confessed. "Four of their friends are feared murdered as well, although there are no bodies to identify. But the blood's enough to make us believe they were killed."

"Where? How?" were the first two questions he thought of.

"We don't know how without bodies. But we found blood, bone and brain matter in Mr King's and Miss Kelly's home, and traces of bleach mixed with saliva and blood, which indicates that one of them might have been forced to drink it. Plus we found a funnel on the floor. We also found rope next to two chairs. We believe they were tied up and bludgeoned to death, using this baseball bat."

Coates observed the bloodstained bat in a photo. "Shit! This is what I was afraid of. He's not even trying to hide it." Willis shook her head. "And he's not scared of getting caught either. He's not afraid of prison. In fact, he probably considers this a little holiday before he's locked up again."

The Chief Superintendent clapped with sarcasm. "Wow! I see why they sent you now. My detectives wouldn't have made those judgements. I'll be singing your praises to your superintendent; you can count on that."

Refusing to bite, Coates smiled. "Would you, sir? That would be smashing." He let his face drop in a heartbeat. "Sergeants Willis and Kennedy, would you walk me through the two other crime scenes, please?"

49

Georgina couldn't tell what time it was, with her hands bound to the metal pole, a rag in her mouth and her fingers and thumbs wrapped in duct tape, she could neither call out for help nor set herself free.

She screamed into her gag for the hundredth time, desperate for an urban explorer, or cop, or anyone to find her and take her away from this graffiti-covered nightmare.

Why her? What had she done to deserve this? Georgina thought of herself as a good person; she didn't treat people badly. She raised money for charities. Maybe this was the cost of fame? It seemed a bit harsh if she had to lose her boyfriend and two best friends. Then she reasoned karma wasn't to blame. Georgina didn't have a bad word to say about anyone; she wouldn't hurt a living creature. Her mum would have something to say if she did.

The heat cut through her. Clammy from all the tugging on the cable ties and screaming into her gag, which didn't help keep the bities away, she continued fighting her restraints. Thirsty, she looked over at Elf Man's side of the mattress and tried to grip a bottle of water with her foot. She missed the first time. The second time she hit the top of the cap, and the bottle fell on its side and rolled away from her. She wanted to cry.

Although petrified of Elf Man, of what he planned to do with her, he hadn't touched her, yet. There would come a time when he wanted to touch her. The way he gazed at her, with those lust-filled orbs, terrified her.

Elf Man had left her gagged and tied the previous day. In the evening, she'd asked him how his day went, making small talk. He informed her that he spent the day tailing the police, watching them work his case. He told her that two cops drove to the airport to meet some guy in a suit Elf Man took to be a detective. He was very smug when he told her that they'd found Shane's body. Georgina tried to kick him, but he moved. Then he'd slapped her, splitting her lip for the second time.

According to Elf Man, she forced him to hit her, not that it stopped him from begging for her forgiveness after the fact. He scared her because of his lack of self-control when angry. Elf Man released his anger immediately, lashing out at what he deemed a threat. He appeared not to have any boundaries.

After spending the day alone, the Brit returned to feed her, cold baked beans. The only food on offer, she'd wolfed them down.

A buzzing in her ear made her try to break the cables ties for the hundredth time. How were the thin plastic ties so strong? She should be able to break them. The buzzing increased and the mosquito landed on her face. Sweaty, hot and bothered, she shook her head until the bloodsucker flew away. Mosquitos were the least of her worries; there were plenty of deadlier insects in these woods that she knew of.

Rustling in the bushes made her stop. There were so many wild animals around these parts, she thought, it could have been anything, or worse... Elf Man. Staring at the doorway, surrounded by brambles that had grown through the walls and in the one glassless window, she waited, breath held.

"Honey, I'm home," Elf Man said, carrying a white bag.

He stepped up to her, bent over, and took the rag out of her mouth.

With her stomach growling, she had to find out what he was carrying in the plastic bag. Two tablespoons of baked beans was all she'd eaten since Wednesday evening. Even if she managed to escape, she would be too weak to run... Or maybe he wanted that. "What've you got there?"

Her smirking captor pulled a cardboard container out. "What do you Aussies call these?" It wasn't the first time he had mocked her language.

"Sangers." Her hope shone bright, as he tore open the pack and took out a triangular sandwich. She ate heartily, taking huge bites out of it every time he presented her with the delicious tuna mayo treat. Being fed by his hand was humiliating, but it didn't stop her scoffing the sandwich.

"You are hungry," he said, placing the second half in front of her.

"Water, please," she begged. Georgina shuffled in anticipation of hydration, her mouth so dry she found swallowing difficult. She drank greedily from the bottle he placed in front of her mouth. By the time he took the bottle away, she had swallowed almost two thirds of a two-litre bottle of water. "Thank you!"

Elf Man sat on the mattress next to her and dug out his meal, which consisted of a sandwich and a six-pack of beer. Picking up a bottle, he grinned at her. "And this?"

"A coldie, or stubby." The British seemed so taken by the Australian language, not that she understood why.

"And a toilet?"

"Dunny."

Bored of the conversation, she turned away from him and stared at her bound hands. How was she going to free herself? All afternoon, she'd tried to tear the tape, except he had wrapped at least three layers around her fingers and thumbs.

Georgina baulked when Elf Man touched her back. It didn't deter him; he continued stroking her. "You are so beautiful," she heard him say in a soothing voice. A scared sob escaped her, and he withdrew his touch. With her eyes closed tight, she prayed for him to go away.

"For fuck's sake, my love, I pay you compliments, I feed you and keep you hydrated. What more do you want from me, huh?" His voice was on the cusp of angry.

"To go home."

"And you will," he said, getting up and crouching in front of her. "We'll build a home. Doesn't that sound good? We'll pick a small town where no one knows us, yeah? Our house will be private, just the two of us in a vast sprawl of land, where we can roll in the fields together. No one will come visit us; we'll be this happy unit, oblivious to the outside world. How does that sound?"

Delusional, she thought, scared of his expectant eyes, the hope they held. With one word she could destroy his dream and send him into a violent frenzy. "Lovely," she said, her small, wavering voice a clear indication of the fear she felt.

"Really?" A frown appeared. "You wouldn't be humouring me, would you? Otherwise, why did you say it like that? Where's the enthusiasm, huh?"

He stood, towering over her, his glare boring into her.

"I'm sorry!"

"You're sorry?" His voice grew in volume. "My ex is sorry. Don't be like her."

Attempting to change the subject, Georgina looked up at

him and gave him her loveliest smile. "You had a girlfriend? What's her name?"

"What, you don't believe me?" He pulled his mobile out of his shorts pocket. "Here. Her name's Tara."

She studied the photo of a gorgeous girl, who she guessed was in her late twenties, maybe early thirties. The poor girl and Georgina had similarities in looks. Tara had lovely, shiny black hair, just like she did. And they both had silky smooth, tanned skin. They were similar builds, petite, with little in the way of cleavage. "She's beautiful. What happened?"

"I loved her so much, and I thought she loved me. We shared time together; I told her things about my life, intimate, secret details. Oh, she understood me, you know? Have you ever had that before?"

He began to relax, she thought, listening to him reminisce about this poor woman. Did he mean the question rhetorically or not, she wondered. Shane understood her more than anyone else. Just the thought of him lying on their living room carpet in a pool of his own blood made her angry.

"Then I find out she was humouring me all along," he said, his anger simmering to the surface again. "She didn't mean the lovely things she said. All I want is someone to be nice to me, to care about me, that's all. And that bitch lied to me. But she won't lie to anyone else, not now."

He flicked through his photos and shoved it in front of her. Georgina turned her head upon viewing the bloody image of the dead woman. She felt sick. Closing her eyes, she had to be smart. If he became angry with her, he might kill her. Opening them, she looked up at him. "I'm not humouring you, Danny, I promise. Our new home together does sound lovely, the way you tell it, with the rolling hills."

"Really?" He crouched down and met her stare. "You really

think it'll work? You think we'll be happy? And it will be just you and me forever?"

The hope returned. "This is what I want, Danny. Just you and me." Her smile almost convinced herself.

When Elf Man moved in for a kiss, she turned her head and his horrible lips met her dirty cheek. His touch almost made her recoil. He might get mad, she thought, if she flinched at his affection. "We're not there yet though, Danny. We've still got to prove to each other that our love is true, don't we? I mean, I don't know about you, but I only want the real thing."

Excited, Elf Man backed away. "I want that too." He moved closer. "So, how do I convince you of my love?"

"Unwrapping my hands would go a long way." She saw the excitement flash across his face. "It hurts, Danny. What harm can freeing my fingers and thumbs do, huh? I can't go anywhere; my hands are still cuffed to this pole."

Without thinking, he started unwinding the sticky duct tape. "This last bit might hurt," he said to her, whipping it off in one smooth motion, taking the fine downy hairs with it. "There. Do you see how much I love you?"

"Thank you, Danny, thank you so much," she said, moving and flexing her hands, letting the blood circulate. "I can see now how much I mean to you." Having her hands free was in no way progress to getting out of this alive. From now on, she had to placate his fractious ego, or he might do some serious damage.

50

"I wouldn't pay him much mind, inspector," Sergeant Willis whispered. "He feels responsible for this. Kennedy's not good at letting things go, so in his eyes, handing this case over to you makes him a failure."

Coates inspected the phone's photo of the bed in front of him. On screen, the covers were soiled, particularly on one side. Spatter marks sprayed the wall behind it. The bed was a shell, the mattress and sheets taken in as evidence, until such a time as they could be destroyed. The carpet beneath, however, still had bloodstains. "What do you mean? How can he be responsible?"

Janae Willis leaned in closer to his ear. "We interviewed Mr Tua after his assault on the Metro. We identified Peebles, or rather Elfman, but couldn't locate him. Then Mr Daley showed us footage taken by Elfman showing him inside their home while they slept. He held a knife against Mr Daley's throat, before... pleasuring himself at Miss Shaw's bedside."

"Pleasuring himself?" Coates raised his eyebrows.

"Yeah, you know." She gestured with her hand.

"You mean in their home?" His question sounded naïve.

"In their *bedroom with them in it*. The creepiest thing I ever saw, I swear. Anyway, we met them on Tuesday, and we scheduled an installation of a panic button for Thursday, but then this happened on Wednesday night or the early hours of Thursday morning, so you can understand why Kennedy's a bit, shall we say, off?"

"Wait! You didn't offer them any protection?"

"Yes, the panic button," she reiterated. "Weren't you listening? We tried asking the brass for manpower, but they wouldn't go for it. Our super said security was a waste. You know as well as I do how little protection we can offer victims of stalkers. I hate it, but–"

"Of course. I apologise; I didn't mean to make it sound like I was blaming you. We practically have to catch them in their home, I appreciate that." For the first time since meeting Sergeant Scott Kennedy, Coates sympathised with the man. His inaction had indirectly caused five murders. He and Willis were tasked with protecting Shaw, Daley and their friends. They failed.

Willis was about to respond, when Coates' mobile vibrated in his pocket. "Gary, this is a surprise. What've you got for me?" Before he left the UK, he asked Packard to keep digging into Peebles. As much as he was a luddite, Coates believed the answers lay in the ether.

"I've been scouring Peebles' online activity for days now, sir, and I may have found something interesting. Of course it might be nothing, but I thought I'd let you judge that for yourself."

Turning his back on Sergeant Willis, he walked to the rear of the bedroom. "Go on, man, tell me what you found. These calls cost a fortune. What've you got for me?"

"He's shown a keen interest in a place called Waterfall Sanatorium. He looked it up no less than eight times on his laptop before he left. It's an abandoned tuberculosis hospital just outside of Heathcote, a small town about an hour's drive from Sydney."

Coates took out his notepad and pen. "Can you repeat that please."

"Waterfall Sanatorium. According to Wikipedia, the hospital was home to some two thousand TB patients before they died, and the buildings have been left abandoned for thirty-odd years now. I thought you'd appreciate the heads-up... Could be worth looking into."

Coates thanked his UK partner and filled him in on the murders, before he hung up and turned to Janae Willis, who was waiting for him. "What have you been told about Waterfall Sanatorium?"

"Forget it!" Sergeant Kennedy strutted into Kereama Tua and Amelia Thomas' bedroom. "The surrounding woods are too thick and overgrown. And besides, the elements made the buildings crumble away. All that's left is rubble."

Wishing the moody sergeant hadn't overheard him, Coates nodded. "I see, worth a punt, I guess. What does my partner know, eh? Silly pom."

"If you want to take a look-see, go ahead. But I'm telling you, even the Urbex lot don't bother with Waterfall anymore. There's nothing to explore, so if Peebles is there, he might as well be camping in the woods."

Coates bowed his head and took Kennedy's comment on board. His Australian colleague must surely have more local knowledge than Packard, Coates thought, turning his attention to Willis, who waited until Kennedy had his back to them and leaned into him.

"Waterfall's not such a bad shout. Two buildings are all but gone. One remains intact, though." She put her finger over her mouth signalling him to keep quiet.

Leaning in closer to her ear, Coates asked, "How do I get to it? If I decide I want to explore the area?" Kennedy glanced at them, then walked away, leaving Coates alone with Sergeant Willis. "Is there a map I can borrow?"

"If you wait until morning, I'll drive you."

"I can't leave it overnight. Miss Shaw's still with him."

"I understand, but it'll be dark soon. You won't find the remaining building at this time, inspector. All you'll end up doing is getting lost in woop woop. Nothing but miles of bush around, I promise you. Nah, the best thing to do is wait until morning. She'll be right; I'll get you to Waterfall."

"Thanks." He held his hand out. Willis had a strong shake and an attractive smile. He could imagine she scrubbed up well out of uniform with that long red hair and those dazzling blue eyes. "I'll take you up on that."

"Take you up on what, Janae?" Kennedy beckoned them over.

"Ah nothing, sir." Willis stopped talking.

"If you say so. You seen enough now, inspector? You're attracting reporters, it seems. There are heaps of them outside."

Coates cursed quietly. "Let's go!" he suggested, his colleagues walking down the stairs in front of him. When they reached the door, they all made sure they avoided the bloodstains near the doormat.

On the driveway, uniforms held back the throng of reporters, who called out to him, asking him if he had any leads. They all seemed to know he was British, and that he had flown over. He didn't say a word to any of them; he focused on getting from the house to their car, which was parked across the road.

"Inspector!" a female shouted from behind him.

Coates turned in the street to find a petite woman stood in front of him, her eyes determined. The woman was attractive with long grey hair; he put her in her late fifties, maybe early sixties. With the journalists waiting behind her, he glanced sideways at Willis. "Ma'am?"

"This is Mrs Thomas, inspector. Amelia's mother."

Kennedy was enjoying the awkwardness, Coates thought, wanting to punch him.

"Are you going to find my daughter, inspector?" she pleaded.

All eyes on him, the journalists didn't need to ask him questions; all they needed to do was watch and listen. Two cameras filmed him. "We're doing our best, Mrs Thomas. If you come by the–"

"Is it true you were called in because Shane's killer is British?"

Kennedy was wearing a smug smile that Coates wanted to wipe away. What could he say? His primary objective was to bring Peebles back to the UK quietly. This wasn't on the quiet, and he was pretty sure Kennedy had leaked the information to Mrs Thomas. "We believe the suspect's British, yes," he said, to murmurs from the news people. "Please, come with us and I'll explain everything."

"I'm not a stupid woman, inspector. In all likelihood my Amelia's probably dead, butchered by that animal, but I have a task for you: bring me my daughter, and catch this mongrel."

"That's why I'm here, Mrs Thomas." He stepped forwards and touched her shoulder. "If you'll join us, I'll discuss this with you back at the–"

"Just do as I ask, please, Inspector Coates."

When she turned and walked away, the journalists barraged her with questions, and after she left without saying a word, they focused on him. They asked him about Elfman, and one reporter asked if the suspect was in fact Arthur Peebles. At this, Coates caught eye contact from Sergeant Kennedy, who shrugged.

"You son of a bitch! You leaked it, didn't you?" Coates

growled when he'd joined the others in the car. Leaning forwards in the rear passenger seat, he saw the stocky officer smiling in the mirror.

"The Australian public have a right to know, inspector."

If he had his way, he would have taken the sergeant outside and smacked some sense into him. In reality, he sat back, unable to vent his anger. He punched the door panel.

51

At ten the following morning, DI Coates stood at the back of the room, his arms crossed, listening to the senior officers explain the situation to their subordinates. Sergeants Willis and Kennedy were either side of him. Chief Superintendent Bradley was front and centre, controlling the hundred-strong crowd of cops. "We're not going to find them here. When can we go?" Kennedy shushed him.

"After this." Willis made sure her partner couldn't hear.

Bradley mentioned Coates' name and asked him to step forwards and address the room. He received a phone call only an hour earlier from DCI Morgan, who was less than impressed that the news stations were reporting Peebles' escapades over here. His cover was blown.

"I'll tell you what I know," he said to eager faces, some young, some old. "Arthur Peebles was released from prison little over eighteen months ago after serving fourteen years for the rape and murder of fellow student, Zoe Evans. He and his co-defendant, Michael Ince tried blaming one another at the trial, but the jury convicted them both and they were sentenced to life imprisonment and sent to HM Full Sutton Prison after being retained at Her Majesty's pleasure for the first four years at Werrington Young Offender Institution in Stoke-on-Trent.

"After speaking to the governor of the prison, I believe Peebles committed two murders while in custody. Brutal and bloody, an inquiry was held on both occasions, yet no evidence was ever found against him. Upon early release, and against the recommendations of the governor, Peebles was given a new name and relocated to Brighton. He chose Danny Elfman as his moniker and began his new life working as a customer service representative at an insurance company. According to the company's CEO, Elfman was a valued employee.

"Reading the messages between Shaw and Elfman, he started following her a little over a year ago, liking most of her cheeps but never contacting her, until on Friday the fourth of January, when he sent her a message asking where he should visit on holiday in Sydney. By Shaw's own admission, one of her friends, possibly Mr King, or Mr Tua replied on her behalf as a prank. I think we can assume that he took her confession badly."

"There you have it, ladies and gentlemen," Bradley said, taking over. "Mr Daley was a registered firearm owner and one of his handguns is missing, a Beretta M9. We're considering Elfman armed and dangerous. If you encounter him, call for assistance first. We've set up a helpline in the next room with volunteers answering calls from the public. I need you all to be vigilant and alert."

"If you find him, radio in," Coates interrupted. "Elfman doesn't care. He didn't try to hide his DNA on Tara Henson's body, which means he's either too dumb, or getting caught doesn't scare him. He's not frightened of prison. He won't feel guilty about shooting you dead, so please, please, please stay safe. You see him, call for backup before approaching him."

Coates walked to the rear of the room and stood between Willis and Kennedy. Bradley continued his briefing, where the map of Sydney and the surrounding area was split up into squares. They were going to fan out and search the city and its neighbouring towns and villages. "Superintendent," he said, attracting his super's attention, "Sergeant Willis and I would like to take Waterfall Sanatorium." Chatter and laughter filled the room.

"I thought you wanted to catch him," Bradley joked.

"Sir... I–"

"You're not from around here, Inspector Coates, so I'll let you in on a little local secret: the hospital doesn't exist anymore. The buildings have collapsed, but if you're suggesting he's lying out there in the woods with all those bities, go and look for yourself."

"My partner over the pond is looking into Elfman's search history and he looked up Waterfall Sanatorium a bunch of times. It's worth a try, isn't it?"

"I have a list of places far more likely to yield results right here in my hand," Bradley said, smirking.

The room laughed at him.

A man in civvies walked up to the superintendent carrying a clipboard.

"We're spreading out the width and breadth of New South Wales, as far north as Lightning Ridge, east as Byron Bay, as far south as Albury and west as Broken Hill. If anyone has any preferences, now's the time to tell me."

The chorus of voices drowned out anything Coates was going to say. Instead of shouting above everyone, he leaned against the wall and folded his arms. By the time their search zone was given out, they would be given the dregs. Elfman and Shaw were at Waterfall Sanatorium. Why else would his charge research the abandoned hospital on Google Maps? And the sanatorium was only a forty-five-minute drive.

"I told you he wouldn't go for it. But don't worry, she'll be right. I'll ask for a decent place to search."

Coates had never wanted to punch a colleague as much as Scott Kennedy before. On the flight over, Coates had wondered what kind of reception he would receive. Apart from Willis, everyone he had met so far seemed to hold him in contempt. "Can we go?"

"No way, mate. If he finds out we've gone behind his back, he'll bump me down to constable. No, I am sorry, inspector, but I have my limits. You'll need to convince some other poor mug to drive you."

The noise level dropped. Coates tried to identify the reason.

A couple, a man in his fifties or sixties and an aborigine woman entered the room. He noted the woman had been crying. Bradley introduced them as Mr and Mrs Shaw, Georgina's parents. In the UK, the relatives wouldn't have been invited to a police meeting like this. But he was in Australia, not the UK.

Everyone quietened down and waited for Mr Shaw to speak.

"Please help us. Find our daughter, I beg you. She's only a dainty little thing, please bring her back to us." His mouth crumpled as his wife buried her face in his shirt. "And kill that piece of shit, too. Make him wish he was never born."

The room erupted. Coates couldn't believe the Chief Superintendent didn't have anything to say about it. After Shaw's parents left the room, Coates hung around until Kennedy came back with a sheet of paper in his hand. Their search zone: Ambarvale. "What's this?"

"A favour," Kennedy announced. "Ambarvale's just west of Dharawal National Park. Dharawal blends into Heathcote National Park. And guess what's near Heathcote? If you're patient and help us in Ambarvale, I'll drive us to Waterfall. How about that?"

Coates didn't have much choice. He would rather leave now, but without a guide, he would no doubt get himself lost; he didn't possess the best inner compass. "You've got a deal. But I have to ask, why are you doing this? You said yourself I'm wasting my time."

"Yeah well, I can be a hothead at times," Kennedy admitted. "If your partner says Peebles searched for Waterfall a lot, there might be something in it. I meant what I said. The hospital's gone, nothing but ruins from where the bush has grown through."

Willis smiled at him and extended her thumb without her senior partner spotting it.

Coates held out his hand.

Kennedy took a few seconds deciding whether or not to shake it. He did.

52

Georgina tried to tear the duct tape he replaced around her fingers and thumbs for the eightieth time. Feeling dizzy from lack of food and water, she grappled with the cable ties, desperate to free herself and run away. To her relief, he left her alone for the third day in a row. He would be back soon, she thought, believing it to be late afternoon. "Help!" she cried into her gag, her words nothing more than muffled noise.

Mosquitos had made a meal of her, being tied up allowing them the chance to sink their teeth into her. Bites littered her legs, arms and neck. Of all the wildlife around her, mosquitos were the cute teddy bears. Earlier in the morning she had to move when a Sydney funnel web, the deadliest of the indigenous spiders, crawled past her. She only wished one would bite Elf Man.

The sun was beaming outside, not that she had seen any over the last three days. It was dark in her room, and hot, the perfect climate for funnel webs and all manner of other nasty insects that would love nothing more than to take chunks out of her. Georgina had her captor and the elements to be afraid of.

Straining to break the cable tie, her wrists bleeding from her clawing at it. No use. The plastic was too strong. Giving up, she studied the metal pole. It was screwed into the ground.

Then she looked down at her taped hands. There was no getting to the screws. Panicking, she screamed into her gag, half out of fear and the rest frustration. Elf Man was due back any time, she thought, sawing away at the cable tie with the metal in the vain hope it would somehow snap. "Help!" The rag made her choke.

She heard voices!

Georgina stopped moving.

Rustling bushes; she heard the wind tickling the leaves.

Her raised hopes dropped.

She screamed into her gag as loud as she could for as long as she could until she coughed. A mosquito bit her on the arm. "Help!" she spluttered for a third time.

The voices grew fainter.

With a sense of hopelessness consuming her, she let out a sob. Elf Man would come through that doorway any moment. The previous nights she'd avoided his advances, but she wasn't sure about this evening. In keeping up the appearances, she had not flinched when he kissed her cheek goodbye. She'd let him kiss her, for Christ's sake. If she had any chance of getting out of this alive, she had to free herself now.

The voices came back! Two guys.

Her throat dry, she screamed into her gag until she coughed.

They continued, only louder.

Desperately yanking on her wrists, she yelled again.

"Did you hear that, mate?" a faint voice said.

Georgina did all she could to scream again, her voice hoarse.

"Hello? Is someone here? If you can, call out."

She didn't need to be told twice. Georgina kept calling between coughing fits. The guy's voice grew louder with each attempt at drawing their attention. Still yanking on the cable ties, her wrists bleeding, she held her focus on the doorway until a man's silhouette stood before her.

"Holy shit!" The first man entered and walked up to her. "She's that girl, the one from the news, mate. That surfer chick. Quick, call the police." He squatted before pulling the rag out of her mouth. "You'll be right. We've got you."

Watching the second silhouette on his mobile, she glanced at the doorway, expecting Elf Man to enter. "Please help me. He'll be back any minute. Cut me loose, I beg you."

The silhouette stood and reached into his jeans pockets. "I don't understand, I had my pocketknife on me when I left."

"Shit! No signal, mate," said the second shadow.

Georgina looked up in desperation at her supposed rescuers. "Quick, find something to cut these ties with, please. He'll be back soon."

"I had my knife on me, I know I did."

When one of them laughed, she understood why. "Are you high?" They were here getting stoned, she thought, pulling on the plastic. "Please, you have to listen to me! Find something to cut with. There must be something you can use."

"Like what?" one asked, putting his mobile away.

"Like glass, anything, something sharp," she snapped. "Use your imagination. It has to be strong enough to slice through this cable tie."

"Oh holy shit! It is you! I remember now, Georgina Shaw," the phone silhouette said, seeming to forget the seriousness of the situation. "You're a badass bitch! What're you doing here, babe?"

"Sunbathing, what does it look like!" she hissed, staggered that he couldn't understand she had been abducted. "Are you kidding me? I need rescuers, and what do I get? A couple of space cadets. Please look for a cutting implement."

"Right." He slapped his forehead. "Like what?"

Space Cadet's friend laughed.

"Listen up, drongos, a psycho pommie who's already murdered my boyfriend and four of my friends kidnapped me, do you get it? He's on his way back, and if he finds you here, *he will kill you*. Do I need to spell it out for you? Now please, please, please find something to cut me free."

They both got to work scouring the floor for a cutting tool.

"Hey! Did she just call us drongos?"

53

S at in the back of Kennedy's police car, Coates was sweating. He had wet patches around his armpits and one starting on his back. Being British, he wasn't acclimatised to the intense heat, and he had been out in the sun all day, searching for Elf Man and Shaw in a tiny place called Ambarvale, going door-to-door with photos. Of course they'd left empty-handed because their suspect was at the sanatorium. "How far is it?"

"Keep your pants on, mate, we're coming up to Waterfall now. We've just passed Heathcote. Should be there in a few minutes. She'll be right."

"Should we discuss arming him?"

Kennedy regarded his partner, he noted. Were they seriously thinking about handing him a gun? He didn't want one.

"Not on your life! No way! Uh-uh. He can come along, but I'm not giving him a piece. And besides, they won't be here, Jan. I'm doing him a favour by taking this detour."

"Hey! I don't want one," Coates confessed. "Don't argue on my account. I never needed a gun before, and I don't plan on carrying one in the future."

Silence wedged itself between them for a moment.

"I bet you haven't done much sightseeing since you flew in, have you?" Kennedy's voice had a natural, pleasant tone. "I tell you, Sydney's one of the best cities in the world. We've got everything you need. And the beaches, mate. Oh my God! What you got back home? Brighton, is it? Pebbles? Ours are all golden sand. Man, I love this place."

Coates smiled at his colleague's bravado. In his own way, Kennedy was being nice, even if done in his backhanded, insult the British way. "Sorry, mate, nothing beats Brighton Beach. Hands down the coolest place in the UK. Even Bondi pales in comparison. Have you even been?"

Kennedy stopped talking and glared at him in the mirror. "The hell you saying? No way Brighton's cooler than Bondi. I ought to throw you out the car for saying that. You can't come to Sydney and start slagging it off. That's not friendly."

"Ease up, Kennedy," said Willis, the voice of reason. "He's allowed an opinion."

Coates wanted to cultivate the uncomfortable silence.

"We're almost there, inspector." She turned in her seat to look at him. "The woods leading to the hospital are just up ahead."

Suspicion in Willis' eyes made him turn and glance out of the back window.

"What's this arsehole doing?"

A car behind them sped up, then pulled up beside them on their right.

The passenger's window opened.

A loud bang reverberated through the car as Kennedy's window shattered.

It all happened so fast, Coates' brain didn't register that a bullet had been fired until his side window splintered, and shards of glass went all over him.

Their car swerved to the left when the other car smashed into them.

By the time Coates realised that their attacker was Elf Man, he looked through the windscreen to find they were heading for an embankment, and a tree. "Watch out!" He braced for impact. Willis screamed.

The collision was a blur. Both airbags deployed when the bonnet hit the tree, fortunately not at great speed, yet fast enough to jar Coates' neck on the seat belt. He could walk. His colleagues seemed unhurt.

"Shit!" Kennedy picked up his radio. He called in the attack to HQ, who told him to stay put and wait for backup. "Arsehole!"

Not wanting to wait, Coates opened his door.

"Where the hell do you think you're going?" Kennedy asked.

"Elf Man! He's here, which means Shaw's here, too. Now he knows we're nearby, he's more likely to move to his endgame and kill her. We can't wait!"

Despite Kennedy's protest, Coates got out of the car and started walking towards the entrance to the woods. Elf Man's car was up ahead, where he had jumped out and was making his way to shoot Shaw. Somehow Coates' leg had caught the brunt of the crash.

Behind him, footsteps made him smirk. "I thought you had your orders to stay put?"

Willis walked next to him, her Glock 22 out and by her side. "And let you have all the fun? No way!" She smiled.

He exchanged glances with her. "You call this fun?"

54

"I think I've found something," Silhouette One said, bringing over a huge shard of glass.

It was a good size and sharp. "Quick, try it!" Keeping her hands as far apart as she could, Georgina looked away, as her rescuer tried slicing through the plastic. "Is it working?"

"Give me a chance," he replied, sawing at the cable tie. "I'm going as fast as I can, dude." He turned his head and stared at her. "You're fit as–"

The bang behind her shook the room.

Georgina felt liquid on her face, only realising it was blood when Silhouette One's body slumped to the floor, a massive hole in the back of his head. His legs twitched.

She screamed.

The shard of glass was right by her hand.

Silhouette Two stood and faced Elf Man.

In fear, she picked up the shard and sawed at the cable tie, while her stoned hero faced off against Elf Man.

With Elf Man fighting her rescuer next to her, she studied her bind.

She was almost through when Silhouette Two lunged at Elf Man, knocking the pistol out of his hand.

The pistol hit the ground a few feet away from her.

Speeding up the sawing, itching to pick up the gun and shoot Elf Man, the ties broke.

Spying the pistol on the floor, she flew across the room, narrowly missing it by a centimetre, when Elf Man reached out and grabbed it while Silhouette Two grappled with him on the concrete. "No!"

Two muffled shots rang out.

Silhouette Two fared as well as his buddy. Georgina watched as the gunshots entered through his stomach and exited through his back. Her rescuer lay motionless on top of her captor, who struggled to push the dead weight off. "You bastard!" she screamed, then ran into the corridor before he raised his pistol.

"Georgina! Get back here, you bitch, or I'm going to fucking kill you. Don't you leave me!"

In the long hallway, she saw nothing but doorways to more rooms, the concrete flooring chipped and cracked. In front of her, a massive hole where the ground had collapsed identified itself. Hearing him shout, she jumped over the hole that led to the basement.

The windows along the corridor had no glass in them. Filled with brambles and ivy, security bars prevented her from jumping out of them. If only she could find one without bars; she would be outside, in the woods. "Shit!" She sensed him behind her.

A loud bang made her dive to her left, into a doorway. He was right behind her. On the ground, she picked herself up, and ran across the room to another door. Part of the floor had collapsed, so she stuck to the walls, shimmied across to another door.

The building was a maze of rooms and corridors. If she sprinted through enough hallways she would lose him eventually, she thought, closing a fifth door and entering yet another corridor. It felt like she'd been running for ages.

In front of her another hole further along the corridor appeared.

Making a note of it, she walked past a doorway and saw movement to her left.

Before she could brace herself, she was in the air, Elf Man on top of her.

When she landed on her back, the floor gave way and a huge chunk of concrete dropped. She screamed mid-air.

Elf Man, heavier than her, landed on his back first, breaking her fall.

55

The woods thick with bushes, brambles, undergrowth, Coates caught himself on the spiky thorns a few times, cursing into the ether. He understood why Kennedy and the superintendent thought it was a waste of time. If a huge abandoned hospital existed nearby, the building was well-hidden. "How much further?" He wiped his sweaty forehead. "We need to get inside, now."

"We're not far." Willis pulled a fat bramble back and waited for Coates to walk through. "It's around here."

Coates tripped over a piece of brick wall. Picking himself up, he dusted himself off and scanned the area ahead. Bricks and chunks of wall lay everywhere. "Christ! No kidding about the ruins." One chunk had graffiti scrawled over it.

"There's one building left," she said, leading the way.

"How do you know?"

"I'm an urban explorer in my spare time."

He followed her through the thick forest, flitting mosquitos away with his hand. Having heard the shots, he was beginning to regret not asking for a firearm. Elf Man had one. "There! I can see it."

Up ahead, Coates made out a large four-storey building. Derelict didn't do the place justice: indigenous vegetation was attempting to take over, with ivy growing up the walls and penetrating them, competing with the prickly brambles. "Shit! How do we get in?"

"Up here, a door," Willis suggested, her gun out in front of her.

Pushing the rotten wood back, Coates waited behind his colleague, who took a torch out of her pocket and held it up, along with her pistol. It was dark inside the crumbling building. The floor was dangerous. "Watch your step, sergeant."

56

Georgina picked herself up. Looking down at an unconscious and injured Elf Man, she scanned the nearby vicinity for his gun. It couldn't have gone far, she thought, checking the surrounding area. If she found the pistol, she would be safe.

Hearing him groan, she panicked and sprinted into the darkness of the basement, ignoring the pain in her knees. They'd fallen far and hard. Splinters of glass embedded themselves in her bare heels as she ran.

"Georgina! I want you back here, you bitch!"

The basement almost as maze-like as the rest of the building, complete with corridors and multiple rooms, she hoped she would find the stairs up to the ground floor before Elf Man caught her. With her life on the line, there would be no talking him down.

With her eyesight adjusting to the darkness, she found a doorway leading to a corridor. Sidestepping along a wall, all she could hear was her own breathing, strong and often. Using her fingers as guides along the wall, she smelt something, like a dead animal. Rotting flesh. She wrinkled her nose.

"Georgina!" came his voice, closer than before.

In a blind panic, she jumped through the doorway, the stench growing with every step she took; she didn't want to be in this room. A buzzing noise in the distance caught her attention. When his voice carried past her again, only louder, she swallowed and headed further inside the room.

The buzzing intensified, until a fly flew into her face.

Flitting it away, her foot hit something soft and cold.

Not wanting to look down, she closed her eyes.

"Please God, no." Crouching, she looked closer: a body.

A woman lying on her back, wearing nothing but a long T-shirt, her bare legs on display.

Georgina inspected further up the body until she came to the face. "No! Isla," she cried, her friend's head beaten in, with nothing left of her forehead or eyes. All she had to go on: Isla's gorgeous mouth and half of her beautiful nose. Her body was cold and hard to the touch.

Next to Isla's body lay the corpse of a man. Georgina didn't need to check: Oliver. She could tell by the shape of his muscular body. She couldn't help but sob, the sight of her murdered friends too much.

"Georgina! Where are you?" Elf Man enjoyed the game.

Forcing herself to stop sobbing, she pulled herself up and walked further into the darkness, away from his voice.

A noise spooked her, and she turned a walk into a run.

After no more than five paces, her right foot hit something, tripping her.

Georgina landed on her front next to a body of another woman.

"Amelia," Georgina wailed, grabbing her best friend's head and cradling it, not caring that her skin felt cold. "Why?"

"Are you mental? You don't cuddle corpses," Elf Man said from behind her. "Our time together is up, I'm afraid."

He was stronger than he looked, picking her up.

She wanted to say goodbye to her friends.

Stood in front of Elf Man, his face confident and strong, rage built up inside her, raw and powerful. She had to release the power.

"Too bad." Elf Man raised the pistol and pointed it at her forehead. "We could've been so great together."

Georgina flew at him, grabbing his gun arm and tackling him.

Two shots fired close to her ear.

Focused, determined, she whipped her leg around his and pushed him to the ground with a thud. And seizing her opportunity, she fell on top of him and punched his face.

Elf Man attempted to protect himself, to block her.

Screaming at him with every punch she landed, the rage inside grew until her fists were red with his blood.

There was no stopping his arm raising, the pistol held aloft.

The handle of his gun struck the top of her head.

Stunned for a moment, Georgina found herself on her back, with Elf Man trying to stand, the gun in his hand. His face covered in blood, she had done some damage at least. She shook her head, thinking how to get out of this, when she saw the handle of his knife sticking out of his shorts.

With him wiping blood from his face, she lunged forwards, grabbed the blade's handle and turned it in, towards him, feeling the blade slide into his groin. She wanted to hear him scream in pain more. No amount of his suffering would compensate for him butchering her friends. "Fucking die, you bastard!"

On the floor, the knife stuck in him, Elf Man lay, writhing in agony.

Sensing his retaliation, Georgina turned and sprinted into the darkness, hearing two gunshots.

She ran as fast as she could past Isla and Oliver, vowing to have their bodies buried once this was over. She ran through so many doorways and along too many corridors to count.

Only when she finally stopped running and the adrenaline had worn off did she notice the blood on her dirty T-shirt. In all the excitement, she had not noticed the bullet graze her shoulder. It stung, but she was too wired to care.

Almost high-fiving the air, she climbed the stairs leading up to the ground floor. They were on the verge of collapse, although she traversed them with caution, holding on to the banisters.

"Georgina Shaw!" a voice said as she arrived at the top.

"Sergeant Kennedy, thank God!" She flew into his arms, the light blue shirt and gun in his hand her safety net against the psycho.

57

"You're safe now," Kennedy said, his muscular arms around her.

"He was right behind me." Georgina broke the embrace. "He's injured, though. I managed to stick him with his knife."

"Good girl." Kennedy trained his Glock on the doorway she had just come out of, and told her to stand behind him. He crouched, gun ready. "Stay low, understood?"

"Got it." More scared than she had ever been, even with a cop on hand to save the day, after a lengthy wait for him to appear, she leaned into his ear. "Maybe he's not following. Maybe he's too badly injured."

"We're not going anywhere until backup arrives," he answered.

It felt like she had held her breath for three days. It surprised her that she hadn't fainted from lack of oxygen to the brain. Having Sergeant Kennedy there helped, more than she would ever tell him. "He butchered them all, you know."

"I know." He paused, his gun still up. "We searched their houses after we found Mr Daley... Shane, in your living room. I'm sorry for your loss. Ah hell, I'm sorry about a lot of things.

I'm sorry we couldn't help you before… I'm sorry I didn't believe you about your friends' texts. I'm never going to be able to make it up to you, you know."

"I tell you what, you get me out of here, and you're halfway there."

"You've got a deal." He tensed, leaning into his gun.

"What is it?"

"I thought I heard something." He remained silent for a minute.

"Never thought I'd love that sound." The sirens grew louder with every passing moment. "Can we go now, please?" Ten minutes and no sign of Elf Man. She'd wedged the knife right in him. "Come on, I'll lead." She stood, with Kennedy in front of her, his gun still pointing at the entrance to the basement. "I have to get out of here."

Georgina held her hand out, turned the other way, and began pulling him along. He still faced the doorway, until she forced him to join her. "He's got to be dying down there with a stab wound that bad."

"You don't get rid of me that easily."

The volume loud enough to make her ears ring, the bullet hit the back of Kennedy's head and exited in a shower of crimson, mostly over Georgina, who turned in the turmoil and fell backwards screaming, as Elf Man continued firing, each bullet hitting the policeman's back.

With Kennedy on top of her, she searched around her for a way out.

By her right hand sat Kennedy's Glock.

The knife sticking out of his groin, Elf Man fired twice more while hobbling in her direction, his face a terrible grimace, his eyes full of hate.

As the bullets tore into the policeman's back, Georgina

picked up the pistol, aimed it at Elf Man's chest and squeezed the trigger.

The gun erupted in her hand and spat out its red-hot projectile.

She fired another two times.

When Elf Man fell back, she dropped the Glock and attempted to slide out from beneath Kennedy, her T-shirt soaked in his blood.

"Miss Shaw?" The voice came from behind her.

"Sergeant Willis," she said, managing to push Kennedy off her. "I'm so sorry! He tried to save me." A man she didn't recognise came striding up to her, crouched down and introduced himself as Detective Inspector David Coates from the UK. Why was a British cop involved, she wondered?

"Scott!" Willis then spoke into her radio. "Officer down; I repeat, officer down. We need an ambo here asap. Suspect is also down."

The sirens stopped.

"It'll take them a good half hour to walk here," Willis said, stroking Kennedy's bloody face, tears streaming down her cheeks. "And this is all your fault!"

Georgina moved when Willis stood and strode over to where Elf Man lay.

"Look out!" She picked up the Glock when she saw his arm rise.

The discharge hit the ginger officer on the bridge of her nose, tore through her brain and exited through the back of her skull. In a shower of blood, Willis fell on her back.

"Willis!"

Elf Man's laugh filled the corridor.

As soon as Elf Man changed the trajectory of the pistol and aimed it at her and the British cop, she fired three times, hitting her target each time, once in the groin, once in the stomach and once in the chest.

After the noise had abated, he laughed still.

He still had Shane's gun in his hand.

Getting up, Georgina kept her Glock on Elf Man, making sure he didn't raise his arm.

"Do the world a favour and finish this, would you? Or I will," Coates said.

Slowly, she stepped towards her tormentor. "I loathe you," she said, pointing the gun at his face. "Why did you butcher my friends? Shane, why murder my boyfriend? Explain it to me, you piece of shit, or so help me God."

"Because," he said, gargling a blood bubble over his face, "I could."

His laugh angered her. Images of Amelia flashed in her mind. Memories of Isla, Oliver and Kereama, too. And then a recollection of Shane made her squeeze the trigger.

The bullet blew a hole in Elf Man's cheek. Georgina heard the faintest laugh still, prompting her to fire the gun a second time.

The bullet hit him in the centre of his forehead, scattering his brain over the concrete. His dead eyes stared skyward, but at least she couldn't hear him laugh.

Satisfied that Elf Man was dead, she dropped the gun and fell to the floor, exhausted.

Coates caught her.

58

Coates peered inside the private hospital room. Sunday morning and the sun shone outside. "Knock, knock," he said, his voice soft.

"Inspector, please come in," Shaw's father said. "Take a seat."

Shaw didn't look at him; she stared into the air, past her parents. Coates guessed she had much to process, what with the deaths of her long-term boyfriend and close friends. He nodded and walked to the opposing side of Shaw's bed, flowers in hand. "These are for you. I'm sorry! I didn't know what you like."

"You're not supposed to bring flowers to hospitals," Shaw's mother said. She reached out for them. "I'll take them home with me and put them in water. Thank you from Georgina. She's not spoken since waking up."

Coates sat opposite her father and regarded her mother. "How is she?"

"Exhausted. She stayed in overnight on a drip. The bastard shot her in the shoulder; plus, she has bruises everywhere. The doctors had to take glass out of her feet. Basically a mess, but she'll mend." She held her daughter's hand. "We'll be here to help her make sense of it."

"I'm not sure there's a person on the planet who could do that." Coates shook his head. "Make sense of it, I mean."

"Who is this Danny Elfman, detective?" Shaw's father asked. "Is it true his real name's Arthur Peebles? And is it true he should still be in prison for rape and murder?"

"I'm afraid so, sir, yes," he confirmed, unable to lie. "He had every opportunity in life. Peebles was one of four born to wealthy parents who doted on them. His two brothers and sister are all upstanding, well-rounded pillars of the community by all accounts. And his mum is a respected physician while his dad owned a printing company. There is no earthly reason why he should go on to enjoy hurting others. At the trial he tried blaming his co-defendant."

"So much for nature. I always was a big believer in nurture."

"Oh, I don't think it's as simple as that, sir. We now know Peebles instigated everything. At the age of fourteen, he raped a young girl; beat her to death with a brick before burying her with his co-defendant's help. At school, he might as well have been Mr Invisible, according to his classmates. Never a high-achiever, he never did anything worthy of note. In prison, he murdered two fellow inmates, but the governor couldn't prove it. Peebles has never been friendly enough with someone to be influenced by them, so I think nurture's out."

Mr Shaw stared at him. "So, what then? If not nature or nurture, why did he murder my daughter's friends?" Shaw's father welled up.

"You really want to hear it?" He waited for the parents to nod. "It's controversial, and I'm no criminologist, not by any means, but I think he had bad wiring. Put simply, his brain bypassed his conscience. He couldn't feel empathy, or anything, really."

"That would explain it," Mr Shaw agreed.

After a lengthy silence, Coates went to stand. "Right, on that note, I think I'll leave you to help your daughter heal." He looked down at Shaw's pretty face – liking the fact she was wearing a hospital gown instead of a bloody T-shirt – and said goodbye to her as softly as he could manage.

"Thank you, inspector, for everything."

He stopped at the door, turned and smiled at her. "For what? I should be thanking *you* for saving *my* life." He looked at the parents. "That's one tough cookie you have there, Mr and Mrs Shaw."

He jumped in a taxi outside the main reception doors and asked the driver to take him to Bondi Beach. He wanted to see what Kennedy had been raving about. In honour of him, he guessed.

The seventeen-minute drive from Sydney Hospital and Sydney Eye Hospital to the beach relaxed him. With the case solved, Coates could enjoy the rest of the day, his return flight not until mid-afternoon on Monday. He planned on buying an ice cream and sitting on the sand to eat it. Then he might have some beers at one of the café bars, either at The Starfish, Lush or The Bucket List.

Sergeant Packard had sold him on trying the food at Lush, having been to Australia a few times himself. Coates only regretted his family wasn't with him. "Thanks," he said, paying the taxi driver and heading in the direction of the beach.

It was busy with everyone from young families to hardcore surfers. Strolling up to the bar at The Starfish, he ordered his ice cream, paid for it, and walked, still wearing his suit, to a free spot on the sand. Careful not to drop his ice cream, he rolled up his trouser legs and sat, the sun beaming down on him. He took his shoes and socks off.

Yeah, he could get used to this, he thought, finishing his cone. Why didn't he bring swimmers? Not caring, he stood, then strolled to the water's edge. The water warm, he waded in, up to his knees, and laughed when a bigger wave whooshed up to his midriff.

Coates submersed himself. He understood why Kennedy had loved Bondi Beach so much; it was wonderful. And he loved Sydney. Scott Kennedy had sold it to him. He vowed to bring his family here as one of their big holidays. Treading water, he tried to put Elf Man out of his mind; he didn't want to be wasting thoughts on him... Instead, he turned his thoughts to Georgina Shaw, glad she would in time recover.

THE END

ACKNOWLEDGEMENTS

I'd like to thank, first and foremost, you, the reader, for taking a chance on reading my book. Without you picking it up and reading it, there would be no need for me writing it, or the publisher releasing it. So, thank you. If you enjoyed Mr Invisible, please consider leaving a review. And if you'd like some behind the scenes information, please follow me on Instagram: @dcbrockwell or my Facebook page: DCBrockwell Author. In addition to writing, I like gardening and making cocktails, so you'll find quite a mixed bag on my Instagram account.

I would also love to thank the team at Bloodhound Books. Betsy and Fred, for taking a punt on my story, thank you so much for this opportunity to showcase my work; it's more appreciated than you know. Morgen Bailey, my editor for shaping it up, ready for publication. Also Heather Fitt and the publicity team. Thank you all for your contributions. I hope I don't let you all down.

And I can't sign off without thanking my beta readers, who often pull me up on poor choices with storylines. Extra special mention has to go to Donna Morfett, Lesley Lloyd, Pauline Render Byron, Beryl Murrell, Lynda Checkley and Ang Lamb.

All members of my group, Brockwell's Betas have been a source of invaluable support, so thank you from the bottom of my heart.

Duncan Brockwell can be found here:
Instagram: @dcbrockwell
Facebook Page: DCBrockwell Author
Twitter: DCBrockwell

Lightning Source UK Ltd.
Milton Keynes UK
UKHW041059240521
384274UK00001B/233